KILLING PLAIN

"Put the woman aside and let's get down to business," said Sam.

"Sounds good to me," said Jake. He gave Florence a rough shove away from him. In doing so, he aimed the tip of his barrel away from her head and pointed it squarely at the ranger. "Whoa!" he said, raising his brow in feigned surprise. "Now we're evened up, Ranger! What do you think of that?"

"That was clever. . . ." Sam stalled as if caught off guard, letting his words trail, watching Florence scurry away to safety.

"What about it, Ranger?" McAllister asked. "Are you all out of smart mouthing?"

"Yep," Sam said grimly. "I'm all out of everything, Jake. I came here prepared to die. I hope you're prepared as well. . . ."

KILLING PLAIN

Ralph Cotton

A SIGNET BOOK

SIGNET
Published by New American Library, a division of
Penguin Group (USA) Inc., 375 Hudson Street,
New York, New York 10014, USA
Penguin Group (Canada), 10 Alcorn Avenue, Toronto,
Ontario M4V 3B2, Canada (a division of Pearson Penguin Canada Inc.)
Penguin Books Ltd., 80 Strand, London WC2R 0RL, England
Penguin Ireland, 25 St. Stephen's Green, Dublin 2,
Ireland (a division of Penguin Books Ltd.)
Penguin Group (Australia), 250 Camberwell Road, Camberwell, Victoria 3124,
Australia (a division of Pearson Australia Group Pty. Ltd.)
Penguin Books India Pvt. Ltd., 11 Community Centre, Panchsheel Park,
New Delhi - 110 017, India
Penguin Group (NZ), cnr Airborne and Rosedale Roads, Albany,
Auckland 1310, New Zealand (a division of Pearson New Zealand Ltd.)
Penguin Books (South Africa) (Pty.) Ltd., 24 Sturdee Avenue,
Rosebank, Johannesburg 2196, South Africa

Penguin Books Ltd., Registered Offices:
80 Strand, London WC2R 0RL, England

First published by Signet, an imprint of New American Library,
a division of Penguin Group (USA) Inc.

First Printing, March 2005
10 9 8 7 6 5 4 3 2 1

Copyright © Ralph Cotton, 2005
All rights reserved

Ⓓ REGISTERED TRADEMARK—MARCA REGISTRADA

Printed in the United States of America

For Mary Lynn . . . *of course*

PART 1

Chapter 1

————

Ranger Sam Burrack had slipped quietly into Cottonwood through a back alley. From the shadowed edge of that same alley, he'd kept an eye on the Topp Dog Saloon for the past hour, having to keep watch above the bustle of wagon and buggy traffic. He stood leaning against the clapboard wall of a mercantile store in his brush-scarred riding duster, his pearl gray sombrero low across his forehead. Beside him, standing close to the wall, Black Pot twitched his ears and let out a low puff of breath.

"Don't worry, fellow," Sam whispered to the big Appaloosa stallion. "It won't be much longer." He ran a gloved hand down Black Pot's dust-streaked muzzle. "We'll mark his name off the list and head home."

As soon as Sam said the word *home*, he stopped for a moment, repeated the word to himself and let his hand lay motionless on Black Pot's nose while he contemplated just were his home might be. *The ranger outpost . . . ?*

No, he told himself, the outpost was only a stopping-off point—it wasn't home. He pictured the long, dusty adobe ranger barracks, a tall saqauro cactus providing the only strip of shade in a yard littered with rocks the size of melons and plentifully strewn with cholla cactus, brittle mesquite and scrub juniper. It was to and from that outpost that he and the other territory rangers came and went between assignments. Sam smiled slightly to himself. He had heard the barracks called many things during his trips there, but never *home*.

Sam looked at his worn saddle atop the big Appaloosa's back, the butt of his rifle standing up from its leather boot, his canvas-wrapped canteen hanging from the saddle horn. "Home is where you make it, Black Pot," he murmured, more to himself than to the stallion. He turned his face back to the street, then lifted his eyes and gazed out across the bleak endless land to the northwest. The badlands. Was that home for him? He didn't think so. Or perhaps he just refused to think so. Nonsense, he told himself, quickly putting aside such idle contemplation, seeing the batwing doors of the Topp Dog Saloon swing open as Stone Eddie Deaks stepped out onto the boardwalk.

"Time to go to work, Black Pot," Sam said quietly over his shoulder. He tugged slightly on the reins and led the big stallion out to the nearest hitch rail, only a few feet from the alley, unnoticed in the busy street.

Following Stone Eddie Deaks, a gunman named Max Thurston cut a quick glance in all directions along the street traffic, his hand near his gun butt as he stepped out and let the bat-wing doors slap back and forth behind him. "The sooner I can give Lonzo your answer, the sooner he can start planning our next job."

"Tell Lonzo I'll think about it, Max," said Deaks, not sounding too attentive to the conversation, which had started twenty minutes ago at the crowded bar and followed him out the doors. "I always seem to work better alone." He put a long black cigar to his lips, took a long draw and blew out a thin stream of smoke, his right thumb hooked into his ornately trimmed vest. Only inches from his thumb stood a double-action Colt Thunderer in a sleek shoulder harness beneath his black linen suit coat.

A woman passing by caught the lingering wisp of cigar smoke and fanned it from her face with an expression of disgust. Stone Eddie Deaks gave her a thin smile and touched his fingers, cigar and all, to the brim of his black flat-crowned hat. "Evening, ma'am," he said. But the woman ignored his attempt at charming her and huffed off along the crowded boardwalk.

"I believe the day of the loner is dead and gone, Deaks," said Max Thurston. "It might be time you hooked up with a gang like ours. Remember the old story about a bundle of sticks being stronger than a stick by itself?"

"Of course I do," Stone Eddie replied, not giving

the gunman so much as a glance of encouragement. "Tell Lonzo Greer if I ever go into the *stick* business, you Black Moon boys will be the first to know."

Max Thurston gave him a smoldering look and started to say something. But before Max could speak, he noticed a young man lurking on his right and jerked around facing him, his hand instinctively going to his gun butt.

"Whooa! Begging you pardon, sir!" the young man said, taking a step back, his hand also going to his gun butt, just as quick and easily as Thurston's. "I heard the bartender say you're none other than Max Thurston. I just couldn't help trying to meet you and introduce myself. I'm Norbert Lamb. Everybody calls me the Kid. Get it?" He smiled.

But Max Thurston didn't return Lamb's smile. Instead he looked the young man up and down with contempt. "Maybe that bartender needs his jaws boxed for having a big mouth," he said.

Stone Eddie had turned enough to see what was going on. He watched intently, his thumb still hooked in his vest. "I've heard of you, Kid," he said, cutting in.

The young man looked awe-stricken for a second. "You have?"

"I sure have," said Deaks. "You're from up Cimarron way, right?"

"Yeah, that's right," said Lamb, taking on an air, looking both proud and surprised at the same time.

"Shot one of Burt Thompson's brothers dead?" said Deaks. "It was Dowdy Thompson, I believe." He seemed to be recalling the facts as he spoke. "Judge called it self-defense because Dowdy drew first."

Lamb nodded with rapt attention each time Deaks revealed more knowledge of the incident.

"But you still nailed his buttons to his chest." Deaks pointed his cigar at the young man for emphasis.

"Yeah! My goodness, mister," said Lamb, "who are you?"

"I'm Eddie Deaks," Stone Eddie said quietly, lowering his voice almost instinctively, his eyes making a quick sweep of the space around him.

"Oh . . ." Norbert Lamb's easygoing smile turned instantly into an expression of somber respect. "Mr. Deaks, I hope I didn't intrude here. I just wanted to meet Max Thurston and tell him that I'm looking for work—"

"No intrusion at all, Kid," said Deaks, cutting him off with a wave of his cigar. "Right, Max?" He turned his eyes to Thurston and saw the sour look on the gunman's face.

"Looking for work, huh?" said Thurston, making no effort to keep his contempt from showing. "What sort of *work* did you suppose I might have for an upstart like you, Kid Lamb?"

"No," said Lamb, shaking his head, correcting Thurston, "it's either Kid *or* Lamb, but not Kid Lamb." Without changing either his expression or the position of his hand on his gun butt, he added matter-of-factly, "I believe I'd have to shoot a man who called me that after me setting him straight about it."

Thurston looked stunned for a second; but then he caught himself and said, "Oh, would you, now?"

Deaks almost chuckled, seeing how quick Lamb had turned Thurston's belligerence around and shoved it in his face. "Easy now, fellows," Deaks said calmly. "It's a beautiful afternoon. Let's not spoil it by shooting one another full of holes—"

"Stone Eddie Deaks! You are under arrest!" the ranger called out loudly above the den of squeaking wagons and horses' hooves along the street. At the sound of the ranger's voice, the town stopped for a second, as if suspended while the townspeople came to the realization of what was happening.

"Oh my God!" said a voice as all heads turned as one toward the ranger walking straight ahead with deliberation, his eyes fixed on Deaks. Then, as suddenly as the town had stopped in place, it sprang back to life. Along the boardwalk, doors opened and slammed shut as people scurried inside and sought peeping positions at the large windows. Wagons, buggies and horsemen veered away, as if making room for a speeding bullet to find its mark. Before another second had passed, the street had cleared and fallen silent except for the barking of a shaggy stray dog whose afternoon nap had been interrupted.

"Well, well," said Deaks, "speaking of shooting one another full of holes, look who we have here."

"Damn it," Max Thurston growled under his breath, "if he's on to you, he's on to me too."

Seeing the situation that was about to unfold, Lamb sidestepped away from Thurston and Deaks. He made it a point to raise his right hand away from his tied-down Colt. No sooner had he stepped away than Max Thurston shouted, "That's close enough, lawdog!"

Sam kept walking, his right shoulder slightly stooped, his hand holding his bone-handled Colt down against his thigh, already cocked, his thumb on the tip of the hammer. In his left hand he held a wrinkled piece of paper above his head. Ignoring Max Thurston he waved the paper slightly, saying, "Stone Eddie Deaks, you are charged with three counts of murder in the deaths of Warren Knox, Andrew Stampler and Herbert Thorn."

"Murder?" said Deaks, bemused. "Ranger, I should have received some sort of Good Citizen's Award for killing those three snakes!"

"I'm warning you, Ranger," Thurston raged, "don't come any closer!"

"They might have been snakes," Sam said to Deaks, still ignoring Thurston, "but that's not my call. You're charged with murder. I'm bringing you in, head up or facedown. Decide which one suits you, right now."

"That must be *the list* that's becoming so famous in these parts," said Deaks, gesturing his cigar slightly at the list in Sam's hand. The ranger noted that Deaks' other hand remained poised, his thumb still hooked in his vest.

"Don't put me off, Deaks," Sam warned him. "I

know your reputation with a gun. I didn't come here
to—"

Before he could finish his words, Max Thurston's
hand streaked upward, his pistol cocking on the up-
swing. But he didn't get his shot off before Sam's Colt
came into play. Raising no more than the tip of his
gun barrel at his side, the ranger sent a bullet through
Thurston's forehead and knocked him backward
through the bat-wings doors.

"To put up with you resisting arrest," Sam said,
finishing his previous sentence, the Colt smoking in
his hand, the tip of the barrel now aimed at Deaks'
belly.

"Good God!" cried a voice inside the saloon.
While the doors batted down to a halt and Norbert
Lamb stood wiping blood and pulp from his cheek,
Deaks carefully gazed around at one of Max's boots
left lying on the boardwalk.

Looking back at the ranger, Deaks said, "I'm sure
Max would agree, there are worse places to die than
the Topp Dog."

"You heard me, Deaks," said Sam. "What's it
going to be? Are you going to unhook your thumb or
am I?"

"You heard the ranger," Deaks said over his shoulder to Lamb. "What would you do if you were me in
this situation?"

"He's got you cold," said Lamb, his voice sounding serious, a streak of Thurston's blood smeared
down the side of his face.

"Yes, that's true," said Deaks. "But don't forget

what a reputation I have for being a fast draw." His eyes seemed to grow dark on the ranger's. "Of course the ranger here doesn't seem to need a fast draw. He arrives already drawn, cocked, and pointed. And as serious as a pocketful of hornets, I might add." He offered a thin trace of a smile. "Am I reading you about right here, Ranger?"

"To the letter," Sam said, not returning Deak's cordial attitude. "I'm not asking you again, Deaks. The next thing you'll hear is me killing you."

"That is grim," said Deaks. But even as he spoke he eased his thumb slowly from his vest and kept his fingers wide apart, lowering his hand to his side in clear view. "But since I don't believe there is a jury this side of hell that would convict me for killing those three . . . I'm going to allow you take me back to a trial."

"That's a wise decision on your part, Deaks," said Sam, letting him continue with his air of superiority. He had his man without any innocent bystanders getting hurt. That was the main thing. "Step down here nice and easy-like so I can lift that gun from its holster.

"What about me?" Norbert Lamb asked, keeping his hand away from his gun butt.

"What's your name?" Sam said for future reference.

"Norbert Lamb," the young man said, "but my friends call me Kid. Get it?"

"I get it," Sam replied flatly.

"In my case, I call him *Kid Lamb*," Stone Eddie

said. He cut the kid a glance as he stepped down from the boardwalk and spread his arms for Sam to lift the Colt Thunderer from his shoulder holster. "Right, Kid Lamb?" Deaks offered a wry smile.

Lamb's eyes flared, but then immediately settled, realizing that this was Deaks' offer of friendship. He nodded, saying, "Yeah, in his case, he calls me *Kid Lamb*. But nobody else does."

"Mr. Lamb," said the ranger, shoving Deaks' Colt down behind his belt, "as far as I'm concerned, I'd just as soon never have to call you anything." He looked Lamb up and down, eyeing his low-slung tied-down holster, the butt of a Colt sticking up from it. Nodding toward the body of Max Thurston lying inside the saloon doors, he added quietly, "But judging from the company you keep . . . I expect I will."

Lamb looked surprised, almost disappointed. "You mean, I'm free to go?"

Sam gestured sidelong with his head, saying, "Yes, go on. . . . Get out of here."

Still looking surprised, Lamb gave Deaks a glance, shrugged and said, "It was good meeting you, Stone Eddie."

"Same here, *Kid* Lamb," Deaks said, offering a taut smile.

Lamb eased through the bat-wing doors back into the Topp Dog Saloon. As a precaution, Sam nudged Deaks away from the saloon doors before pulling a pair of handcuffs from the back of his gun belt. He clicked the right handcuff on first, then the left one, as Deaks looked down at his wrists.

"Cuffs?" Deaks said, realizing it was really too late for him to resist. "There's no need for cuffs, Ranger." He jerked his wrists back and forth as if testing the cuffs. "Like I said, no jury is going to convict me for shooting those snakes."

"Maybe you're right, Deaks," said the ranger. "In that case, it'd be a shame for you to do something stupid and get yourself killed before you get a chance to clear your good name."

"You think you know all the answers, don't you, Ranger?" Deaks commented.

"No, not all," Sam said bluntly. "Just the one about whether or not you're going to wear these cuffs."

Deaks let out an exasperated breath. "What if I just give you my word that I won't try getting away from you?"

"That would be good, Deaks," said Sam. He gave Deaks a slight nudge toward the hitch rail.

"But it won't gain me anything, will it?" Deaks asked, going to the horses without stalling. He stopped and stood beside his big dust-streaked dun.

"It keeps your hands cuffed in *front* of you, instead of *behind* your back," the ranger replied. "Believe me, Deaks, that's no small thing."

Deaks chuckled, indicating that everything he'd been saying was nothing more than his way of feeling the ranger out. "I've got a hunch riding with you is going to be one of those long, dull trips, Ranger."

Sam holstered his Colt. "I hope so, Deaks. That's the kind of trip I'm looking forward to."

Before Sam could unwrap the reins to Deaks' dun

horse, he saw the town sheriff and a deputy hurrying along the middle of the street toward him. "Hold on, Ranger! Not so fast!" the sheriff called out in a gruff, demanding voice. He carried a thick, three-foot-long hickory club in his big right hand. The deputy carried a shotgun at port arms across his chest. Coming to a halt and giving a quick glance at Max Thurston's boot soles and his blood splattered on the wooden frame above the bat-wing doors, the sheriff growled, "You're not leaving me to clean up your mess!"

"Afternoon, Sheriff Hundley," Sam said in a mild tone. "I was just coming to see you before leaving town."

"Oh, were you, now!" the sheriff said sarcastically. "You might have had the respect to come see me *before* shooting one man dead and taking another man prisoner right under my nose!"

"I looked around some, Sheriff Hundley," said Sam. "I was told by your deputy here that you couldn't be disturbed." He nodded toward the deputy and added, "I'd appreciate you lowering that scattergun into a more friendly position."

"Is that true, Parker?" The sheriff asked, turning a frown to the deputy.

"Hell no, Saul! That ain't how it was, and he knows it!" The deputy's eyes darted back and forth between the two with a worried look. "I told him you was involved in important business! He never even asked me to come along with him! Next thing I know, I heard a gunshot! That's when I came running to get you! Did I do wrong, not telling him where to find you?"

Sheriff Hundley looked embarrassed, as if he'd rather his whereabouts not be discussed. "You did all right, Parker," he said. His eyes went back to Sam. "The ranger should have handled this different, is what I'm saying." He slapped the hickory club up and down against the palm of his hand. "I don't like being overlooked in my own damned town!"

Sam took his prisoner by the forearm and backed him up a step. Then he looked at the deputy and said, "I only ask a person once to lower a scattergun," he said to the deputy. As the shotgun drooped toward the ground, Sam turned his gaze to Sheriff Hundley, saying, "Sheriff, I didn't *overlook* you. I just didn't figure on meddling into your private business." Nodding at the hickory club, he said sternly, "But slap that head buster against your palm one more time, you're not going to like what I'll do with it."

The hickory club stopped abruptly. Sheriff Hundley lowered it to his side, his attitude seeming to cool down. Sam allowed his expression to turn more pleasant as well. "I can assure you, Sheriff, I meant no disrespect. Next time if you want me to, I'll come find you first, no matter where you are."

Before the sheriff could respond, on the boardwalk a tall elderly man stood leaning on a brass handled cane. "Enlighten us all, Sheriff Hundley!" the man called out, a dark scowl on his weathered face. "Tell everybody where you were . . . as if we don't already know!"

"Stay out of this, Bertram!" Sheriff Hundley barked.

"He was laid up with one of the whores above the barbershop!" the elderly man said loudly, turning his head along the boardwalk as if to make sure the whole town heard him.

"That's enough out of you, Bertram!" the sheriff shouted, seeing more and more people beginning to gather along the boardwalk and the dusty street. "All right, Ranger," he said hastily to Sam, "you and I got off on the wrong foot here. Take your man and go. No hard feelings, far as I'm concerned."

Sam nodded toward the blood above the bat-wing doors. "What about the *mess* I'm leaving behind?"

The sheriff looked embarrassed, saying, "Don't worry about it. I'll have the deputy here take care of everything."

"Me? Why me?" the deputy asked.

"Damn it, Parker! Just go along with me here!" the sheriff bellowed, hearing Bertram Elsie telling the townsfolk about the sheriff's frequent trips to the rooms above the barbershop.

Seeing a good chance for him to leave, Sam gave Stone Eddie Deaks a slight nudge toward the horses again. Deaks grinned, looking around the street. "Do you cause this sort of trouble everywhere you go working your *list*, Ranger?"

"I try not to," Sam replied, the two of them swinging up into their saddles, Sam holding the reins to Deaks' big dun. "But I work my list, one way or the other."

Chapter 2

———

Sam and his prisoner rode until the final glow of smoldering red sunlight wreathed the western horizon. When the two did step down and make camp, the ranger gathered loose scrapes of mesquite and dried juniper brush into a mound and started a small fire while Stone Eddie Deaks lay flat on his dusty stomach to keep his black suit coat from burning his back. On his elbows in a short bed of wild grass, he fanned his face with his wide-brimmed hat. He moaned aloud, then said, "Jesus, Ranger! Can you tell me why the hell we had to travel this far before making a camp? Is somebody chasing you?"

"Not me," said Sam, his eyes and ears tuning toward the long shadows stretched across the darkening land. "What about you? Is anybody chasing you?"

Seeing the look on the ranger's face, Deaks' interest piqued. "Hey, is there *really* somebody out there?"

"You tell me," Sam said, in a no-nonsense tone of voice. "You're the one who brought it up."

"Whoa, now, wait a minute, Ranger," said Deaks, himself getting more serious, judging the ranger's expression. "I was just making conversation. If there's anybody following me, it's without my knowing it. I told you, this charge against me isn't worth the paper it's written on. I'm not up to anything."

"I'm going to take your word for it," Sam said. He looked all around in the darkness again. "I'm making you my lookout while I fix us up some coffee."

"*I'm* keeping a lookout?" Deaks asked as if he'd heard him wrong.

"That's right," Sam replied. "Anybody comes upon us without you warning me, I'll just figure you're in cahoots with them."

"Now wait a minute, Ranger," Deaks protested. "You can't make me responsible! I don't know who might be following you . . . or for what reason!"

Sam offered a wry grin. "It's good to have an extra set of eyes, Deaks. Scoot yourself over there against those rocks and pay attention, while I fix us some grub." He walked back to the campfire, seemingly no longer concerned about who might be out there on their trail.

"Whatever you say, Ranger," Deaks responded, moving across the dirt and grass. Once against the rocks he also looked out across the shadowed land, searching for any sign of horse, rider and drifting rise of dust.

Moments later, when the ranger carried a tin cup

of coffee to him, Deaks took the hot cup in his cuffed hands, blew on the steaming liquid, then sipped it.

"Hear anything?" the ranger asked quietly.

"No, not for a while," said Deaks. "I thought I heard something a few minutes ago, but then it stopped."

"Like somebody was following us, but somebody else must've scared them off?" Sam asked.

Deaks gave him a peculiar look. "Yeah, that could've been it. Maybe, now that I think of it." He considered, then asked, "Is that what you think it was?"

"That's what I think it was," Sam said with finality. "Are you hungry?"

"I could eat a horse, hooves and all," said Deaks. He nodded at salt pork frying in a small skillet. "Looks like you cooked plenty."

Sam didn't answer. Instead he walked back to the campfire, stooped down and stirred the salt pork around in the sizzling grease. In a few minutes he returned with a tin plate of salt port and pan-fried bread. He set it down on the ground beside Deaks and asked again, "Have you heard anything else?"

"Yes, just now," said Deaks. He nodded out toward the trail they'd ridden in on. "It sounded like a horse's hooves scraping on rock."

Sam gave him a look of satisfaction, stood up and walked back to the fire. From beside the fire, he raised his Colt from his holster and fired two shots straight up. Deaks flinched in surprise.

Within a second, the ranger's shots received an an-

swer from the desolate terrain. One single pistol rang
out within a hundred yards of the campsite. "That's
my partner, Jonesie," Sam said to Deaks, who sat
watching curiously.

"You mean to tell me that all this time, you've been
on lookout for someone you *knew* would be coming
in tonight?" Deaks asked, sounding put out.

"I thought it might be a good idea to see how you
stand," Sam said, "since we'll be traveling together
the next week. You just made a good impression for
me to pass along to the judge."

"What if I hadn't heard somebody riding in?"
Deaks asked. "Would that have looked bad? Looked
like I was letting you be set up?"

"We won't worry about what didn't happen,
Deaks," said Sam. "You just keep acting like an innocent man should. You'll be surprised how much better off you'll be."

Deaks let Sam's words sink in. He shook his head.
"All right, Ranger, I give. You're calling the shots
from here on in."

"Much obliged, Deaks," Sam said wryly, the
sound of two horses coming closer through the brush
and braken.

"Say, Ranger," Deaks asked as if it had just
dawned on him, "I thought you always worked
alone. What's this about a partner?"

"I do always work alone," said Sam. "But Hadley
Jones is a friend of mine. We're making a few pickup
runs together . . . just until he learns his way around
out here."

"Oh, a *new* man, eh?" Deaks stared at him.

"No, he's not new at being a man," Sam remarked. "But he just started rangering this past year."

"But you've taken him under you wing, so to speak?" Deaks asked.

"Nobody takes anybody under their wing in this business, Deaks," the ranger said, his voice taking on a slight edge, as if some dark memory had crossed his mind.

"No offense, Ranger," Deaks commented, seeing the subtle change come over him. "I suppose I'm having a hard time seeing how you and this man work together."

"None taken," Sam murmured, watching the two horses come into sight from out of the darkness beyond the circle of firelight. "Keep your eyes open, you might see how we work together tomorrow at Marshal Springs. We're making a stop there."

"I'll be watching for sure," said Deaks.

"Hello the camp," said the young ranger, stopping and turning his big roan gelding sideways at the edge of the campsite.

"Hello, yourself, Jonesie," Sam replied. He noted the lead rope in the young ranger's hand. The rope ran back to a sweaty brown pinto on which two dusty prisoners sat staring blankly. The prisoner in front wore a floppy hat pulled low across his forehead, his hands cuffed in front of him. The other prisoner sat slumped behind the saddle, a large bloodstained bandage wrapped around his head. His hands were cuffed behind him; his boots were missing. His dirty big toe stuck out through a hole in his wool sock.

"Any trouble?" Sam asked, nodding toward the prisoners as the two stepped down from the pinto. The one with no boots stepped carefully back and forth until his feet adjusted to the rough ground. He touched his fingertips to his bandaged head.

"None worth mentioning," said Ranger Hadley Jones. "Marvin here is a runner, just like you said he'd be." As he spoke, Jones gave the prisoners a nudge forward toward the campfire. "But once I took his boots, he settled right down."

"Did you have to crack his head for him?" Sam asked looking at the bandage on Marvin Steller's head.

"No," Jones replied. "It was dark when I arrested him. He took off around the side of the boarding-house and ran smack into an iron pole that holds a dinner bell.

Sam winced, getting a picture of the incident. "Goodness," he said quietly.

"You could hear the bell ring halfway across town," Jones added. "It knocked him cold. I had to get Decker here to help me carry him to a doctor."

The other prisoner pushed up his low hat brim and said, "Don't forget you're going to mention to the judge how much help I was." Then he turned his attention to Sam and said, "Evening, Ranger. I figured it would be *you* coming after us, like last time."

"Jones and I are working together for a while," Sam said.

"Oh . . ." Stanley Decker looked at Jones as if appraising him. "Well, if you want my opinion, he did all right. Nobody got kilt or even shot, for that matter. Hadn't been for that iron pole, everything would have been smooth as a ribbon." He glanced at Steller with contempt. "You can't keep a stupid sonsabitch from knocking his brains out, I reckon, once he's bent of doing it."

"My head's busted something awful," Marvin Steller mumbled, paying no attention to Decker. "Who the hell would put an iron pole in the ground that way?" He looked at the ranger for sympathy. "Ain't there already enough stuff stuck in the ground out here as it is? Where's it all going to end?"

Sam shook his head. "I told you last time—don't run once you're caught. It never works out well for you."

"I know," said Steller, his fingertips once again going to his bandaged head. "But running's part of my nature. It always has been."

"You better redefine your nature then," said Sam, "before some lawman shoots you down. You're lucky it was Jones here who came to arrest you."

"You wouldn't have shot me down, would you, Ranger?" Steller asked.

"I don't know, Marvin," Sam replied, not wanting to give the man any ideas about making another run for it. "Shooting might be a part of *my* nature. It's best we don't test each other, I suppose."

Jones had walked back to his horse and taken two tin cups from his saddlebags. He came back to the

fire, stooped down and filled them both, passing the
first one to Joe Decker. "You boys will have to share
that cup," he said. "It's the only extra I've got."

Jonesie set his cup of coffee off to the side, letting
it cool while he walked back to the roan. He loosened
his saddle and pulled it from the horse's back.

"How did the trail look riding in?" Sam asked.

"There was a rider out there," Jones replied, taking
the saddle from the pinto's back and dropping it as
well. "Did you think I had missed seeing him?"

"No," Sam replied, "I figured you saw him . . . either him or his tracks." He smiled to himself, watching Jones drop the bridle from the pinto's mouth.
"You must've scared him off."

Jones walked back toward the campfire, carrying
the bridles from both horses over his shoulder. "Is it
just some passerby or somebody dogging you?" he
asked.

"There's a young gunman named Lamb who was
with Deaks here when I arrested him. It might be
him."

Deaks cut in, saying, "It could be one of the Black
Moons. Max Thurston is one of them. So is his
brother, Calvin. You could end up in big trouble with
those boys, Ranger."

Without acknowledging him, Sam said to Hadley
Jones, "Sounds like my prisoner is concerned about
me."

"Want me to ride out, scout around some, Sam?"
Jones asked. "Maybe he's right. Maybe it's worth
being concerned about."

"Oh, he's right—about the Black Moons and about Calvin Thurston too. But they're not out there tonight. If it was them, we'd already be fighting. If it's anybody, it's Norbert Lamb. He calls himself Kid. He acted like him and Deaks are long-lost brothers." He looked at Jones closer and said, "Besides, we've got to get back to the outpost. There's a wedding about to go on in a town near there . . . remember?"

Jones grinned, stooped down and picked up his coffee. "You bet I do." He sipped the coffee. "This is one wedding I *better* remember."

Lonzo Greer rode at the head of the seven horsemen along the middle of the dirt street that ran the length of Barstow. Looking around in distaste at the nearly deserted town, he said to Paul Metlet, who rode beside him, "Is this Max Thurston's idea of a joke?"

Paul Metlet also observed the small town in disgust. "I've never known Max to joke much about anything." Just out of the middle of the street, a sow lay in a fly-covered puddle of black water and horse urine, nursing her litter of piglets.

"As soon as Max gets back from Cottonwood, remind me to kick the living shit out of him," Lonzo said, swatting flies from his face with his gloved hand.

Metlet let go a stream of tobacco juice and said, "Will do. What the hell is taking him so long anyway?"

"Drunk, most likely," said Lonzo.

Metlet looked at him, watching him stare straight

ahead. "You never did say why you sent him to Cottonwood, did you?"

"Nope, I never did," Lonzo replied, tight-lipped.

"Then I figure it must be something to do with the
bank there?" Metlet probed.

"Nope," said Lonzo, giving him nothing.

"Look, if it's none of my business, just say so,"
Metlet said, sounding exasperated by Lonzo's secre-
tive air.

"If I did, you'd just want to know *why* it's none of
your business," Lonzo said, finally offering a trace of
dark smile.

"That ain't so," said Metlet. "It's just that if I'm
supposed to help keep this bunch in shape, I need to
know what's going on with Max . . . or anybody else
you send to scout out a place for us." He gave a nod
back toward the other riders. "You know how these
men are. They like to know what's waiting for them
around the next bend. To tell you the truth, so do I."

Lonzo stopped his big buckskin in its tracks so
suddenly that it caused the rest of the men to bunch
up behind him. Metlet looked startled, but he caught
himself and stared at Lonzo, as if wondering what
came next from the outlaw leader. "All right, Paul,
listen up," Lonzo said. "I sent Max to talk to a fellow
I've been wanting to join us. He's a big gun out of
Missouri."

"Yeah?" Metlet's expression appeared mixed. "Is it
anybody I know?"

"Could be," said Lonzo, teasing his right-hand
man a little. "Who do you know?"

"Come on, Lon!" Metlet said, sounding put out. "Who is it?"

"All right, it's Stone Eddie Deaks," Lonzo said, almost in a whisper. "Now do you feel any better?"

"Stone Eddie! Jesus!" said Metlet, contemplating the idea of riding side by side with a gunman like Deaks. "I never knew he was a robber!"

"See? That's one more thing you didn't know yesterday that you do know today," said Lonzo. He nudged his horse forward again. "Hell, tomorrow you might just know something else if you try real hard."

"Hear that, men?" Metlet said to the others. "Max is bringing Stone Eddie Deaks with him. A big gun out of Missouri!" He gigged his horse and caught up to Lonzo, wanting to know more. The men looked at one another in mild surprise.

In a soft voice, an aging gunman named Vernon Wilcox said to the man riding nearest to him, "Buck, what's a gunman like Stone Eddie got in mind, wanting to ride with a bunch like us?"

Buck Simpson replied in the same quiet tone, "Who knows? Maybe he's got debtors hounding him."

"That's what it was brought me here," a man named Ernie Shay said, giving a short chuckle. Muffled laughter rippled, then fell quiet as Paul Metlet looked back at the men with a sour dark frown.

"What about you, Owen?" Reverend Vernon Wilcox asked. "Is that what you put you on the owl-hoot trail?"

Owen Reager said, staring straight ahead without cracking a smile, "No. I came from what's called *a troubled childhood*."

"I thought it was all those young'uns you fathered," Calvin Thurston said from the rear of the riders.

"It was that too, once I was grown," said Reager. "It got to where every time I looked at my woman another baby showed up. She finally had so many I had to leave her, go make my living on the trail . . . couldn't stand it at home. All them wild young'uns running around, screaming all the time, *eating* all *the damned* time! It finally turned me into an outlaw. It would anybody I expect."

The men nodded in sympathy. "Lord, yes, it would," said Wilcox.

"What set you afoul of the law, Reverend?" asked Reager.

"Me?" Reverend Wilcox straightened in his saddle and stalled for a moment as if having to consider it. "Well, now, I'm just not sure. A combination of things I reckon."

Buck Simpson cut in, saying, "One night we was drunk, you told me it was because you couldn't make a living preaching."

"Did I sure enough?" Wilcox grinned. "Well, if that's what I said, I guess I best stick to it."

"Was you really a preacher, Wilcox?" asked Reager.

"Hell, yes, I was!" Wilcox said defensively. "I still

am for that matter. Once *Reverend* hooks on to your name, it stays hooked for the rest of your life."

"The Most Reverend Vernon Wilcox," Buck Simpson said, trying out the sound of the name. "I always said it sounds like it fits." He grinned looking Wilcox up and down as if for the first time. "What made you quit?"

"Who said anything made me quit?" Wilcox replied. "I just run out of what to say one Sunday, took off my collar and walked out . . . in the middle of a sermon. Never went back."

When the men offered no comment after a moment of silence, Wilcox shrugged and said reflectively, "Boys, preaching is a hard way to make a living."

"You think *stealing* is easy?" Reager chuckled.

"No, but it's easier than preaching any day," said Wilcox.

"Some say the two are the same," Buck offered, giving Reager a wink. The men chuckled again.

But Wilcox saw no humor in what Buck had said. "That's not true, Buck," he said seriously. "All the time I preached, I never laid a hand in the collection plate. I never took from the building fund, the widow's relief or nothing else."

"Come on now," said Simpson as if he didn't believe him.

"That's the truth, so help me God," said Wilcox.

At the head of the riders, Lonzo stopped and stepped down at a long hitch rail in front of the town's largest saloon. "Drexal's Silver Slipper," Paul

Metlet said, reading a battered overhead sign. He grinned and said to Lonzo, "Sounds like a gentle, fun-loving place to me."

"Yeah, me too," Lonzo replied. He pitched Metlet a leather pouch filled with gold coins and said, "Get the first round on me while I go get rooms for all of us."

"Rooms?" Metlet looked shocked. "For all of us?"

"That's right, segundo," said Lonzo. "No more sleeping on the hard ground for this bunch. We've arrived at the peak of our profession."

"Hear that, men?" said Metlet. "We're all sleeping in rooms tonight!"

As a cheer went up, Lonzo looked at the men, who had began to gather around him. "Boys, we're going to be here for a couple of days. So everybody enjoy themselves." His gaze hardened a bit as he added, "But don't forget what we came here to do and don't go telling our business to every wide-eyed whore you meet." He stepped down amid the cheers of the men, wrapped his horse's reins around the hitch rail and started walking toward a dusty clapboard siding hotel a half block away.

"This is all good, Metlet," Calvin said, stepping up beside the second in charge, "but what about my brother, Max? How come we ain't heard nothing from him like we should have by now?"

"I don't know, Calvin," said Metlet, "but don't worry about it. He'll show up. If he doesn't, we'll go looking for him."

"We better," said Calvin with a bit of a threat in his

voice. "Anything happens to my brother, some-body's going to pay up for it with their life. Do you understand me?"

"Jesus, yes!" said Metlet. "I understand. Now come on let's relax and wash some of this desert out of our bellies."

Chapter 3

In the silvery hour of dawn, Sam and Jones led their prisoners quietly along the back trail into Marshal Springs. They stopped in a litter-strewn alley behind the jail and Sam slipped down from his saddle and knocked on the jail's wooden back door. When a moment passed without a response, he knocked again, this time louder. Another moment passed. "Wait here, Jonesie," Sam said. "I'll go and check around front."

Jones nodded, backed his horse into a position where he could better keep an eye on the three prisoners and sat with his hand on the Winchester repeating rifle lying across his lap. No sooner was Sam out of sight than Stone Eddie Deaks nudged his horse forward an inch closer to the young ranger. "If you don't mind me saying so, Ranger Jones," he said, "you look a mite nervous this morning. Are you sure you have the stomach for law work?"

"Find out for yourself," Jones replied calmly. The

Winchester swung up from his lap without hesitation and cocked toward Deaks, causing the gunman to nudge his horse back into place.

"Whoa!" Deaks chuckled. "I was only making a little conversation!"

"Don't," Jones said flatly.

Deaks gave the other two prisoners a glance. Seeing that they had no interest in helping him goad the young ranger, he shook his head and sat slumped and silent until Sam reappeared around the corner of the building. Beside Sam, a thin man in a white merchant's apron carried a ring of keys. While he nervously sorted out the back door key, Sam said to Jones, "This is Alvin Hack, the mercantile owner." To Hack he said, "This is my partner, Hadley Jones."

"Pleased," said Hack, his attention going back to the key almost before Jones could tip his hat in reply. He stuck the key into the back door lock, turned and swung the door open. "Here you are, Ranger," Hack said to Sam, jerking the key from the lock and handing the ring to Sam. "I'm glad to hand these over to a real lawman."

"We're not going to be here long, Mr. Hack," Sam said. "Just long enough to do our job."

"I understand that, Ranger," said Hack. "But if you rid this town of McAllister and his rats, you'll be doing more than Sheriff Eiler ever could—not meaning to speak ill of the dead of course."

"Mr. Hack told me that three days ago McAllister and his friends killed the town sheriff," Sam explained to Jones, who sat with his rifle covering the three prisoners while they dismounted.

"That's too bad," said Jones, stepping down himself. "I wish we'd gotten here sooner."

"The sonsabitches—if you'll pardon my language," said Hack. "They made poor old Eiler dance in the middle of the street, like some sort of fool!" He watched Jones lead the prisoners through the door, then followed Sam inside, saying, "Whatever you do to them won't be harsh enough, Ranger. If you want to string them up from a barn rafter, I'll provide you with brand-new rope, free of charge!"

"We don't hang, Mr. Hack," said Sam matter-of-factly. "We just arrest."

"Well, just so you know," said Hack, "this town is behind you fellows one hundred percent."

"Obliged," said Sam, looking all around the sheriff's office, three cells with their iron doors standing wide open.

"We had the town drunkard, Curtis Renfrow, in jail, working off a fine for relieving himself off the edge of the boardwalk. But with Sheriff Eiler dead, we told Curtis to go on home."

"How many days did he have left?" Sam asked. He watched Jones step aside and motion the prisoners into one of the cells and close the iron door behind them.

"Just two or three is all," said the storekeeper.

"When you see him, tell him to get back over here," Sam replied, taking a look around the office, seeing that the place could use a good cleaning. "I want those two days worked off."

"Yes, sir!" said Hack. "I'll tell him straight away! He's usually at the saloon door, waiting for the place to open."

"Where will we find McAllister?" Jones asked, lifting his dusty hat and slapping it against his leg.

"They stay at the only hotel in town. The Royal," said Hack, pointing off toward the far end of town. "Florence Macey will be happy to get rid of them. Her husband died from snakebite last year. She stayed here running the Royal herself. McAllister and his rats have broken three windows and done God knows what all else to the place. They run off all her other guests!"

"That's too bad," Sam commented. "But we'll soon have them out of here." Looking around, he noted the door to the wood stove hanging open and said, "We could use a pot of hot coffee."

"Yes, of course," said Hack, "I'll go get one from Brady's restaurant straightaway." He hesitated before going out the door, saying, "Should I also bring back some breakfast, for both of you?"

"That would be greatly appreciated, Mr. Hack," said Jones.

Deaks shoved his wrists through the service opening in the bars so Jones could unlock his cuffs. "And don't forget us prisoners," he called out to Hack. He stepped to the side rubbing his freed wrists as Jones unlocked the cuffs on Steller and Decker. "I like my eggs unturned, with some thick cut bacon . . . a bowl of hot gravy standing beside them."

Hack gave the rangers a questioning look. "Yes, bring them some food," Sam said, "I'll sign script for it."

"Nonsense," said Hack. "This whole breakfast is on me."

"Then we are obliged, sir," said Hadley Jones.

"It's the least I can do," said Hack, "you gentlemen coming all the way here to help us rid ourselves of this murdering vermin. God bless you both." He backed his way out the door and hurried off toward a restaurant across the street.

"That's the part I'm still having trouble getting used to," Jones said. "It still feels like I'm taking advantage some way, letting a town give me a free breakfast."

"Don't worry, Jonesie," said Sam. "He knows the whole town will feel like it's been paid back in full when they all see us taking McAllister out of here."

"Shouldn't you be saying *if* you take Jake McAllister out of here, Ranger?" Deaks cut in, including himself in the conversation. He stood with both hands wrapped around bars on the cell door, a smug grin on his face.

"We'll be taking him out of here all right," said Jones. "Don't you worry about that."

Sam didn't answer.

"You sound awfully cocksure of yourself, Jones," said Deaks. "I know Jake McAllister well enough to tell you that he is no light piece of work."

Jones said confidently, "You're right. I am sure of myself . . . and Sam. We'll take him out of here, one way or the other."

Deaks grinned. "What about you, Ranger Burrack? I don't hear you saying anything. Are you as sure as the new man here?"

"We came here to do a job, Deaks," Sam replied grudgingly. "We'll get it done."

"But you're not saying much about it, Ranger. How come?" Deaks chided.

"Because I don't socialize with prisoners, Deaks," said Sam. "Now shut up and sit down, or I'll see to it you get some cold grits while the rest of us enjoy a hot breakfast."

Deaks made a gesture of surrender, backed away from the iron-barred door and turned to a cot along the right side of the cell, where Stanley Decker sat slumped, rubbing his wrists. "Move it, Decker," he said in a menacing tone.

Decker hurriedly left the cot and sat back down beside Steller on the other cot across the cell. Seeing Deaks bully the man, Sam said quietly to Jones, "Maybe we best separate them out before breakfast. Put Deaks in the next cell by himself."

"Right," said Jones. "I suppose I should have done that to begin with."

"No, you did it right, Jonesie," said the ranger. "The main thing was to get them behind bars. Now that we see how Deaks is going to act, we'll separate them."

Jones nodded, walked to the cell with the key in

his hand and said as he turned the lock, "All right, Deaks, come on. You get a private cell all to yourself."

Deaks grinned, then started to walk out of the cell and to the open cell next to it. He stopped in the open door and said over his shoulder to Jonesie, "Shouldn't you have cuffed me first, making a move like that?"

Jones caught the goading sarcasm in Deaks' voice. Giving him a nudge into the cell he said, "Keep it up, Deaks."

"Now that sounded like a threat to me," Deaks said, grinning as he looked all around his new cell before flopping down on a cot. He swung himself back flat, threw his forearms beneath his head and crossed his boots. "Ranger Burrack," he called out, "maybe you better inform your helper that I'm going to be going free as soon as I stand before the judge. I wouldn't want him confusing me with these common criminals."

"He's trying his best to get under my skin," Jones said just between the two of them.

"Don't let him." Sam walked to the front window and looked idly back and forth along the street.

"I won't," said Jones. "But what's the whole story on him, Sam?" He walked up and stood at Sam's side.

"When it comes to being smart, Stone Eddie is a cut above the average gunslinger, and he knows it," said Sam. "Word has it his pa was an attorney in Philadelphia. Some of it rubbed off I suppose. Stone

Eddie is smart and he's slick. He's always finds a way to be in the right when it comes to a shoot-out."

"Even this time?" Jones asked.

"Especially this time," Sam answered, still searching the wide, empty street in the early-morning light. At the mercantile, a wagon had pulled up in the grainy light and begun loading sacks of flour and supplies. Two men in business suits appeared out front of a land titled office, one checking his pocket watch.

"He's right in what he said about no jury convicting him for killing those three snakes," Sam continued. "Every judge west of Missouri wanted to see them stretch rope. They were murderers and cattle thieves, but no witness ever stayed alive long enough to testify against them. But then they made the mistake of rustling from Carl Landsford Tappensfeld, the president of the West Plains Cattlemen's Association."

"The association hired Deaks to hunt them down?" Jones asked.

"Yep," said Sam, "which they had every right to do, for the purpose of bringing them to trial anyway."

"But Tappensfeld didn't want these men brought to trial," Jones said, figuring the situation out as they went along.

Sam nodded slightly. "That's right, not after these three had gotten off so many times before. Men like Tappensfeld say the only thing time is good for is fattening cattle. He wasn't about to waste his in court, just to watch these men go free. He paid Deaks to kill them. So Deaks did. In broad daylight, in front of the whole town. Not because of the cattle they stole, but because they supposedly picked a fight with him and drew first."

Jones looked around at Deaks, seeing his dirty boot soles propped up on the cot. "He's that fast, huh?" He turned back to Sam. "Fast enough that he could let three men draw on him, then shoot them down?"

"He's alive, they're dead," Sam responded. "That says it all."

"That must take some nerve," Jones said, "to stand there and wait until the other man has already made his move before going for your gun."

"Yes, it does," Sam said, turning and taking a glance at Deaks himself, then looking back out the window. "But if a man has that kind of confidence in himself, and his nerves will let him hold out that long, he walks away from the hangman's noose every time." Sam paused, then added, "It's perfect for a killer like Stone Eddie Deaks."

"The law never wavers on its position?" Jones asked.

"Not that I've ever seen," Sam replied. "Once a man's hand begins raising his gun toward another with the clear intent of bringing bodily harm, the court says anything you do to defend yourself is justified."

The two stood in silence for a moment as if letting a variety of possibilities cross their minds. Finally, Sam asked, "Does that sound fair enough to you?"

"Yes, it does," Jones said. "How do these badges play into it?"

"They don't," said Sam. "If you ever draw first and kill a man in front of witnesses, you're in some serious trouble."

"A lawman could hang for doing his *job*?" Jones asked quietly.

"Killing for no reason isn't a lawman's *job*," Sam replied.

"But you know what I mean," said Jones. "How have you managed to get so much done, stay alive and not get yourself in trouble?"

"The law gives the criminal an advantage going in," Sam explained. "The criminal knows it, and he uses it. The first thing I do is take that advantage away from him. I try to always go in with my Colt already in hand, cocked and ready to fire. The law doesn't say I have to carry my gun in a holster, just that I can't be the first to grab it."

"So it tells the criminal where you stand," said Jones.

"Yep. He knows that he *had* the advantage of making the first move, but that I just took that advantage away from him." Sam smiled flatly. "He knows that I have fulfilled the letter of the law and have come prepared to do some killing if need be."

"What if you ever had to draw, one on one, Sam?" Jones asked.

"I've had to a couple of times," Sam replied. He gazed off again along the street.

"Are you—" Jones hesitated, then said, "I mean, *are* you fast?"

"I'm alive, Jonesie," Sam said.

"Yes, but I mean, how fast is that?" Jones pressed.

Sam didn't answer. Instead, something up the street caught his attention and he said, "Four riders coming in from the south."

A moment of silence passed as the two stared through the lifting gray of morning. "Is that McAllister?" Jones asked quietly.

Another moment passed while the four riders reined their horse to the front of the Royal Hotel and stepped down from their saddles at the hitch rail. "Yes, that's him," Sam said in a calm voice, his hand slipping instinctively to the butt of his Colt. "I was hoping this would wait until after breakfast."

Chapter 4

Stepping onto the boardwalk in front of the Royal Hotel, Jake McAllister came to an abrupt halt and stared down at his black suit, his dress shirt and three pairs of socks lying in a loose pile on the dusty planks. "What the hell is this?" he asked no one in particular.

Along the boardwalk lay three more piles of clothes, half-empty whiskey bottles and dusty saddlebags, personal belongings of the other riders. "We've been tossed from the premises!" said Rodney Floyd, a bemused look on his whiskey-lit face.

"Well, by God, now!" said an older gunman named Giles Pruitt. "This place has better taste than I thought!" He laughed aloud at his joke.

"Shut up, you fools!" Jake McAllister shouted at the two drunken gunmen. Over his shoulder he said to the third gunman, a serious-looking man wearing a dried human ear on a golden watch fob, "Fox! Check the street!" Pruitt and Floyd both stopped laughing instantly and stepped back and looked all around the empty street. Porter Fox stepped down from the boardwalk and turned a slow complete circle, checking doorways and alley entrances.

"What's the matter, Jake?" Rodney Floyd asked.

"I'll tell you *what's the matter*!" McAllister growled in reply. "This stupid she-bitch wouldn't have enough guts to throw my belongings out like this unless she thought somebody was in town to protect her!" He glanced all around again warily and said in a lowered voice, "I smell *law*, something fierce!"

"That's right, you bastards! There is a lawman in town!" Florence Macey called out through an open peep panel in the locked front door of the hotel. "He's Sam Burrack, the same men who killed Junior Lake and his whole rotten gang! He's here to kill you pigs for everything you've done to me!"

Rodney Floyd called out in reply, "You've enjoyed every minute of it, you white-livered bitch!"

"Shut up, Bobby!" shouted McAllister. To the face in the peep panel he said, "Florence, if you know what's good for you, you'll get your house man out here to get my belongings off the street!"

Fifty yards away, hearing the argument between Florence and the gunmen, Sam said to Hadley Jones, "Well, there goes any element of surprise." He glanced at the shotgun Jones had picked up from the gun rack. "Take the scattergun and disappear. Be ready to come out and throw down on the other three when I start tangling with McAllister."

"Right, Sam!" Jones veered away and ducked into an alley.

At the same time, Sam saw McAllister's fist crash through the peep panel in the hotel door and heard Florence Macey scream, "Turn me loose, Jake!"

"Unlock that door, damn you!" Jake raged. "Or so help me God, I'll empty your brains all over that carpet!" He held his cocked Colt up beneath his arm that stretched inside through the open panel, his hand holding Florence by her flaming red hair.

"Wait, Jake, *please!*" Florence pleaded with him. "I'm unlocking it! There, see?" The door opened slowly, until Jake McAllister reached in with his gun still in hand, grabbed her by her dress and jerked her out against him, the tip of his gun barrel under her chin.

"Now, then, whore!" he shouted, making adjustments, his free hand once again grabbing her by her hair. He pressed his pistol barrel against her temple. "Tell me how some ranger is going to kill me!"

"Jake, please! I didn't mean it!" she shouted.

"Turn her loose, McAllister!" the ranger demanded from the middle of the street, twenty yards away and still advancing. He held his big Colt down against his thigh, his thumb on the cocked hammer.

McAllister and his men jerked their attention toward the sound of Sam's voice. Even though they had been scanning the street, they had somehow missed the single figure approaching them. "Where the hell . . . ?" Rodney Floyd murmured.

"Turn her *loose,* you say?" Jake McAllister drew

Florence Macey tighter to his chest. "That's not at all what I have in mind for this sow!" With his pistol jammed to her forehead, he said, "Spread out, boys, unless you want to get her brains all over your clean shirts!" He shook Florence and said, "I'll teach you to bring the law down on me!"

"She didn't bring me, Jake," Sam said coolly. "I was already on my way here to kill you."

"To kill me?" Jake laughed at the idea. "First of all, you couldn't kill me on your best day!" The other three men chuckled as they spread out, Porter Fox stepping farther away from the boardwalk and moving wide around Sam, putting Sam in a half circle among them. But to the gunmen's surprise, the ranger kept advancing slowly. "Second," McAllister continued, "whatever happened to a man getting a fair trial?"

"Come on, Jake, a court trial?" Sam said, as if they were old acquaintances. "I'm disappointed in you. I only put you on my list because I figured a man like you would want to go down fighting." He glanced at the other three men. "Same goes for your men here. What about it, boys? Wouldn't you rather I killed all of you right here than dragged you before a judge? Have to spend a day or two just sitting, hearing what no-accounters you are?"

The men didn't answer, but Rodney Floyd said out the corner of his mouth, "He's still coming, Jake!"

"Yeah, I see that, Bobby!" said McAllister, looking a bit pressed by this single ranger walking him down, giving no regard to the numbers against him. "That's close enough, Ranger!" he shouted.

Sam stopped and looked around, standing no more than fifteen feet from the boardwalk, where McAllister stood. "Yes, I believe you're right, Jake," he said. As he spoke, Sam raised his Colt as calmly and as naturally as a man might raise an arm to point directions. McAllister didn't seem to realize what the ranger was doing until he stared into the black hole of the gun barrel.

"Now how the hell did you do that?" McAllister said, looking impressed at how the ranger had suddenly gotten the drop on him.

"That's only half of it, Jake," Sam said. "Put the woman aside and let's get down to the rest of this business."

"Sounds good to me," said Jake. He gave Florence a rough shove away from him. In doing so, he aimed the tip of his barrel away from her head and pointed it squarely at the ranger. "Whoa!" he said, raising his brow in feigned surprise. "Now we are evened up, Ranger! What do you think of that?"

"That was clever. . . ." Sam stalled as if caught off guard, letting his words trail, watching Florence scurry away to safety behind a stack of empty wooden shipping crates.

"Looks like the cat's got his tongue, Jake," Rodney Floyd said.

From the corner of an alley, seeing Sam and McAllister standing with their Colts out at arm's length, cocked toward each other with little room between them, Ranger Jones raised the scattergun to his shoulder. "Jesus, Sam!" Jones whispered to himself. "That's too close!"

"What about it, Ranger?" McAllister asked. "Are you all out of smart mouthing?"

"Yep," Sam said grimly. "I'm all out of everything, Jake. I came here prepared to die. . . . I hope you're prepared as well."

Something flickered in McAllister's eyes, a dark realization brought on by the ranger's words. The ranger was right. At this distance, neither one of them would come out of this alive. Jake saw that fact so clearly that it gave him pause. For only a second, a hesitancy swept across his mind. But the ranger saw it in his eyes, and that second was all he needed. His hammer fell.

Jake McAllister's eyes crossed as the red bullet hole appeared between them and lifted him backward against the front of the Royal Hotel. In reflex, the dead gunman's hand squeezed off a shot that nipped at Sam's shirtsleeve. But Sam ignored it as he turned quickly, disregarding Porter Fox, and put his next shot in Rodney Floyd's chest, dropping him dead. Even as his shot exploded, Sam heard the scattergun bark loudly from the alley, picking Fox up from behind and slinging him forward, facedown on the dirt street.

"Wait! Don't shoot!" Giles Pruitt shouted, raising his hands high as the ranger swung his Colt toward him. "I'm out of it! I'm out of it!"

"Then keep your hands raised high and turn your

back to me," the ranger demanded, seeing Jones come out of the alley with the scattergun still against his shoulder, pointing it quickly from one downed gunman to the next.

"Are you all right, Sam?" Jones asked, seeing the hole in the ranger's shirtsleeve.

"I'm good. What about you, Jonesie?" While Sam spoke, he stepped forward behind Giles Pruitt, lifted the other man's pistol from its holster and shoved it down into his belt.

"I'm all right too." Jones shook his head, looking around at the dead gunmen. "Sam, that was a risky thing you did, walking into them like that."

"I know," Sam replied. "But they had a woman held hostage. I saw no other way." He looked over at Florence Macey, who stood straightening her mussed up hair while she stared at the bodies on the ground. "Are you all right, ma'am?" he asked.

"Yes, Ranger, thank you," Florence replied coolly, glancing toward Jake McAllister's body. "I'm fine now that *this* bastard is dead."

"I never harmed her," Pruitt pointed out, glancing over his shoulder at the ranger.

"That's right, he never," said Florence. "He was a gentleman compared to these lousy sonsabitches." She spit at Rodney Floyd's body.

"I'm glad to hear that," said Sam, seeing the woman had bounced back quickly from her ordeal. He smelled the odor of sour whiskey as he lifted a pair of handcuffs from behind his back, cuffed Pruitt's hands and turned him around.

"Ranger, I just want to let you know that I ain't wanted by *anybody* anywhere," Pruitt said quickly, his breath reeking of cheap rye.

"We'll see about that, Giles," Sam said. "If you're not, we'll let you go."

"You two know one another?" Jones asked.

Before Sam could answer, Pruitt cut in saying, "Oh, hell, yes! I know Ranger Sam Burrack. That is, I seen him in action last year in Bentonville. That's why I didn't go for my gun."

"That was a wise move on your part, Giles," Sam replied. Then matter-of-factly he asked, "Why did these other two make such a strong stand for McAllister? I never knew of him having so many loyal friends."

"I don't know, Ranger," said Pruitt, shrugging. "I reckon they felt like they owed him something."

Sam gave him a questioning stare. "Come on, Giles, you'll have to do better than that."

"I swear, Ranger, I have no idea why they backed him. We both know that Jake McAllister is—that is, he *was*"—he corrected himself as he gazed over at the dead gunman—"the most unlikable sonsabitch the devil ever spit out of Hades." Pruitt shook his head. "I remember once, when me and him were up the Wind River country, my horse came up lame and I said, 'Jake, why don't we—' "

"That's enough, Giles," Sam said, realizing the gunman was only talking to keep from giving him any sort of answer. "Just remember that the more you stall around and lie to me, the longer it's going to take for me to *telegraph* around and see if you're on anybody's wanted list."

Giles shrugged again, this time in an appeal for sympathy. "Ranger, you know what happens when a man gets to talking about the wrong fellows out here! You don't want to get me killed, do you?"

Sam looked him up and down, seeing nervous sweat form on his forehead. He looked down at Pruitt's cuffed hands, noting the slightest tremor in his thumbs. "All right, Giles, forget it. For your own good I'm going to keep you in jail for three days. We're going to see to it you get some good wholesome food in your belly."

"Obliged, Ranger," said Pruitt, "but I ain't really hungry. I eat like a bird, as they say."

Sam continued talking, as if he hadn't heard the aging gunman. "We'll get some hot water and a bathing tub. Let you soak all that whiskey out of your system. It'll be good for you."

"Good for me?" Pruitt swallowed a knot in his throat, looking terrified at the ranger's suggestion. "Ranger, I don't *want* to get sobered up. I've managed to stay on an even drunken keel more than the past two years! I'm good right where I'm at, not too drunk, not too sober. If I drink any more or any less, I'll start unraveling like a wool sweater! Believe me, I know!"

"Come on, Giles, let's get started," Sam insisted, nudging him toward the jail, as if he hadn't heard a word he'd said. "You're going to feel like a new man in no time at all."

Pruitt stopped in his tracks. "All right, Ranger, ask me whatever you want to ask me. I'll cooperate."

"That's better," said Sam, stopping, Jones stepping in beside him, listening as he replaced the spent shotgun load. "Now tell us why you men spent last night sleeping out when you had rooms waiting at the Royal Hotel."

"All right," said Pruitt. He looked back and forth warily, then said in a lowered voice, "We met with Bobby Caesar and his boys. The fact is we were talking about throwing in with them and robbing a place or two." He nodded toward the three bodies on the ground. "I expect you've soured that notion for us."

Sam gave a sigh, saying, "Bobby Caesar, Leon Maddox, Purple Joe Croom." He shook his head. "Every rock we turn over leads us to another den of snakes."

"Are we going after them, Sam?" Jones asked.

"Not this time, Jonesie," said Sam. He gave Pruitt another nudge toward the jail.

"You ain't going to make me sober up now, are you, Ranger? I've told you everything straight up."

"I'll get the telegrams sent off this morning, Giles," said Sam. "If you're not wanted anywhere, you'll be riding out of here before nightfall."

"Obliged, Ranger," said Pruitt. "Do you suppose I could get just a little shot of rye . . . enough to keep my eyes from watering?"

"Don't push your luck, Giles," Sam warned him.

Chapter 5

By midafternoon, Curtis Renfrow had the street in Marshal Springs looking as if nothing had happened. The only signs of the earlier gunfight were the three bodies of the gunmen that the townsmen had tied to rough oak boards and propped up in the shade of the boardwalk in front of the barbershop. The town photographer had shown up within minutes of the shooting and taken pictures of each gunman individually and one larger picture of all three for the town newspaper.

When the photographer had gathered his camera and equipment and left, the town fell back into its routine, the only difference being that arriving wagons and horseback travelers alike veered in close to the barbershop for a better look at the grim exhibition. On the front of the Royal Hotel, Florence Macey's handyman had quickly posted a sign that read in bold letters, the paint still wet and shiny:

NO BUMMERS, GUNMEN, OR DRUNKARDS
ALLOWED.

Standing in front of the sheriff's office, Sam sent the telegraph delivery boy away with a dime tip and read the message he'd brought him. He folded the telegram and gazed off at the Royal Hotel, watching Florence Macey welcome a young couple inside the hotel with a wide sweep of her arm. As the couple stepped inside, Florence looked over at the ranger and gave a friendly smile and a slight curtsy. Sam touched the brim of his sombrero in response and turned his gaze across the sky toward a dark storm cloud on the distant horizon.

"I bet you'd be more than welcome to spend the night there with Florence, Ranger," said Curtis Renfrow, who stood smiling wistfully toward the Royal Hotel. He stood down in the street, a long-handled broom in his hands. "I must say, that is one fine, handsome woman! If her hair is as red all over as it is on her head, my goodness, I bet a man could just about fall—"

"Curtis!" Sam said, cutting him off.

Curtis' smile faded as he looked up and saw Sam give him a flat, cold stare from the edge of the board-walk. "Are you about finished up?" Sam asked, ignoring the comment about Florence.

"Well, I suppose I am," Curtis said, quickly lifting his broom and shaking it as he looked all around the freshly cleaned street, "unless you have more you want done this evening."

"No," said the ranger, "that's all for today. Go on home. Tomorrow will be your last day for working off your fine."

"Whew, I'm glad of that," said Curtis. He wiped a hand across his forehead. "It ain't that I mind working. It's just that I hate taking on added responsibility. I can't stand having people rely on me! It gives me the willies, just thinking about it." He shivered all over for a second, as if suddenly stricken with a chill. Then he propped the broom against the boardwalk, tipped his fingers to his bare head and walked away. No sooner was he out of sight than Ranger Jones walked out of the sheriff's office and stood next to Sam.

"Any word back yet about Giles Pruitt?" Jones asked.

"Yep," said Sam, handing him the telegram he held in his hand. "I just had this delivered to me a couple of minutes ago."

"Well," said Jones after reading it, "what do you want to do?"

"We'll have to let him go for now," Sam said.

"That seems like a shame," said Jones, "especially after him telling us they were all about to go on a robbing spree."

"Pruitt has been a criminal his whole life," Sam said. "His name will show up again sooner or later. When it does, we'll get him."

"I know," said Jones, nodding in agreement. "He's told us everything he knows about what Bobby Caesar and his Lost Canyon gang is up to. That's worth something."

"You bet it is," said Sam. "Next time we see him, he might tell us something about another hard case or two he's been riding with. He gets around well among the kind of men we're hunting for."

"You're right," said Jones. "Still, I wish we could get more done this trip."

"We can't though," said Sam, "not if we're going to get you back in time for your wedding." He turned to the office door, Jones following him. "Don't worry. There'll be plenty of lawbreakers left for us on our next trip. Crime is a booming business. I don't look for it to fall off anytime soon."

Inside the office, Sam held up the telegram for Pruitt to see from his seat on the edge of a cot in the cell with Stone Eddie Deaks. "Guess what this says, Pruitt?" Sam called out.

"Is that about me?" Pruitt asked, standing up with an anxious look on his face. "Good news, I hope?"

"As good as can be," said the ranger. "He walked over with the key to the cell in his hand. "We're letting you out of here."

"You mea—mean, it came back saying I'm not wanted anywhere?" he stammered with a surprised expression on his face.

"Isn't that what you said too?" Sam asked. "Didn't you say you weren't wanted anywhere?"

"Well, yes, I did say that." Pruitt still looked surprised. "But when you've been drunk as long as I have, you often forget things. A fellow never knows when somebody might be falsely accusing him of something he ain't even aware of."

"Not in this case, Giles," Sam said, turning the key in the lock and throwing open the iron-barred door. "You're clean as a cat's whiskers." He paused for a second, then said, "Unless there's something you want to tell us about, that is."

"Nope, not a thing that I can think of," said Pruitt, shaking his head vigorously. He walked out of the cell and stopped and turned at the oaken desk, where he saw his pistol lying atop a stack of papers. "Can I?" he asked, nodding at the pistol. He stood nervously rubbing his hands up and down his trouser legs.

"Sure you can," said Sam. He closed and locked the cell door, then stepped over to pick up the pistol from the desk and hand it to Pruitt, butt first. "It's not loaded anymore, Giles." Reaching into his pocket, Sam lifted the six bullets he'd taken from the Colt and handed them to Pruitt. "Don't load it until you get outside of Marshal Springs." Sam took an envelope from his shirt pocket and handed it to the eager gunman.

"All right by me, Ranger," Pruitt said, tearing open the envelope and counting the seven dollars he'd had in his pocket when the rangers had brought him to jail. Putting the money away, he motioned for Sam to step farther away from the cells. Once Sam did so, Pruitt leaned in close to him and said, "Ranger, I'd appreciate it if you wouldn't go telling anybody that I mentioned Bobby Caesar or what we were planning to do."

"Don't worry, Giles," Sam assured him. "I won't mention anything about it so long as you keep letting me know what's going on out there from time to time."

"You mean keep on telling you everything I know about fellows I ride with?" He looked stunned and said in a guarded tone, "Ranger, I can't do that! What kind of man would go around telling on his friends all the time?"

"The kind of man who doesn't want me to let his friends know that he told me about them in the first place," Sam said barely above a whisper himself.

"Oh no!" said Pruitt, rubbing his forehead. "What kind of pact have I made with you law devils?"

"The kind you want to be very careful not to break, Giles," Sam said, patting his shoulder as he ushered him to the door. "Your horse is still saddled and waiting at the rail."

"You don't treat a fellow half bad, Ranger." Pruitt turned for a moment with a grin, throwing his hand in the air toward the other three prisoners. "*Adios!*" he called out.

Deaks stood with both hands wrapped around the bars on the cell door. He shook his head, chuckled to himself and said to the ranger, "I hope you haven't believed a word that old rummy told you about any-*thing* or anybody."

"Oh?" Sam feigned a surprised look. "Who says

Giles Pruitt told me anything about anything or anybody?"

Deaks grinned, saying, "Come on, Ranger, everybody out here knows that McAllister and his boys were trying to join forces with Bobby Caesar. I figure Pruitt started putting that into your ear no sooner than you snapped the cuffs on him, seeing if he could make things easier for himself."

Sam gave Jones a glance, the two of them realizing that if Pruitt hadn't told them about Bobby Caesar and his gang, Deaks just did.

"Then why don't you set me straight, Deaks?" Sam replied. "Tell me all about Bobby and his boys so I won't be chasing off in the wrong direction when I have to go after them."

"A man would have to be a fool to tell you something like that, Ranger," said Deaks. In the next cell, Steller and Decker nodded their heads in agreement. "But I'll tell you one thing. Whoever Pruitt runs into first out there will hear every detail about you shooting down Max Thurston. You can count on that."

Sam hooked the key ring to the cells on his belt and said, "I *am* counting on that, Deaks." Ending his conversation with Deaks, he turned to Jones and said, "Looks like we've got a storm coming down on us tonight. We might just as well spend the night here, let everybody rest up and head out first thing in the morning."

Sheriff Anderson Goins looked out through his office window toward the sound of cursing, laughter and gunshots in front of Drexal's Silver Slipper Saloon. "Forrest, grab yourself a shotgun," he said over his shoulder to his deputy, Forrest Bidson, who sat relaxed with his boots propped up on a battered oaken desk, as if nothing were going on.

"*A shotgun?*" the deputy responded, becoming suddenly alert, his boots coming down to the floor. "What the hell for, Sheriff?"

"They're taking this town apart, Deputy," said Sheriff Goins. "One of them just threw a whore out the window atop the Silver Slipper." He drew his Colt and checked it quickly. "Now get that shotgun and let's get moving here."

"Is she dead? Is she *hurt*?" the deputy asked, still sitting, watching the sheriff continue to prepare himself for battle.

"She's alive," said Sheriff Goins, slipping his Colt back into its holster and sliding it up and down, loosening it up. "She's limping back inside the saloon, nothing covering her but the washcloth that fell with her."

"Really?" That got Forrest Bidson's attention. He stood up and stepped over quickly, hoping for a look. But all he saw was a glint of white skin as the young woman disappeared through the bat-wing doors into a loud round of whistling and clapping of hands. "Damn, I missed it," Bidson murmured to himself.

The sheriff looked at him, narrowing and hardening his gaze. "Are you with me, Deputy, or not? This is the day that we find out just how much wearing a badge means to you. These are the kind of men the town of Barstow hired us to go up against. I can't let this town down when it needs me, can you?"

Bidson grinned. "Oh, hell, yes, I can! And I'm glad to do it. Remember last month, the town counsel spent two hours deciding whether or not they needed me any longer? Well, looks like it's time they find out the hard way that they *do*."

"For God's sake, Deputy," said the sheriff, "if you won't do it for the town, do it for me. If you don't take up that shotgun, I'll have to do it myself. Is that what you want?"

"It suits the hell out of me," said the deputy. He hurried to the gun rack, took down a shotgun, checked it, clicked it shut and shoved in into the sheriff's weathered hands. "There you go, Sheriff, all loaded and ready for you." He grinned widely. "I'll just watch from the window here and see how things go for you."

Sheriff Goins looked at the shotgun in his hands, then back at the deputy, letting the words sink in on him. Finally he said, "Why, you cowardly son of a bitch. You stay here then. I don't want a scared bastard like you dying beside me."

"That makes *two* of us, Sheriff," Bidson beamed. "Now go out there and give them hell." He walked to the door, opened it and made a sweeping gesture with his arm. "God bless you and the fine work you do!" he said in a sarcastic tone.

"I'm not going to forget what you did to me today, Deputy," Goins said. "Soon as I get back, I'll be taking that badge from you."

"Oh no! Not my badge!" Bidson chuckled, watching the sheriff walk past him onto the boardwalk. "Whatever will I do now?" He slammed the door behind Sheriff Goins and laughed to himself, saying, "You stupid old turd!"

Chapter 6

———

Inside Drexal's Silver Slipper Saloon, Thomas Drexal stood terrified against the back wall, hearing the sound of a knife blade slice through the air and thump into the wall only an inch from his ear. He wore one of his saloon girls' dresses and a flowery woman's hat. At gunpoint he'd been forced to pull a pair of red net stockings up over his hairy legs and squeeze his feet into a pair of glittery silver slippers. Fifteen feet away stood Ernie Shay, a mug of foamy beer in his left hand, four sharp throwing knives on the bar near his right.

"That wasn't so bad, was it?" Ernie asked, laughing drunkenly.

Drexal let out a breath in relief, but that was only for the moment. He watched Ernie turn up a long swig of beer and wipe his shirtsleeve across his mouth.

"Do it blindfolded!" Buck Simpson called out.

"No, please!" Drexal shrieked. "I can't take any more of it!"

"Awww," said Ernie, "listen to you carry on. It ain't you having to do all the work here—it's me!" Without warning, he sent another knife flying through the air, this one thumping into the wall dangerously close to Drexal's other ear. The barkeeper nearly swooned, his legs bucking under him. But he managed to catch himself and stay upright.

"If you think you can't stand up, let me know," said Ernie. "I can pin both shoulders of that dress to the wall for you!"

"Don't you ruin my good dress!" one of the saloon girls called out.

"Don't encourage them, Candy," said a large woman standing behind the bar.

"I'm not trying to encourage them, Bertha," said Candy Crawford. "But it *is* my good dress. I don't want it ruined!"

From the bat-wing doors of the saloon, Lonzo called out to the others, "Looks like that sheriff finally got his bark on, boys. Everybody pay attention here."

The men set their beer and whiskey glasses aside and moved over to the doors beside Lonzo, checking their pistols and readying themselves for battle. "Don't you go away," Ernie Shay said to Drexal. "We ain't finished yet!" He sent another knife whistling through the air; this one nailed the dress to the wall between the terrified man's legs. Drexal stared down at his trembling legs for any sign of blood. Upon seeing none he let out another sigh of relief.

In front of the saloon, Sheriff Goins stopped fifteen feet away from the boardwalk and poised his hand above his tied-down Colt. "All right, Greer," he called out to Lonzo, "let's get it over with. You knew I'd be coming sooner or later."

Lonzo took a short black cigar from between his teeth and grinned slyly. "Why, Sheriff, whatever do you mean? My men and I have been on our best behavior ever since we rode into this little shit hole of yours."

"You've all been drunk and loud and belligerent, Greer," said Goins. "It's the same way you've done a dozen different times in a dozen different towns. I know what comes next. It's my job to stop you. Let's get on with it."

Lonzo stared coldly at him and said, "Well, you've certainly managed to take all the fun out of it." He looked around at the other men and said, "I suppose there's nothing left to do but *get on with it*," he said mimicking the sheriff.

The men shook their heads and sighed as if in disappointment. "Oh, but wait," said Lonzo, staring past the sheriff back along the dirt street, seeing another lone figure coming toward them from the sheriff's office, this one carrying a shotgun. "What have we here?"

Goins grudgingly turned his head enough to see Deputy Forrest Bidson approaching at a steadily deliberate pace. The trace of a proud smile same to

Goins' lips. "That's my deputy, Lonzo," he said. "If you knew him, you'd know that right now he's just itching to empty that scattergun in somebody." Goins looked from one man to the next, hoping that his words and the sight of the shotgun might make a difference.

Lonzo stared at the deputy as he drew nearer. When Bidson stopped five feet to the sheriff's right, he said to the outlaw leader, "I don't know what he's telling you, but I never came here to help him fight you."

Goins looked as if he'd been kicked in the chest.

"Oh?" said Lonzo, "Then what *did* you come here to do, Deputy?" He stuck the cigar stub back between his teeth, taking on a renewed interest.

Bidson stood tall with his chin lifted, saying, "I know all about you, Lonzo Greer. I know there's not going to be much left here after you and your men leave. I'm hoping I can come with you."

Lonzo and his men stood in bemused silence for a moment; then Lonzo let out a chuckle and said, "I'll be damn. He's come looking for a job!"

"That beats all," said Metlet, his hand resting on his gun butt. "Then why is he carrying a shotgun. That doesn't strike me as very friendly."

"Me neither," said Lonzo, eyeing Bidson closely. "Why the shotgun, Deputy? And how do I know you're on the level?"

Bidson shrugged. "For all I knew I'd have to shoot my way to you." While he spoke, he reached up and unpinned the deputy badge from his shirt.

"This is a terrible thing you're doing, Bidson," Sheriff Goins said in a lowered tone. "You'll shame your name from now on. You'll be reviled by outlaw and lawman alike—"

"Aw, shut up, Goins," said Bidson. He cocked the shotguns hammers, swung it sideways and emptied both barrels into the old lawman's face, sending him flipping backward in a spray of blood, bone and brain matter.

"Hot damn!" said Lonzo, stunned for a second at the deputy's viciousness. "You lit him right up!"

"Is that on the level enough for you?" Bidson asked, wiping yellow-streaked blowback blood from his cheek, looking at it, then wiping it on his trouser leg.

Lonzo seemed to consider for a moment. "Well, yeah, I expect it does at that." He said to his men over his shoulder, "Anybody got any objections to this deputy joining us?"

"No," said Metlet, speaking for the rest of the men, "so long as he holds up his end."

"My name is Forrest Bidson," Bidson said, cradling the shotgun in his arm as he stepped over and stooped down to unbuckle the sheriff's gun belt from around his waist.

"Not anymore, it's not," said Lonzo. "I believe we're going to all call you *Deputy*. What say you, men?"

"Yeah, Deputy is good," said Metlet while the others nodded in agreement.

"Suits me," said Bidson, standing up and slinging

the sheriff's gun belt over his shoulder. He took out the Colt, checked it, and twirled it on his finger while the rest of the men watched him warily until the Colt slid back into the holster.

Pointing at the deputy badge Bidson had pitched to the dirt, Lonzo said, "Pick that up. I want to see you wearing it." He grinned. "I think that would just be the berries. Don't you, Paul?"

"Yeah, the berries," said Metlet, looking Bidson up and down. "It looks like that shotgun blast sent all the townsfolk running. I hope they haven't armed themselves so they can pick us off while we ride out." His eyes went up and along the roofs.

"You can put that out of your mind," said Bidson. "These are the most cowardly, miserable sons-abitches you'll ever come across." He raised his voice loud enough to be heard by anyone in the doorways along the boardwalk. "They make me sick, the bastards!"

Lonzo gave Metlet a look and said, "We sure don't want *Deputy* here to get sick! Let's break this place down and put the torch to it!"

"Can I grab me a whore to take with me?" Buck Simpson asked, getting excited.

"Well, hell, yes, Buck," said Lonzo, "if that makes you happy. Grab me one too." He raised his pistol from his holster and walked slowly toward the town bank, seeing a CLOSED sign swinging back and forth on the front door. "I think it's time I mosey over and see how much this bank officer thinks his sorry life is worth."

"All right!" Buck Simpson shouted. He bounded from the street back to the boardwalk and burst through the bat-wing doors. He stared hungrily at the two saloon girls who had gathered around a table, nursing the naked girl who had been thrown from the window. Drexal had torn his dress loose from the wall and stood at the bar with his face buried in his hands, his silver slippers on the floor near his bare feet. "You two whores are coming with us!" Simpson shouted.

"Just hold your horses, Buck!" said Candy Crawford, holding a wet rag near the injured girl's forehead. "Can't you see Madeline's injured here? What kind of lunatic throws a woman from an upstairs window?"

"I expect Calvin must've done that," Buck said. "I've seen him do worse." He lifted his pistol and waved it at the women. "Now you two come on. We've got some hard riding to do."

Bertha hurried around from behind the long oak bar and said, "Damn it, man! Leave these girls alone. If you have to drag somebody along with you, take me!"

"Stop your fat ass right there, Bertha," Buck said, leveling the pistol toward her. The large woman halted in her tracks. "You stay here and take care of that *fallen dove*." He grinned at his humor and turned his gun toward the other two again. "Now I'm only saying this one more time. You two are coming with us."

"Please, mister!" Drexal said, raising his head, his

eyes teary and red. "These girls are like daughters to me. Take Bertha!"

"I bet they're like daughters to you, Drexal, you dirty old son of a bitch." He cocked the pistol toward the saloon owner.

"Wait!" said Candy. "We're coming, but put the gun down, Buck. Rolena won't come if there's a gun pointed at her. Will you, Rolena?"

"Hunh-uh," said the other girl, shaking her head. "Guns scare me."

"There now, big boy," said Candy, putting a hand on her hip, "what's it going to be?"

Buck lowered his pistol an inch. "All right then, come on. We've got to get going."

"One more thing," said Candy, raising a finger for emphasis. "How much are we getting paid for this little ride-along?"

"Paid? You're being snatched away from here! You ain't getting paid for nothing, you stupid whore."

"Like hell we ain't," said Candy. "We're whores all right, but we ain't stupid. We go with you, we get paid, and that's final."

"Damn it," said Buck, feeling pressed. He rummaged through his shirt pockets and pulled up a wad of dollar bills. "All right, here! It's all I've got! Now come on, or so help me God, I will shoot you both."

Candy and Rolena hurried to him, Candy snatching the money from his hand, eyeing it quickly and making it disappear up under her dress. "Now we both feel more like riding," she said, tweaking Buck's beard-stubbled cheek.

"One thing though," Buck said, hesitating before rushing them out the doors.

"What is it?" Candy asked.

"I need to carry one of yas out of here over my shoulder. Maybe you can kick and carry on some, like I'm being real—"

"Say no more. I know what you want," said Candy, cutting him off. "Here, take me." She reached up and pulled one shoulder of her low-cut dress even lower, revealing a firm white breast. "How does that look to you, Buck?"

"Oh yeah, that's wonderful!" Buck said, wide-eyed, leaning out toward her.

She allowed him to stoop down and lift her up over his shoulder. "Here we go," Candy said, waving to Drexal and Bertha as Buck hurried out the doors.

From the lobby of the bank, Lonzo, Metlet and the others heard Candy screaming and cursing. Ernie Shay looked out the open front door of the bank and said, "Looks like Buck is bringing along a little company for us, boys."

"How many?" asked Owen Reager.

"Two of them," said Shay. "One over his shoulder, the other tagging along behind them like a lost calf."

"There would have been three had Calvin not tried to see if that one could fly!" said Reverend Vernon Wilcox.

"Listen, old man," said Calvin Thurston, "what I

do with a woman in private is none of your damn business."

"Of course it's not," said the reverend, "and I certainly beg your pardon for implying otherwise." Even as he apologized, Wilcox kept a hand on his holstered Colt, staring hard at Calvin.

Calvin spit and murmured under his breath, "Backsliding sonsabitch."

At the large safe behind the bank counter, Lonzo reached down with his pistol barrel and tapped the trembling bank president on his shoulder. "Get it open, moneyman, if you don't want your helper here to see your brains run down the wall."

"Please sir, I'm hurr—hurrying!" the bank president stammered, his fingers working the brass dial frantically. Three feet away, a young clerk lay facedown, his arms spread out, his nose and forehead pressed against the hard wooden floor.

"Yeah, hurry it up!" said Metlet, kneeing the man in his back. "We've got whores waiting for us!"

Finally the large steel door swung open. Lonzo and Metlet gasped quietly at the sight of trays filled with gold coins and shelves stacked full of bills. "This is when I love what we do for a living," Lonzo whispered as if in awe.

"Ain't it the truth," Metlet whispered.

Over his shoulder, Lonzo said, "Boys, bring some saddlebags!" Then he asked Bidson, "Deputy, have you reloaded that scattergun?"

"Yes, I have," Bidson answered from the other side of the counter.

"Both barrels?" Lonzo inquired.

"Yep, both barrels," Bidson replied.

"Then get in here, you rascal," said Lonzo. "Do some more killing for me."

Chapter 7

The town of Barstow fell quickly and easily into the hands of Lonzo and his men. Within an hour the town appeared to have never been inhabited. A small force made up of store owners and clerks had armed themselves at the first sound of gunfire, but three of their bodies now lay strewn in the dirt in the middle of the street. With the bank money stuffed into a large canvas bag, and most of the buildings ablaze, Lonzo and his men unhurriedly walked to the hitch rail, mounted their horses and formed up in a loose column, the two saloon girls bringing up the rear.

Forrest Bidson stepped his restless horse back and forth in the littered street, a torch still blazing in his hand. Along the boardwalk, stores and businesses stood engulfed in a long roaring fire. "I just want all of you to know how bad *I hate* you sonsabitches!" Bidson cried out to the few remaining unseen townsfolk who had taken shelter anywhere they could find it. "How bad I've *always* hated you! If I ever come back to this hole in the dirt it'll be to kill every one of you lousy bunch of bastards!" He hurled the torch toward the burning buildings.

Behind Bidson, Lonzo and the rest of the men sat atop their horses watching. Lonzo smiled and said to Metlet, who sat beside him, "You have to admit, somebody here has done something to ol' *Deputy*, as stoked-up as he is."

Metlet replied, "I think he's just one of them wild, hot-tempered fools you run into every once in a while."

Lonzo chuckled and said, "Don't worry, Paul. He ain't taking your place."

"I never thought he was," said Metlet. "But you have to admit, he seems to have a real mad-on at the whole damn world."

"Well, that's true," said Lonzo. He stepped his horse forward and called out to Bidson, "Hey, *Deputy*! Are you coming with us or not?"

"You're damn right, I'm coming!" said Bidson, his voice sounding enraged at the hidden townsfolk. "*Adios*, you sonsabitches!" he called out to the bellowing flames.

Bertha the bartender lay behind the low adobe wall of an old dried well, her large arm around Drexal, holding him to her bosom as if he were a terrified child. She watched the band of gunmen turn their horses and ride out single file toward the flatlands surrounding Barstow. On the last two horses, Candy and Rolena rode along with Buck Simpson leading their horses by their reins. Candy turned in her saddle and once again waved goodbye.

"You poor girls," Bertha murmured, shaking her head.

"Are they gone?" Drexal asked in a trembling voice muffled by Bertha's smothering breasts.

Waiting a moment before answering him, Bertha finally said, "Yes, I believe they are."

"It's about damn time," said Drexal, his demeanor already beginning to change. "I've got to get out of this dress."

Bertha pushed herself to her feet, bringing Drexal up with her.

"I can stand on my own!" Drexal said, sounding a bit testy now that the danger had passed. He shoved himself free of the large bartender and straightened the soiled torn dress down the front of him. He looked all around and said, "I've got to find myself something to wear before anybody sees me like this."

"Oh my, look!" said Bertha, pointing out along the street in front of the burning bank.

In the heat of the raging fire, a dust devil filled with dollar bills danced along the street. "Whooie!" said Drexal. "Come on, it's rebuilding capital! Help me gather it up!" He gave only a quick glance toward his burning saloon, then ran off toward the flying money.

When Giles Pruitt left Marshal Springs, he rode steadily northeast until darkness overtook him. At a thin stream that ran near the base of a low stretch of hills, he stepped down from his horse and collapsed flat on his back for a moment, raising the last swig of whiskey from a bottle he'd purchased before leaving town.

"Now what will become of me?" he asked the dark sky above him. He let out a despairing breath, pitched the empty bottle away and heard it crash on the rocks alongside the streambed.

No sooner had he heard the glass break than he also heard a frightened voice call out from the darkness, "Who goes there?"

Struggling quickly up into a crouch, Pruitt pulled his gun and pointed it in the direction of the voice. He called out loudly, "We're four cattle buyers over here. We're traveling to Barstow. Who might you be?"

"We're two new whiskey peddlers, delivering our first load all the way from Whitley City, Kansas," said the voice that Pruitt now judged to be no more than fifty feet away. "The sound of glass breaking makes us nervous."

"*New* whiskey peddlers? Delivering their *first* load?" Pruitt mouthed the words silently to himself. "Thank you, Jesus!" He tossed the words skyward, then said aloud, "You've no cause to be nervous. We are peaceful businessmen. Are we welcome in?"

After a moment of silence, the same voice called out, "Yes, come on in, but keep your hands away from any firearms."

Pruitt grabbed his horse's reins and jerked the tired animal toward the sound of the voice. "You know, you could build a campfire," he called out. "There're no hostiles around to speak of."

"There's some kind of hostiles out there," said the voice. "Our mules have disappeared on us."

Pruitt ran it through his mind; a load of whiskey, no mules to pull it. He liked his possibilities here. "Mules wander off worse than any animal I ever seen," he called out. "Did you hobble them?"

"Hell no," a voice said in disgust.

"Then there you are," Pruitt said. "You can build a fire. There's no hostiles."

"We were not sure of that," said the voice. Before Pruitt gained another three steps, a match flared up, followed by the glow of an oil lantern.

"That's better," said Pruitt, attempting a pleasant smile. He stopped and looked at the two bearded faces staring back at him in the lantern's circling light.

Seeing the Colt still in Pruitt's hand, one of the men called out, "He told you to keep your hands away from your guns!"

"Did he?" Pruitt shrugged. "I must not have heard him in the course of things."

"Well, you just stop right there and holster it before you come any closer, mister!" the same voice said. "And where are the other three men?" His eyes searched the darkness back and forth.

"They are surrounding you right now," Pruitt said, still walking toward them, leading his horse, his Colt leveling up at them instead of going into his holster.

The two frightened faces probed even more warily into the darkness for any sign of the other three men. As they did so, Pruitt shot each of them in turn without missing a step.

The glow of lantern light fell flat for moment until Pruitt quickly stepped forward and picked up the lantern before it went out. He adjusted the wick and looked around in the renewed light at the two men lying on the ground at his feet. One face stared blankly up into the endless sky. The other stared at him, wincing in pain, and said in a strained voice, "You—you lied to us, mister!"

"What the hell did you expect out here?" Pruitt chuckled. "This ain't no place to invite strangers in, this time of night." He idly fired another round into the dying man's face, then holstered his pistol and held the glowing lantern out toward a canvas-covered freight wagon, saying, "Lord, *please* don't let them be as big a liar as I am."

He reached out, hand shaking in anticipation, loosened a corner rope and flipped up the canvas, revealing wooden whiskey crates stacked three deep in the wagon bed. "Looky here!" he said, his voice quavering a bit with emotion at the sight of crate upon crate of hard liquor. He wiped an eye and looked down at the two dead men on the ground at his feet. "You wonderful men got here just in the nick of time."

After a few moments of staring in awe at the whiskey, running his hands over crate after crate, Pruitt found a pry bar lying in the wagon and opened one of the crates. He raised one of the bottles in his hands, examined it in the lantern light, uncorked it and tipped in a toast to the two dead whiskey peddlers. "God bless you both!" he said aloud before throwing back a long, gurgling drink.

At the end of his drink, he let out a whiskey hiss, wiped a dirty sleeve across his mouth and leaned back against the side of the wagon, giving his situation some thought. He realized that with daylight came the possibility that someone traveling the same trail would come upon him and his newly acquired trove of drinking whiskey. He couldn't have that happen, especially with two bodies lying on the ground in full view. He threw back another long drink, corked the bottle and stuck it inside his shirt.

Using his tired horse and a rope he took from the wagon, Pruitt dragged the two bodies to the stream and rolled them into the water. But contrary to his plans to watch them float away down stream, the bodies only lay in the shallow water and bobbed up and down. "Damn it!" Pruitt said.

He took the bottle of whiskey from inside his shirt and had another long drink. Then he dragged the bodies back out of the water and back to the wagon. Again using the horse and rope, he gathered a large pile of downed wood from along the streambed and built a roaring fire, careful not to build it too close to the wagon. While the fire raged, he pulled a fresh bottle of whiskey from a crate and stuffed it inside his shirt, taking the other one out and finishing it in two long swigs.

Staggering a bit, he walked off in search of the mules and found them standing in a stretch of wild grass, quietly grazing, a lead rope dangling from their necks. "There's a good mule," Pruitt said soothingly in a drunken tone, trying to slip up on the animals without spooking them.

But the mules would have none of it. They waited until Pruitt got within four feet of them; then they quickly bolted away a few feet and stopped, going back to their grazing. "You sons of bitches," Pruitt growled.

Instinctively his hand went to his pistol butt before he could stop himself. But then he calmed down and started over, walking slowly, talking to the skittish animals in a low, soothing voice. "Come, mules. Come to ol' Giles. We've got some whiskey to haul out of here." Again the mules waited until he was within four feet, then bolted away. "To hell with yas!" Pruitt cursed.

He turned and walked away, raising the bottle to his lips, deciding to let the mules graze a while longer. He would come back in the daylight, hoping that by then the animals would have finished their grazing and perhaps even walk up to him. *Patience,* he reminded himself.

Yet, as he sat at the roaring fire a half hour later, drinking from his third bottle of whiskey, he kept thinking about the mules and the bodies on the ground and everything he had to get done. He wasn't about to let the mules get the best of him, and he wasn't about to get caught out here with two dead men wearing his bullets in their chests. After downing another long swig of whiskey, he struggled to his feet and staggered for a moment, waiting for the earth to stop tilting beneath him. "All right, Giles, ol' pard," he said aloud to himself, "it's time to go to work."

Throughout the night the fire glowed for miles across the flatlands. Metlet was the first of the gang to see it when he and Lonzo crested a low rise and stopped their horses for a moment while the others caught up to them. Lonzo Greer had dozed off in his saddle, the bag of bank money riding safely on his lap. But the sound of Metlet's voice saying, "Lonzo, wake up!" brought him out of his sleep and caused him to tighten his grip on the bag.

"What is it?" Lonzo asked, straightening up in his saddle.

"Over there, a campfire," said Metlet, pointing off toward the glowing firelight.

"Yeah," said Lonzo, rubbing sleep from his eyes with a free hand. "But how far is it?"

"It's a good ways off yet," said Metlet. "But what does it matter? We're heading that way anyway."

Lonzo grinned. "Nothing like riding all night, and come morning find a nice warm fire and breakfast prepared and waiting for you, I always say."

Metlet returned his grin. "That's what I thought you'd say." They nudged their horses toward the glow on the distant horizon.

CHAPTER 8

———◆———

Dawn lay cloaked in a silver-gray swirl as Lonzo led his men the last yards toward the smoldering fire. A harsh-smelling wood smoke permeated the air and partially hid the wagon from sight. Lonzo and Metlet stared at the grim bowed figure sitting perched on a pile of driftwood and brittle mesquite brush. "What the hell is that smell?" Metlet asked.

"I had nothing to do with this!" Giles Pruitt called out in a low gravelly voice before Lonzo could answer.

"Lord God, look at this!" Reverend Wilcox called out, having nudged his horse up beside Metlet. "Some terrible evil has manifested itself here."

"They were like this when I found them!" Pruitt insisted. "Why don't you just go on and leave a man in peace. I didn't ask you for nothing! Not a gawddamn thing!"

Nudging his horse closer because he recognized the voice, Lonzo said, "Is that you, Giles?"

"Hell, yes, it's me," said Pruitt, his voice sounding thick and tormented.

Riding closer to the fire, Metlet and Reverend Wilcox looked down at the trunks of the two bodies lying charred and glistening in the bed of glowing coals. "Oh no," said Wilcox, "this poor tortured soul has turned to cannibalism!"

"Like hell I have," said Pruitt. "I told you they was like that when I found them."

Seeing Pruitt's right hand lying in his lap holding his Colt, Lonzo demanded, "Lay that gun down, Giles."

"I can't," said Pruitt. "I've been shot. My hand ain't working."

Lonzo looked closer and saw the blood on the old drunkard's right shoulder, his left hand pressed against the wound caked with dark blood. Stepping down from his horse, Lonzo moved forward carefully, his hand drawing his own gun and cocking it toward Pruitt just in case. "Who shot you, Giles?"

"I shot myself, gawddamn it!" Pruitt cursed. "I got myself too drunk and was trying to kill a couple of mules who wouldn't come to me. I warn people all the time that I can't get *too* drunk or *too* sober. It ain't my fault!"

"There's dead mules over here," Owen Reager called out from a few yards away, having eased his horse around the campfire for a better look at the camp.

"This poor evil bastard will have to be put out of his misery," said Reverend Wilcox, drawing a rifle from his saddle boot. "That's all you can do with a man who has turned to human flesh."

"I didn't turn to human flesh, you damned idiot!" said Pruitt. "I told you, I got too drunk. I killed these whiskey peddlers and couldn't figure what else to do with them. So I cut them up and stuck them into the fire!"

Lonzo and rest of the men looked all around. "Why?" Lonzo asked with a puzzled expression. He reached down and took the gun from Pruitt's hand.

"For all I knew the law could have come along this trail anytime," said Pruitt.

"So he decided to eat his victims!" Reverend Wilcox shouted, cocking his rifle. "I've heard enough!" He raised the rifle butt to his shoulder.

"Lower your rifle, Reverend!" Lonzo demanded. "Giles here is one of us."

Wilcox looked around and saw Metlet raise his pistol from his holster, staring straight at him. Hesitantly Wilcox lowered the rifle a few inches.

"Why does he keep saying I ate these two?" Pruitt asked Lonzo. "Is he crazy?"

"No," said Lonzo, "it's because you've got blood all over your whiskers, Giles."

"Oh, I do?" Pruitt took his hand from his shoulder wound and rubbed it across his bloody mouth. He looked first at the chopped-up body parts on the ground near the fire. "Lord," he whispered. Looking up at Lonzo with a puzzled look, he said, "You don't reckon I did, do you?"

"I don't know, Giles," said Lonzo. "From what you've told us so far, it ain't looking good for you."

Pruitt winced in contemplation. "Damn! I don't *think* I did, but I can't remember." He scratched his head. "I can't even remember being hungry."

Lonzo patted his shoulder, saying, "Let's just let that one simmer awhile before you say for sure one way or the other." He looked at the wagon. "That's all whiskey in there?"

"Yep, it is, and it's all *mine*!" said Pruitt, suddenly getting protective of his treasure. "I found it and I don't owe nobody nothing for it!"

"All right, take it easy, old man," said Lonzo, getting a bit impatient with him. Seeing that some of his men had stepped down from the saddles and eased over toward the wagon, Lonzo waved them back with a gloved hand, saying to Pruitt, "None of us is out to rob you." While he spoke to Pruitt, Lonzo saw Owen Reager slip up on the wagon from the other side and raise a bottle of whiskey from a crate. He nodded to Reager, giving him approval.

"I can't figure what to do next," Pruitt said, staring up at Lonzo through bloodshot eyes. "My brain can't get started or something."

"I understand, Giles," said Lonzo, again patting his back. "One thing for sure, you're not hauling this whiskey wagon anywhere without some animals to pull it for you."

"I know it," said Pruitt, sounding defeated. "But I can't go nowhere until the whiskey's gone. This is one of them once-in-a-lifetime things that only happens to a few men. I ain't turning it loose."

Talking to Pruitt, Lonzo watched Reager step away from the wagon with bottle necks sticking out of his shirt. One by one the rest of the men stepped up to the other side of the wagon and silently stuffed bottles anywhere they could carry them. "Maybe we could share a couple of horses," said Lonzo, "and help you get this load to some town where you can sell it."

"It ain't for sale," Pruitt said sharply.

"There's too much whiskey for one man to drink in a year, Giles," said Lonzo.

"We'll see if it is," said Pruitt. "I'm staying right here until I've drunk every bit of it. I'm not leaving a drop behind."

"You better think about that, Giles," said Lonzo. "We can swap our horses back and forth enough to keep that wagon rolling and help you get it out of here."

"Not if it means I have to share the whiskey with you," said Pruitt.

"You know damn well you'll have to share the whiskey with us, Giles," said Lonzo, getting less patient with the drunken outlaw.

"Then go on and leave me alone," said Giles. "I ain't sharing it."

"Think about this first, you drunken old wretch," said Lonzo. "I'm standing here holding your gun. If I wanted to, I could kill you and take all the whiskey." He gestured with the sweep of an arm. "Hell, we could legally hang you and leave a letter pinned to you saying you're a cannibal! Who would ever question it?" As he spoke, Lonzo kept an eye on the men lifting whiskey from the other side of the wagon.

"I ain't sharing it," Pruitt said firmly, "and that's that."

"I'm through talking to you, Giles," said Lonzo. "I ought to drag you along with us for your own sake. But if you'd sooner die here, so be it."

"He's too drunk to know what he's doing," said Calvin Thurston, walking up beside Lonzo after having walked back to his horse and stuffed his saddlebags with bottles of whiskey.

Pruitt squinted up at the younger gunman, saying, "Yeah? Well, I wasn't drunk when I heard about what happened to your brother, Max."

"What *about* my brother?" Calvin said, both his and Lonzo's attention becoming more intense.

"He's dead," Pruitt said flatly, staring hard at Calvin.

Calvin lunged toward him, saying, "You're lying, you drunken old son of a—"

But Lonzo stopped Calvin by forcing his way in front of him and shoving him back. "Stand down, Calvin!" Lonzo demanded. Then turning to Pruitt he said, "Old man, you better be telling the truth, or I *will* kill you with your own gun."

"I ain't lying," said Pruitt. "The same ranger who killed Junior Lake and his gang killed Max over in Cottonwood. I heard him bragging about it."

Lonzo stood considering it for a moment. "Max

went to Cottonwood. I told him that's where Stone Eddie spends most of his prowling time."

"He ain't prowling there anymore," said Pruitt. "The ranger arrested him, brought him to Marshal Springs in chains. I was there. He gunned down Jake McAllister, single-handed."

"The ranger killed big Jake?" Lonzo asked in stunned disbelief.

"Not *just* Jake," said Pruitt. "He killed Rodney Floyd and Porter Fox at the same time. I saw it from a block away and tried my best to get there . . . but it was all over too quick." He shook his head. "Poor bastards never had a chance."

"What do you mean the ranger was *bragging* about killing my brother?" Calvin asked Pruitt.

"It's all he talked about, over and over," Pruitt lied, staring Calvin straight in the eye. "It was enough to make you sick."

"I can't stand it!" Calvin shouted, stomping the ground in his anger and frustration. "I'm killing that ranger, so help me God!"

"Easy, Calvin," said Lonzo. "We'll all take care of the ranger when the time comes. From everything I hear lately, he's getting to be a burr under everybody's blanket."

"That he is," said Pruitt. "Jake and us were all getting set to throw in with Bobby Caesar and his Lost Canyon boys. The ranger shot that deal all to hell. I expect Bobby Caesar won't be too happy with the ranger either."

"Maybe it's high time all of us out here banded together long enough to take care of this ranger once and for all," said Lonzo.

"I want him all to myself," said Calvin. "The sonsabitch won't be bragging then."

Lonzo asked Pruitt, "How did the ranger get the drop on Stone Eddie?"

"I don't know," said Pruitt. "But Stone Eddie didn't seem to be too worried about anything. He told everybody in the jail there that he'd be set free as soon as a judge heard his case. I reckon he knows what he's talking about." Pruitt shrugged.

Lonzo looked at the body parts piled on the ground beneath a growing number of flies and at the two burned torsos of the whiskey peddlers still sizzling in the glowing embers. He looked at the dead mules and at the dark dried blood on Pruitt's shoulder. Choosing a firm even voice, he said to Pruitt, "Come on, get up from there. You're coming with us."

"I said I ain't going nowhere," Pruitt stated. "Didn't you hear me?"

"You won't last a week out here like this, Giles," said Lonzo. "Look at you! No food, no water! Get up, man, and come on with us."

"I've got all the whiskey a man could ever dream of," said Pruitt. "Now go on and leave me alone."

"Damn right we will then," said Lonzo. He looked around at the men, seeing that they had all made their way around to the other side of the wagon. "Is everybody here ready to to ride?" he called out.

The men had filled their shirts, hats and arms with

bottles of whiskey and carried them back to their horses. Lonzo looked at the horses standing with their saddlebags bulging, bottle necks sticking up from the open flaps.

"We're ready when you are, Lonzo," said Metlet.

"Then let's leave this greedy old bastard with his whiskey," said Lonzo, realizing that his men had taken a larger amount of whiskey than they would have taken if Pruitt had agreed to share it with them.

Mounting their whiskey-laden horses, Lonzo and his men rode away from Pruitt without another word. Pruitt sat staring at them, unarmed, with no provisions. Thirty yards from the grizzly campsite, Metlet looked back at Pruitt.

"He ain't coming," he informed Lonzo.

"I never thought he would," Lonzo replied without looking back.

"The crazy old bastard will just sit there until he dies, I reckon," Metlet said.

"We left him his horse," said Lonzo. "If he snaps out of it, he can always get up and ride away."

"But I bet he won't snap out of it," Metlet speculated, giving one more look back along the trail, seeing a curl of greasy black smoke drift upward.

Lonzo shrugged. "Then I suppose he'll die happy. If all a man wants is whiskey and he dies drinking from a wagon load of it, what's better than that?" He nudged his horse into a quicker pace. "Far as I'm concerned he can drown in it. We've got ourselves a ranger to kill."

PART 2

Chapter 9

———

At the old Spanish mission near the ranger outpost at Haverston, Ranger Hadley Jones and Flora Cruz kneeled before an old priest and became man and wife. At the end of the ceremony, Sam, who had acted as Jones' best man, stood outside the adobe church holding his pearl gray sombrero. His hand toyed with a new hand-tooled silver hat band that Ranger Jones had given him as gift.

Ordinarily Sam would not have worn anything so ornate; but since Jones had forged and tooled the silver by hand, Sam planned on wearing it for a few days before putting it away as a keepsake. Beside Sam, Territorial Judge Winston Martingale looked down at the silver hatband and said in a conversational tone, "Say now, that is quite a flashy piece of silver, Ranger."

Idly, Sam replied, "It's a gift, Your Honor, for being best man."

"Oh, I see," said the judge, realizing why Sam

wore it. Only three days earlier Judge Martingale had presided over Stone Eddie Deaks' hearing and dismissed the three counts of murder against him.

"Ranger Burrack," the judge said, "I thought you would like to know that Stone Eddie Deaks finally left Haverston late last night, headed south."

"I already heard about it, Your Honor," Sam replied.

"I'm certain he only stayed around town for a while hoping the sight of him would irritate you," said the judge.

"Then his time here wasn't very well spent," said Sam, dismissing the subject of Stone Eddie Deaks. "All I've been interested in is my friend's wedding."

"Of course." The judge smiled, taking the hint. "How much longer will it be before we see you taking yourself a wife?"

Sam offered a half smile and answered, "Not anytime soon, Your Honor."

After a pause the judge said in a more official tone of voice, still discussing Deaks, "I hope you weren't too disappointed in my releasing him."

"Not at all, Your Honor," Sam said patiently. "Stone Eddie is headed the same place as the rest of the hard cases. He's just smart enough that it's going to take him longer to get there than some of the others."

"That's a good, positive way to look at it," the judge said, returning Sam's half smile. "At least Stone Eddie has managed to only kill those within his own circle."

"That we *know* of, Your Honor," Sam interjected.

"Yes, that we *know of*," said the judge, raising a brow slightly. "But in my position those we *know* of are the only ones that count. The great imperfection of the law is that we can only act in response to a man like Stone Eddie. He always gets the first move."

"I understand," said the ranger. "But that first move always costs someone their life. Knowing it always causes me a bitter taste."

The two stood watching the newlywed couple come out of the old adobe church and run smiling and waving through a gauntlet of rice and ribbons toward an awaiting buggy. Rangers from the outpost and a few young women from Haverston called out their best wishes, along with a few playful catcalls.

"Shouldn't you be there saying something to your partner, Ranger Burrack?" the judge asked.

"He knows I wish them both the best," said Sam. "Anything else I've got to say will keep till Monday morning." He smiled watching Jones help his new bride into the buggy. Once Flora was seated, Jones rushed around the buggy, climbed up into the driver's seat and took up the reins. Before slapping the reins to the buggy horse's back, Jones looked over at Sam and waved.

"Good luck, Jonesie," Sam murmured to himself, responding with a touch of his fingers to his forehead.

As the buggy pulled away in a low stir of dust, Ranger Captain Earl Martin walked over to Sam and said, "Burrack, since your friend is going to be busy the next couple of days, I want you to take that string of stage horses we recovered back over to Quincy. The relay station needs them right away."

Sam nodded in the direction of the blacksmith shop, saying, "Black Pot is getting new shoes. I'll ride one of the livery horses."

"Carry on then." Captain Martin nodded and walked away.

"Well, it appears you have found yourself a chore for the weekend, Ranger," said the judge.

"Yes, it appears so," said Sam, putting on his sombrero and tipping it slightly to the judge. "Good day, Your Honor." He walked away toward the livery barn while the dust from Hadley and Flora's buggy stood adrift on the desert air.

Within the hour Sam had headed out on the eight-hour trek to Quincy, carrying only short provisions, one canteen of water for himself and a goatskin full of water for the horses. He had picked and saddled one of the livery's spare service horses for his trip, leaving Black Pot behind not only to be newly shod but also for a couple of days' rest out of the scorching desert sun. Behind him, the ranger led the six big, dark bay stage horses that had been stolen from the Quincy relay station three weeks earlier.

By late afternoon, the slow pace of the livery horse beneath him and the pull on the lead rope in his gloved hand told him it was time to make a camp for the night, rest the horses and finish the ride in the coolness of morning. At a clearing atop a high cliff overhang, the ranger tied the horses in the shade of a sparse stand of cedar, took down the goatskin and watered each horse in turn by pouring the water into his sombrero and letting the thirsty animal drink from it.

While Sam watered the animals, at a distance of less than a hundred yards, higher up, Stone Eddie Deaks' eye and rifle sights fixed on the ranger's head. He smiled to himself, lowered the rifle an inch and said, "Bang!" to himself. Behind him, his horse blew out a breath and stamped its hoof on the hot rock ground. "Don't worry, boy," said Deaks, taking off his hat and laying it on the ground beside him. "He's dead. I'm just savoring the taste of it for a minute or so, before I drop the hammer."

Sam propped his saddle, rifle boot and all against the side of a rock. He scraped together enough twigs and scraps of dried mesquite brush to start a small fire and boil a pot of coffee. While he waited for the water to boil, he walked out to the edge of the cliff and looked down at the tops of tall pine and mountain cedar thirty feet below. Before turning away, he looked out across the narrow rocky canyon just in time to see the fading evening sunlight glint off the rifle barrel.

"Deaks!" he whispered, catching a glimpse of the rifle pointed at him. Instinctively he tried to jump out of the way, but he was too late.

"And you never even knew what hit you, Ranger." Deaks lowered the rifle from his shoulder and smiled to himself with satisfaction. "I like that." He watched Sam topple off the edge of the cliff and plunge downward until he disappeared into the thick green treetops below. Then he leaned back, folded his hands behind his head and listened to the quiet whir of wind for a moment. "Neat and clean and with no living witnesses." He chuckled softly.

Twenty minutes later he had ridden his horse down and across the canyon floor and up the other side. When he stepped down from his saddle again it was at the campsite where the pot of coffee Sam had started now boiled over the top edge of the pot. "It's a good thing I got here when I did," Deaks said, looking all the horses up and down, his rifle in his hand. "All this fine coffee was about to go to waste."

Using a tin cup the ranger had set out by the small campfire, Deaks poured himself some hot coffee and walked over to the edge of the cliff and looked down. He saw the ranger lying entangled amid broken branches halfway down the trunk of a tall pine tree. Deaks set the coffee down and raised the rifle butt to his shoulder. But just as he settled his sights on the ranger's exposed back, a breeze caused the trees to sway back and forth. He watched the ranger tumble farther down the tree trunk.

"You're not worth another bullet, Ranger," he said, lowering his rifle. "Now it's over, I'm almost disappointed at how easy it was killing you." He spit off the ledge in Sam's direction, picked up his coffee, turned and walked back to the campfire.

*   *   *

Sam awakened painfully, swaying in the breeze beneath a sky full of shining stars. A hard, deep pain pounded in his head; a slicing, sharper pain started at his shoulder and ran the length of his left arm. It took him a moment to sort through his fragmented thoughts and recollections and realize that he'd been shot. Not only had he been shot, but he had fallen from the cliff ledge that he now saw looming above him through a streak of broken pine limbs. He looked around at his shoulder for the source of the stabbing pain and saw the jagged point of a broken limb sticking out of his upper arm.

"I'm pinned," he murmured to the cool, quiet night. Before attempting to free himself, he looked up and down through blurred eyes, considering his situation carefully. It appeared that his arm being pinned to the tree was all that held him some sixty feet above the sloping rocky ground. At his stomach another limb helped support his weight. He bowed slightly on it, adjusted himself more securely and ventured his right hand up to the large pounding knot on the side of his head.

Blood . . . ? Yes, it was—he confirmed for himself, rubbing his fingertips together. But it was not the thick congealing blood that he would have found if a bullet had struck him directly. He probed the knot again with his fingers, enough to realize that it was no bullet graze. Through the pounding in his head, it came to him. The bullet had struck the silver hatband that Jones had made for him. *That had to be it. . . .* His metal hatband had saved his life.

Pausing for a moment to take a few breaths and try to clear his head, Sam raised a leg, hooked it over the thick limb against his stomach and managed to pull himself astraddle of it. Forcing himself to keep his consciousness, he untied his bandanna, stuck it into his mouth and bit down on it. Grasping his pinned left arm with his right hand, he slowly, methodically, removed the injured arm from the jagged wooden stake, leaving a dark smear of blood behind it.

His arm free, he removed the bandanna from his mouth and wrapped it snuggly around the bleeding pulsating wound. He removed his gun belt from his waist and rebuckled it, making a loop that he could use for climbing. He took his Colt from the holster and shoved it down into his trousers. For a moment he closed his eyes and allowed himself to slump against the tree trunk in preparation for a difficult one-armed climb down to the ground.

A quarter mile away across the canyon floor, an old hermit had heard the gunshot before dark and had hidden himself and his burro deep in the rocks like two creatures of the wilds. He had awaited the cover of darkness before venturing back out. When he did pull the little burro forward, it was with great trepidation, his knobby knees trembling violently beneath his short, ragged trouser legs.

"Keep ye self silent, Bartholomew," he whispered to the burro. "I'll suffer none of ye dumb brute tongue on this terrible night." He crept along silently for another fifty yards, but then suddenly let out a shrill scream when the ranger came tumbling the last ten feet through snapping pine limbs and landed with a thud near his feet.

"Holy *mother of God!*" the old hermit shouted, cringing, throwing both arms across his face.

The sight of the fallen ranger sent the little burro into a braying, kicking frenzy. On the ground the ranger moaned and rolled over on his back, gripping his injured upper arm.

"Don't move, man!" the hermit cried out in warning. He drew back his long walking stick with both hands, ready to swing it at Sam's head. Behind him the burro began to settle down a bit.

"Lower that stick, mister," Sam groaned, struggling to hold onto his consciousness. "I'm Arizona ranger Sam Burrack. I'm wounded." The way Sam held his wounded arm kept the old man from seeing the badge on his chest.

But the hermit wouldn't budge. He only tightened his grip on the walking stick. "You're a lawman! What would a lawman be doing up a tree? You're another prospector! You're spying on me! You think I'll show you where my gold is? Well, I won't! My gold can't be found by fools like you!" Behind him the burro settled even more, but backed away a few feet and stared at the two men curiously.

"Mister," Sam said, feeling himself fade, "if you swing that stick, I'll have to shoot you." He raised his Colt from his belt, but didn't cock it. "Please lower it, and give me a hand."

"Shoot me? Ha!" said the old hermit even as he began to lower the stick. "That seems to be the answer to everything in these last and troubled days." He shook his disheveled head. "Something goes, just shoot somebody! That's supposed to fix everything!" He lowered the stick the rest of the way down to his side, stepped forward and stooped down, taking a better look at the ranger. Finally seeing the badge on Sam's chest, he said, "Oh, then you are a ranger!" Looking closer he added, "And you have a hole in your arm!"

"I know," said Sam, struggling partially up onto his knees, reaching out to the man.

The old hermit took his hand and pulled him to his knees. But no sooner had Sam stood on his feet than he collapsed into the hermit's arms. "Oh my goodness," the hermit said aloud, holding Sam under both arms to keep him from falling back to the dirt. Giving a twisted glance over his shoulder to the burro, he called out, as if scolding the little animal, "Well, Bartholomew! Are ye just going to stand there? Get over here and give me some assistance!" The little burro walked forward as if it understood every word the hermit said. "I know what you're going to say," the hermit said to the animal. "But if he's really not a prospector, let's mend him up and send him on his way." He dragged Sam toward the little burro, saying in a softer voice, "I believe that's what the Lord Jehovah would have us do."

Chapter 10

———

Sam awakened in a shallow cavern and saw morning sunlight shining into the entrance twenty feet away. The throbbing pain in his head had lessened, but was still there. He noticed through a lifting mental haze that his upper arm had been bandaged with strips of cloth. Touching the wound, he noted the bandage was dry and had no bloodstain on it. A small fire burned a few feet from him, and between him and the fire, the old hermit stood stirring a stick in a bed of glowing coals. Sam's pearl gray sombrero sat atop the hermit's head.

"How long have I been out?" Sam asked, his voice still coated with sleep.

Startled by the sound of Sam's voice, the old hermit jumped and let out a short squeal. "Good God, man!" he said, jerking around toward him, stick in hand. "Have the courtesy to announce yourself! Don't scare a body half to death!"

"Didn't mean to surprise you," Sam said, sitting

up on the blanket pallet, seeing his boots standing nearby. "How long have I been out?" He looked all around the clean, well-kept cavern as he spoke. A table with a checkered red table cloth sat near a rough stone wall. A pile of firewood lay stacked in a cord, a small hatchet sticking up from a thick pine chopping block.

"Surprise nothing!" said the old hermit, shaking violently for moment. "You nearly scared the black water out of me!" Lowering the stick, he rubbed his trembling hand on his trouser leg and said, "You've been out nigh on to three days, Ranger."

"Three days . . . ?" Sam touched his fingertips to the knot on his head, feeling the soreness there, but also feeling that the swelling had gone down since he'd first felt it while perched high in the pine tree.

"Yes, three days," said the hermit. "But you haven't gibbered on and on like some I've seen. So you haven't been much of a nuisance, I'm happy to say." For no apparent reason he turned toward the little burro standing near the cavern entrance and shouted, "Shut ye up, Bartholomew!"

Sam gave the burro a curious glance because the timid-looking animal hadn't made a sound. "Are you a prospector, mister?"

"No! No, indeed!" said the old hermit. "At one time I was a craven seeker of gold like all the other fools. But now I have come to loathe and despise prospectors and everything they stand for, including that cursed *devil's ore!*"

Sam stared at him for a moment in contemplation,

then said, "Suppose you can hand me that Colt sticking out of your trousers?"

The old hermit glanced at the gun butt. "I've got no use for it." He pulled it up slowly, walked to Sam and handed it to him. "It was about to pull my britches down anyways."

Sam took the gun, checked it and held it as he looked all around for his holster belt. Not seeing it anywhere, he said to the old man, "I'll need my hat too."

The old man nodded, took off the tall sombrero and handed it over. "I found this right after I found you. I was hoping it wasn't yours, but I must've known that it would be."

"Obliged," Sam said. He examined the sombrero, noting that the silver band was missing, but seeing the clear indention where the bullet had mashed it into the crown before breaking it. "I'm going to need this sombrero for the walk out of here. But as soon as I get to the outpost, I'll send you a brand-new one just like it . . . and anything else you need, for all your help."

The old man shook his head slowly. "No, I expect I better not. A body starts getting accustomed to having things, and pretty soon he has more things than he can keep track of." He looked at the sombrero. "Well, I don't think one tall, handsome sombrero would hurt, do you?"

"I can't see how," Sam replied. He struggled to his feet and stood on wobbly legs for a moment. "I'll have the stage leave it for you anywhere you like along the trail. What's your name?"

The old man concentrated, squeezing his eyes shut. But finally he said, "I just plumb forgot, Ranger."

"I understand." Sam nodded. "If it comes to you let me know. Otherwise, I'll just call you *Mister*."

"Wilson!" the old man said suddenly, his eyes wide in realization. "It's Wilson! There, I remembered it after all!"

"Is Wilson your last or Christian name?" Sam asked.

Wilson concentrated again.

"Never mind," said the ranger. "I'll call you *Mister* Wilson." He carefully put the sombrero atop his head and asked, "Mister Wilson, I had a string of horses atop that cliff I fell from. Did you happen to see them?"

"No," said Wilson, "I surely did not. But we're only a few miles from there, if you're up to the walk."

"I'm up to it," said Sam. "Lead the way."

"Don't you want something to eat first?" Mister Wilson asked.

"No, not until I go see about those horses," Sam replied. "I've been missing three days. By now my partner is probably out looking for me."

"Partner, eh?" the old man said skeptically. "I had one of them things once. I couldn't trust him no farther than I could hurl a wild hog."

"Then you had a bad partner," said Sam. "But I

can trust my partner. Wherever he's at right now, he's wondering what's happened to me."

In moments the two men and the burro had left the cavern and begun backtracking the path Wilson had taken across the canyon floor. They followed the sharp little hoofprints Bartholomew had left behind while carrying Sam three days ago. Less than an hour had passed before they stopped at the base of a steep wall of rock and looked up the trunk of the pine tree through broken limbs and scuffed tree bark. "That fall looks even longer in the daylight," said Wilson, as if in awe.

Sam nodded and looked toward the entrance to a trail leading up into the rocky belly of the land. Within another hour they had topped the cliff and seen where the horses had gotten thirsty and hungry and snapped the thin tree limb they were tied to. On the ground lay Sam's saddle and belongings, untouched, except for his tin cup and coffeepot.

"Strung together, the horses won't be far away," Sam said, looking out across the level stretch of land atop the hill. "I hope wolves haven't gotten them." Even as he spoke, he noticed the string of stage horses standing less then a hundred yards away. "There they are right now, grazing," he said.

"Yep," said Wilson, seeing the stage horses at the same time. "And there's water just beyond them. You drew lucky, Ranger. With graze and water, those horses would've stayed here till kingdom come."

Before heading out toward the animals, Sam walked to the edge of the cliff and stood on the same spot where he'd stood when the bullet had struck him in his head. Searching the rocky ground beneath him, Sam stooped and picked up the broken silver hat band. He examined it while Wilson stood watching him closely. The bullet had struck dead center of one of the silver coins that Jones had forged into a thick rosette.

"Are you thinking what I'm thinking?" Wilson asked, looking at the crushed rosette. "That the fancy hatband might have saved your life?"

"Not *might have*," said Sam. "It *did* save my life." He looked out across the canyon toward where he had caught a glint of sunlight on Deaks' rifle barrel. "This time you made a big mistake, Deaks," he whispered to himself. "You left a living witness behind."

On their way to the string of stage horses, Sam found the livery horse lying stretched out in the wild grass sunning itself. Seeing the two men and the burro approaching him, the big buckskin livery horse stood up, shook himself off and waited patiently for Sam to walk up, take hold of the short length of rope dangling from his muzzle and look him over closely.

"This one is no worse for the wear," Sam commented, rubbing the horse's neck. Looking out toward the other horses he said, "Everything else looks about the same as I left it."

"Then we best gather up and get on back to the cavern," said Wilson. "I'll fix you something to eat and let you get some more rest."

"Obliged, Mister Wilson," said Sam. "But you've done enough already. I'm going to keep my camp right here and wait for my partner to show up. I calculate he should be tracking me here most anytime."

"Ha!" said Wilson, "I don't know who this feller is, but you sure have lots of faith in him."

"That's right, I do," Sam replied, pulling the livery horse along toward the stage horses. "You and Bartholomew can head on back. Keep an eye on the stage that passes through here every week. Soon as I get caught up, I'll be sending you a sombrero, like I promised."

"Ahhh," Wilson said, brushing the idea aside, "it ain't necessary."

"It is to me," said Sam. He tipped his sombrero and walked off toward the stage horses. Moments later, when he took a glance back over his shoulder, the old hermit and his burro had vanished from sight.

Two hours later, Sam had tended the horses and prepared a pot of coffee. He sat waiting with a cup in his hand as Ranger Jones rode into sight along the winding trail. "I knew it," Sam whispered, smiling to himself.

Seeing Sam, Hadley Jones booted his horse up into a trot until he rode in closer. Coming to a halt, he looked down at Sam, saying, "What's happened, Sam? The captain said he sent you to deliver the stage horses and hasn't heard a word since."

"There's the horses," said Sam, nodding toward the string of horses. "They're still not delivered." He lifted his sombrero and revealed the red-purple knot on the upper side of his head. "I got ambushed.

Hadn't been for that silver hatband you made, I'd be dead."

Jones whistled low at the sight of the knot. Then he said, "I don't suppose you caught even a glimpse of the coward who did it?"

Sam leveled his sombrero. "Oh, I caught more than just a glimpse. It was Stone Eddie Deaks," he said with finality. "I saw him plain as day. As far as he knows, he killed me."

Jones stepped down off his horse and walked over to where Sam sat on the ground. "Then I expect he's in for quite a surprise." He reached a hand down. Sam took it and pulled himself to his feet.

"I wish I had Black Pot beneath me," Sam said, "but I guess this livery horse will have to do."

"Whoa," said Jones. "You're not thinking about going after Deaks right *now*, are you?"

"Right *now* is the best time I can think of," Sam replied. "I've got tracks to follow. He's in no hurry, probably not watching his back real close about now."

"But we've got to get these horses delivered," said Jones. "You've got to report what happened to you and get a warrant issued to bring Deaks in."

Sam gave his partner a purposeful stare. "I'm not bringing Deaks in, Jonesie."

"You mean . . . ?" Jones let his words trail.

"I mean that right now is the best time for me to catch up to him. He's never left a living witness before. He thinks I'm dead. Even if he sees me alive, he has no idea that I know he's the one who shot me. I'll tell him when I get ready to drop the hammer on him."

Jonesie looked shocked. "Sam, you mean you're not even going to try to take him in alive?"

Sam didn't answer. Instead he said, "Jonesie, why don't you take the horses on to Quincy? I'll get on Deaks' trail and ride him down."

"We're partners, Sam," Jones said in a somber tone. "If you're going after Deaks, I'm going to be right beside you." He looked down at the ground and off in the direction of Quincy. "Odds are he's headed in that same direction anyway. We can deliver the horses and be back on his trail in no time."

Sam considered, then said, "Don't think that your being along is going to change anything. Stone Eddie Deaks is mine."

"I understand, Sam," Jones replied. "But I wear the same badge as you do. I can't stand by and let you commit murder."

"Murder?" said Sam. He touched a gloved finger to the side of his sombrero covering the knot on his head. "Let's not forget who the murderer is. I'm not the first person Deaks ever drew a long bead on from a half mile away. There's something about that kind of killing that sticks awfully deep in my craw."

"I *know* who the murderer is, but you've got to give him a chance to turn himself in if he'll take it, right, Sam?" Jones asked, still hoping to get some sort of satisfactory answer from his partner before they embarked on a personal manhunt. "Isn't that the difference between them and us? We do things by the letter of the law?"

"That's right, Jonesie," Sam said, taking a deep breath as if reconsidering the matter. "We'll stick by the letter of the law—the same way Deaks has always done it. Let's ride."

"You don't sound like you mean it, Sam," Jones persisted.

But Sam didn't reply as he took the reins to the livery horse and stepped up into the saddle.

Chapter 11

———

Shortly after leaving the ranger's campsite, Eddie Deaks began to suspect that someone was on his trail. But he'd taken his time, circling wide of the trail for the next couple of days, staying close to rock cover, making sure whoever was back there wasn't on his trail purely by coincidence. On the morning of the third day, he decided to spring his trap.

Riding upward along a steep elk path, he found a good place to backtrack through the rocky terrain and wait a few feet above the trail with his rifle in hand. Within moments he saw a drifting rise of dust. Moments later he caught sight of a single rider pushing his horse hard, as if trying to catch up to him.

"So long, stranger," Deaks said to himself, raising the rifle to his shoulder and taking aim dead center on the rider's chest as the man came into full view atop a rise in the trail. But his finger eased back off the trigger as he recognized Norbert Lamb riding closer and bringing his horse to halt. "Over here,

Kid," he called out, seeing Lamb stare down at the fresh tracks left earlier by Deaks' horse.

Startled, Lamb jerked upright in his saddle. His hand went to his gun butt.

"That would be real stupid, Kid," said Deaks, his rifle still raised but not closely aimed.

"Jesus!" Lamb exclaimed. His hand came away from his gun. "You got me cold, Mr. Deaks!"

"Yeah, it looks that way." He lowered the rifle a little more, liking the idea that he'd gotten the drop on the young gunman. "How long have you been trailing me?" he asked, already having a pretty good idea. He just wanted to know if Lamb had seen him shoot the ranger.

"A long ways," said Lamb. "But don't worry. I didn't see anything you have to worry about."

Deaks thought about it for a second, realizing that he could kill Lamb along the trail anytime he chose to. He liked the way the Kid looked up to him. Lowering his rifle the rest of the way, he said, "If you saw me settle up with that ranger, you best learn a lesson from it."

"*What* ranger?" Lamb grinned, denying any knowledge of what Deaks might be talking about. He stepped down from his horse.

"Yeah, *what* ranger?" Deaks said, liking that kind of wise talk. The Kid might be all right. He returned the knowing grin. "I take it you're still trying to hook up with some fast money?"

"You can count on that," said Lamb, walking closer. "I figured on catching up with you tonight to

see about riding along with you." He shook his head.
"Man! You have been wandering all over the place.
Why didn't you just stick to the trail?"

Deaks gave him a bemused look, deciding that
maybe he'd misread the Kid. Was this man a little
thickheaded? He didn't seem to realize Deaks had
been checking things out, leading him along these
past three days. "I enjoy sightseeing," Deaks said, deciding to check the Kid's wits again, just for good
measure. He gestured off across the endless rugged
land.

"Really?" Lamb replied, not seeming to get Deaks'
wry humor. He looked off through the swirling heat,
then shrugged and said, "Whatever suits you, I
reckon. Myself, I prefer watery scenery."

Deaks stared, a bit puzzled, wondering for a second if Lamb himself was joking. If he was, Deaks
couldn't detect it.

Lamb stopped a few feet from Deaks, his arms
hanging loosely at his sides. "So what do you say?
Can you stand some company?"

Deaks looked him up and down as if appraising
him before saying, "I don't know, Kid. Has your
shooting got rusty since Dowdy Thompson?"

No sooner had Deaks got the words from his
mouth than Lamb spun away from him, his Colt
streaking up from his tied-down holster. He fired
three shots in rapid succession. The first bullet
clipped a short juniper bush from its perch a few feet
up the side of a rock slab. As the bush leapt upward,

the next two shots clipped it into three pieces and sent them careening away in the air.

"That's about the best I've got, for a small target," said Lamb, spinning the Colt around backward in his hand and dropping out the three empty cartridges all in one smooth motion.

"That ought to come in handy for gathering fire kindling," said Deaks.

"That's why I learned it," Lamb responded in a serious tone, eyeing Deaks as he poked three new rounds into the Colt and shut it with a brisk spin.

That's why he learned it . . . ? Deaks caught himself staring again, wondering if the Kid had been kicked in the head early on.

Lamb could tell that the shooting had impressed Deaks. "So what do you say? Do I ride with you? Maybe cover your back if the need arises?"

"Sure, ride along, Kid," said Deaks. "I can't see anybody ever getting the jump on me. But you never know when an extra gun might come in handy out here." He stood up from his position amid the rocks and walked to his horse. He shoved the rifle into its boot and stepped up into his saddle. Lamb nodded, satisfied with his shooting performance, and stepped up into his saddle and booted the horse over closer to Deaks.

"If my memory serves me right," said Lamb, "this trail leads straight to Quincy, then over to Sourweed."

"Better known as Dutchman Flats," Deaks commented, "but right you are, Kid. We're riding on to

Dutchman Flats to meet the man Max Thurston wanted me to meet in the first place."

"Before that ranger blew his damn head off," Lamb commented, offering a smile, seeming amused at the picture of Thurston flying backward through the saloon doors with his head shot open. "I bet Thurston never went through a door so fast in his life."

Deaks chuckled at the memory of the quick shoot-out between the ranger and Max Thurston. "I'll say one thing for Ranger Burrack. He was one tough-jawed sonsabitch. Things never turned dull when he was prowling around."

"If you don't want the whole world knowing you killed that ranger, you better quit saying *was* every time you talk about him," Lamb advised.

Deaks studied Lamb's flat expression for a moment before allowing himself to break into a smile. "*What* ranger?" he said smugly, turning his horse and nudging it down toward the flatlands.

Back on the wide trail, the ride into Quincy passed quickly. As soon as the two riders eased their horses along the narrow dirt street they saw the manager of the stage company–owned relay town standing alongside a smoldering pile of ashes. A charred stone chimney was all that remained of a small saloon that the stage company had erected to accommodate thirsty travelers.

"Looks like Lonzo Greer and his boys have been here and gone," Deaks said with a chuckle. "They always like to leave a place a little different than they found it."

"It's a shame they had to burn the saloon," said Lamb, in his serious tone. He looked around at the crumbling adobe stage depot, a corral and a ragged tent. "But I guess there wasn't much else worth burning."

"Yeah, I suppose," Deaks said, giving him a curious look. Nudging his horse toward the man standing beside the pile of ashes, he added, "Come on, let's go hear his sad song."

As the two stepped their horses closer to the relay station manager, the man threw open his black duster and swung a shotgun up, cocking both barrels. "I don't who you are, but if you belong to the bunch who did this, all I've got for you is a hole in the ground!" He raised the butt to his shoulder and took aim.

"Whoa now! Easy old pard!" said Deaks, wearing a smile and raising both hands chest high in a show of peace. "I don't know who this *bunch* is you're talking about, but if we belonged to them, this sure wouldn't be a good time for us to mention it."

"You're damn right it wouldn't!" said the manager. "Now who are you and what do you want here?"

Without answering right away, Deaks stopped his horse, looked all around calmly and said, "I take it you are the station manager, Mr. . . . ?"

"Bertrim!" said the manager, his tone no less gruff in spite of Deaks' pleasant demeanor. "Felix Bertrim!

Damn right I'm the manager here! Now what can I do for you? You don't look like men who came to catch a stage coach. And as you can see, we've no longer got a saloon. So you'll have to go somewhere else to get yourself blind staggering drunk."

"I can see we've caught you in a less than amiable mood, Mr. Bertrim," Deaks said beamingly. "Suppose we might just water our horses and be on our way? I realize how trying it can be, people burning your saloon down around you."

Bertrim seemed to calm down a bit. The shotgun lowered an inch. "Well, it wasn't really *my* saloon," he said. "The fact is I told the company it was a bad idea to begin with, putting hard liquor out here in the middle of nowhere so's every low white and wild red heathen in the territory can get a whiff of it. It has caused us every sort of problem you can think of. We've had everything hit here from smallpox to stolen horses!" As he spoke, he thumbed over his shoulder toward a water trough. "But go on and water your animals. There's no point in me raving to you about the failure of this enterprise."

"Much obliged, sir!" Deaks said politely. Lamb and he turned their horses toward the trough while Bertrim continued to speak.

"I will warn the both of yas though to be on the lookout for the sonsabitches who done this. It was Lonzo Greer and his band of devils."

"Oh, was it now?" Deaks stopped his horse short for a moment. Lamb could see the station manager had just made a terrible mistake.

"You're damn well right it was," said Bertrim. I recognized every one of them. I don't mind telling the proper authorities about it either, soon as I get a chance."

Deaks sat tense in his saddle for a moment, studying the man as if considering something. But then he relaxed, smiled and said, "You, sir, are a man of courage. I admire you for it." Tipping his hat slightly he nudged his horse on to the water trough. Lamb followed quietly, not sure of what to expect.

The two dismounted at the trough and watered their horses in silence. When the thirsty animals had drunk their fill, Deaks looked over at the station manager, who still stood shaking his head, looking down at the pile of cinders and smoldering ashes, his hands on his hips. "Stupid bastard," Deaks whispered, grinning.

"Too stupid to live?" Lamb asked idly.

Deaks didn't answer. But when the two had mounted and ridden a full hundred yards away from the small station, Deaks stopped in the trail, lifted his rifle from its boot, cocked it and took aim at the center of Bertrim's back.

Lamb didn't flinch as the rifle shot ripped across the rocky vacant land. At the charred pile of rubble, Bertrim fell straight forward, facedown into the smoking embers, his hands still on his hips. "There now," said Deaks, still grinning, jacking another round into his rifle chamber, "that's the way I like doing things. Nice and clean and peaceful-like. Hell, he died never even knowing I did it."

"Or why," Lamb added. He stared at the body in the smoking embers as he spoke. "As back shooting goes, that's about as slick as any I've ever seen."

"Yeah?" Deaks replied, looking the Kid up and down, taking a second to wonder if Lamb's words were intended to be a compliment or a slur. "I have to admit, there is a certain art to it."

"I can see that," said Lamb, the intention of his words still unclear to Deaks. "If it's done wrong, you've got a poor sumbitch crawling all around, his back shot out, hot cinders burning hell out of him."

"Exactly," said Deaks, shoving his rifle back down into its boot. Without another word on the matter, he turned his horse back to the trail and booted it out toward Dutchman Flats.

Riding along beside Deaks, Lamb finally asked in a cautious tone, "No offense, but as fast as I've always heard you are with a gun, would you mind telling me why is it you've taken to back shooting?"

"Not at all," Deaks said amiably, seeming not the least bit ashamed of his cowardly act. "I do it because I *like* it!" He chuckled quietly and stared straight ahead.

Chapter 12

"Well, well, look what we've got coming here," Buck Simpson said sidelong to the circle of men without taking his eyes off the two riders coming in off the flatlands. He squinted, watching the riders through the simmering evening heat while in the circle at his feet a battle continued to rage between two bloody exhausted roosters. Reaching his gloved hand up, Buck shoved his wad of dollar bills down into his shirt pocket.

"Somebody better go tell Lonzo," Owen Reager responded, too engrossed in the cockfight to go tell Lonzo himself.

"You're the newest man here. You go tell him, *Deputy*," Ernie Shay said to Forrest Bidson, who stood crouched beside him, his fist also clenching a wad of money.

Bidson gave Shay a cold stare, saying, "Until Lonzo tells me otherwise, I don't take orders from you, Shay."

Ernie Shay started to straighten up from his crouch and say something to Forrest Bidson, but Reverend Wilcox saw trouble coming and cut in, saying, "I've got no money on this fight. I'll go tell him."

"Never mind, Reverend," Lonzo called out from the open doorway of the cantina. He and Metlet stepped through the dusty length of burlap that served as a door. He glared at Shay and the others. "I don't want nobody missing their gawddamn chicken fight just to keep me informed on what's going on around us." Walking straight to the center of the cockfight, Lonzo kicked both battle-locked roosters high into the air, breaking them up.

"Damn it!" Shay groaned. "There goes my last seven dollars!"

An old Mexican cock tender rushed in, snatched up the two roosters as they hit the ground and raced away with them under his arm. *"Gringo bastardos!"* he shouted over his shoulder.

Lonzo ignored the man's insult, his interest now piqued by the sight of the two riders slowing down as they rode onto the street into Dutchman Flats. "Deaks?" he asked aloud, squinting in the harsh glare of evening sunlight.

Paul Metlet stepped in beside him and studied the two riders. "I damn well believe that is Stone Eddie," he said.

"Who's that with him?" Calvin Thurston asked, getting interested, having heard from Giles Pruitt that Deaks had been there when the ranger killed his brother, Max.

"We'll find out who it is, Calvin," said Lonzo. "The main thing is we make Deaks feel welcome. Looks like he must be thinking about joining us if he's come seeking us out."

"Hello the street," Deaks called out when he and Lamb were within twenty feet of Lonzo and his men.

Lonzo stood with his hands on his hips and watched the two rein in close to the hitch rail. "You and your friend step down, Stone Eddie," he said, looking Lamb up and down.

"Obliged," Deaks replied, touching his hat brim. He nodded toward Lamb. "This is Norbert Lamb. If you need a good gun, Lamb here is your huckleberry."

"I'm glad Max Thurston managed to find you before he got himself killed."

"Me too," said Deaks, steeping down and spinning his reins around the hitch rail. "That was a damn shame what happened to your man Thurston—that ranger gunning him down that way."

Beside Deaks, Lamb also stepped down and hitched his horse. He looked around at the faces of the men, noting the way they stared at him, sizing him up.

"Yes, it was a damn shame," Calvin Thurston cut in. He thumbed himself on the chest. "I'm Calvin Thurston, Max Thurston's brother. Was you not able to offer my brother any help that day?"

Deaks gave a cold, thin smile and said quietly, "If I were to answer that question, I would find myself *explaining* my actions to you." His right hand poised at shoulder level, he added, "The fact is, I don't *explain* myself to nobody. Is that all right with you, Calvin Thurston?"

Calvin glowered at him.

"Hold on, men," said Lonzo, his gaze turning harsh as he stared at Calvin Thurston. "Let's not all get off to a bad start here!"

Ignoring Lonzo, Deaks continued staring at Calvin as he said, "But if it's any consolation to you, that ranger who killed your brother is laying deader then hell back along the high trail right now."

"What?" Lonzo's face lit up in bemused disbelief. He smiled. "You mean you *killed* Ranger Burrack?"

Without saying *yes* outright, Deaks offered a crafty smile. "Let's just call his death a little something to show you how happy I am to be riding with you and your boys."

Calvin's expression softened. He shook his head a bit as if having to clear it. "He's already dead?"

"Deader than he ever thought he'd be," Deaks replied. Giving Calvin a quick once-over, he asked, "Now then, are you and me squared up on things?"

Calivin replied in a more humble tone, "Damn, Mr. Deaks, I don't know what to say."

"Just call me Stone Eddie," Deaks said.

"Much obliged to you, Stone Eddie," said Calvin.

"See, men?" Lonzo beamed, unable to control his joy and excitement. "Damn it to hell, I told all of you. Having a man like Stone Eddie Deaks riding with us is not a thing to take lightly! This gang is going places, by God!"

A cheer went up from the men; but Deaks raised a hand settling them. "Now, now, before everybody gets too excited, I need to tell all of yas that Ranger Burrack wasn't the only man there when Max Thurston hit the dirt. There was another ranger there. As far as I'm concerned, he was just as much to blame as Burrack for your man's death."

"Is that right?" Lonzo turned serious. "Would you recognize him enough to point him out to us?"

"What do you think?" said Deaks. "Me and Lamb here saw him from as close as I am to you right now."

"Then I think it's only fitting that we ride over to the ranger post, stop in, blow his damn head off and be done with it," Lonzo said. He liked knowing that soon his gang would be famous for having killed both Ranger Sam Burrack and his partner as well.

Deaks gave him a level gaze and said, "Lonzo, I don't mind killing one ranger, two rangers, or a whole damn barn full of rangers if that's what suits you. But I didn't come all this way just to kill lawmen. I came looking to make some money. That's what Max said this gang does best."

"And by God, Max was right," said Lonzo. "You want to rob something? Hell! We'll start right here!" He half drew his pistol as if ready to begin shooting up the town.

"Easy," said Deaks. "First I want some whiskey to cut the dust from my throat." As he spoke, his eyes went to Candy and Rolena, who had stepped into the open door of the cantina and stood staring at him. "Next," he said, "I want both of those women with me, buck naked in a tub of hot water, and bathing me like I'm their long-lost child." He looked all around the small town, appraising it. "Then we'll gut this place and go kill us a ranger. Is that all right with you, *boss*?" he asked Lonzo.

Lonzo let his gun slip back down into his holster. "I couldn't have said it better myself." He called out over his shoulder, "Candy! Rolena! Go find the biggest tub in town. Let's show Stone Eddie and his friend Lamb some hospitality!"

In the doorway of the cantina, Candy groaned and said to Rolena under her breath, "Come on, let's see if this Stone Eddie is all he's cracked up to be."

At the burned-down relay station in Quincy, Sam and Hadley Jones sat atop their horses looking down at the station manager's charred body. Sam held the lead rope to the recovered stage horses in his gloved hand. "I expected as much when we saw their tracks lead into here," he said. He stared at the charred body of Felix Bertrim lying facedown, his hands on his hips in almost the same position as when Deaks' bullet had hit him.

"Yep," said Jones, "and here comes a stage right now." He sat slumped in his saddle beside the ranger, gazing off toward the big Studebaker coach that had ambled up into sight on the trail north of the station. Two passenger's heads stuck out the windows. The people stared in curiosity at the blackened chimney amid the debris.

Swinging down from his saddle, Sam said, "Go

meet them and keep them back while I drag this man out of sight."

Jones gigged his horse and headed off to meet the stage while Sam led the stage horses aside and tied the lead rope around an iron hitch pole at the side of the trail. Pulling his bandanna up over his nose, he walked back, dragged Bertrim's body out of the still smoking ashes and took it behind a nearby stand of mesquite brush. Then he stepped back into his saddle and nudged his horse toward the stopped stagecoach, where Jones sat talking to the driver.

"Oh dear!" said a matronly woman who sat with her neck craned out the stagecoach window. "I do hope this is not one of the scoundrels who did this!" She held a dainty handkerchief to her cheek and nodded toward Sam, who rode toward them with his bandanna still raised across the bridge of his nose.

"No, ma'am," said Jones, seeing Sam approach them, "he's my partner."

From the leather-bound driver's seat, a gravelly voice said to Jones, "I thought Ranger Burrack always rides alone?"

"Used to be he did," said Jones. He gazed away toward Sam and watched him pull down his bandanna. "But now him and I are partners."

"You must be a hell of a lawman yourself," the driver commented, "if Sam thinks enough of you to let you ride with him."

Too modest to reply to such a comment, Jones only smiled slightly to himself and sat quietly until Sam rode the rest of the way up to the stage. "'Day to ya, Ranger," said the stage driver.

"Good day to you too, Whitey," Sam replied. As he spoke, he took off his sombrero and fanned it widely, as if to blow away the smell of death surrounding him. In the stage window, the woman passenger raised her handkerchief to her nose and stared as if in awe.

"I was just telling your partner here, he must carry some tough bark on him to be able to ride with you," said Whitey Sheppard.

"He's a good man, Whitey," said Sam.

"What's the story in there?" Whitey asked, gazing toward the charred chimney.

"It's just what you see," said Sam. "Everything's burned to the ground. There's water in the trough for the animals, and water in the well for your passengers. You can change horses here. But I'd appreciate it if you led your tired horses on to your next stop. We can't stay here and tend to them. We want to catch up to the ones who did this."

"Let me guess," said Whitey. "Lonzo Greer and his Black moon gang."

"Why do you say it's Greer and his gang?" Sam asked.

Whitey spit a stream of tobacco juice and wiped his cuff across his stained lips. "Why, hell, Ranger, there ain't any meanness gone on out here the past few months that didn't have Lonzo's hand in it."

From the stage window, a male passenger said in a critical tone of voice, "If this Greer fellow is so

widely known as a scoundrel, why is it that you so-
called *lawmen* have let him go this long unchal-
lenged?"

Sam and Hadley Jones ignored the man's remark;
but Whitey Sheppard grew enraged by it. "What
the hell did you say, mister?" he bellowed, jerking the
brake handle back and jumping down from the
driver's seat. He yanked the stage door open and
shouted at the cowering man in a finely creased business suit, "Get your pin-striped ass out of my stage if
you're going to insult my friends! You tinhorn
sonsa—"

"Easy, Whitey," Sam said, cutting him off sharply.
He stepped down quickly from his saddle and put
himself between the angry old stage driver and the
frightened passenger. "I'm sure this gentleman didn't
mean anything by it. Did you, sir?" He gave the man
a look.

"N-no! Indeed, I did not!" said the shaken busi-
nessman.

"There, now, Whitey, you see?" said Sam. He patted the old stage driver's shoulder. "No harm done."
He waited for only a second to let Whitey settle
down, then said calmly, "Why don't you go ahead
and get these horses swapped and watered, then get
on to your next stop? Jones and I need to hurry if
we're going to catch these murderers."

Chapter 13

———

The Black Moons had ridden a full three hours from Dutchman Flats before Buck Simpson finally realized Candy and Rolena had disappeared. "They were with us when we left, weren't they?" he asked Ernie Shay and Owen Reager with a puzzled expression.

"Damned if I know," said Shay. "Once the shooting started I sort of lost track of who was where."

"What's it matter?" Reager asked, shrugging. "It's time we traded the whores in anyways. If I wanted to sleep with the same woman every night, I'd have married me one and stayed home with her."

"I'm going back for them," Buck said with determination, turning his horse away from Shay and Reager and looking back along the trail.

"You best check with Lonzo first," Shay warned. "He might not take kindly to you chasing off after whores, especially going back and looking for them in a town we just robbed."

"Don't tell him I'm gone," said Buck. "I'll get them and be back before you know it."

"I wouldn't count on that if I was you, Buck," Shay warned again. "If them whores don't want to be here, it might be best to leave them be. You'll be on your own, you know."

"Yeah," Reager joined in, "whores can get pretty nasty, particularly if they have a fellow outnumbered."

"Naw, it ain't that way with these whores," said Buck, dismissing their warnings. "These girls wanted to come with us. All that fighting and resisting? Me having to haul them along over my shoulder? That was all part of the game we was playing with one another. Whores like playing games like that." He grinned. "Hell, so do I."

"Oh?" said Shay. "In that case, where are they? Seems to me like that game might be over, else they'd still be here. Since they ain't here, I'm thinking they'd rather just be left alone. We all gave them a pretty hard going-over, if you know what I mean."

"You don't know whores, Shay," said Buck, brushing the matter aside with the wave of his hand. "Keep me covered with Lonzo while I go back, get them and bring them back here."

"Go on then," said Shay, "since you ain't going to listen to reason. We warned you. That's all we can do."

Buck gigged his horse away in a flurry of dust and headed back along the trail at a hard run. He hadn't gone over a few hundred yards before he found the tracks of two horses that had turned back and veered slightly off the trail and into the cover of mesquite and scrub juniper. He grinned slyly to himself and said, "All right, girlies, let's see how well you play hide and seek with old Buck."

Following the sets of tracks through the under-brush another three miles back toward Dutchman Flats, Buck stopped abruptly when he heard Candy call out his name from a rise of rock alongside the trail. "Buck, go away and leave us alone, please!" she called down to him.

But Buck would have none of it. He called out loudly up into the rocks, "I know you fillies don't mean that! I'm coming for yas and taking you both back. I'm afraid I might have to lay my hand to your bottoms if you give me any sass! How would you like that? Huh, Candy? Huh, Rolena? Is old Buck going to have to take a strong hand with yas?"

"Buck, please listen to us. The game is over," Rolena called out. "It's time you go your way and we go ours. Stay away from us. We don't want to hurt you!"

"They don't want to hurt me." Buck chuckled to himself. "Ain't that as cute as a button?" He nudged his horse around the edge of the rock and coaxed it up a steep, narrow trail, following the hoofprints of the women's horses.

"Come out, come out wherever you are!" Buck called in a gruff but playful voice. But no sooner had the words left his mouth than both women stood up and hurled rocks the size of goose eggs out over the ledge above him.

"We tried to tell you, Buck," said Rolena as the rocks descended on him.

"Jesus, look out!" cried Buck, barely ducking the first round of rocks. He jerked his horse sideways just in time to keep more rocks from hitting his shoulder. "You girls could hurt a fellow bad throwing rocks down—" His words stopped short as another large rock sailed down and landed squarely atop his head with a solid *thunk.*

"Oh, my God!" said Rolena, clasping a hand over her mouth. "I've killed him sure enough!"

Buck's limp figure seemed to melt down the side of his horse into the dirt. "Don't worry," said Candy. "You'd never kill Buck Simpson hitting him on the head." She stood up and dusted off her hands. "Come on, let's take him back to the Flats and let the town decide what to do with him."

"Do you think they'll hang him?" Rolena asked, sounding a bit shaky at the prospect.

"If they do, so what?" said Candy. "Buck always knew he'd hang sooner or later. Besides, this could work out good for us. Taking him back will let folks know that we weren't a part of what Lonzo's men did to the town." The two helped each other down from the rock ledge and approached Buck, who lay babbling incoherently by the time they reached him.

Candy reached down and picked up Buck's flat-tened Stetson and the reins to his horse. "Take down that rope, Rolena," she said, nodding at the coiled lariat hanging from Buck's saddle. "We'll have to tie him good tight and lift him over his saddle."

"Tie who?" Buck bellowed, his groggy voice sounding like that of a drunkard. A bloody knot stood up two inches atop his head. "I'll kill . . . you!" he threatened. His hand clawed limply at the gun holstered on his hip.

"Stop it, Buck!" said Candy, stamping her heel down hard on his wrist, causing him to draw his arm back in pain.

"Gawddamn you!" Buck raged, his head still reeling in a half-conscious stupor. "I've been your friend! How can you whores do this to me?"

"Buck, shut up," said Rolena. She had stepped beside the trail and picked up a stout pine limb from a pile of deadfall timber. She came back welding it like a club, the rope from Buck's saddle looped over her shoulder. "We've got a long ride, and I'm not going to listen to you bellyache all the way."

"Bellyache?" said Buck, starting to come around a bit, enough to raise his head and try to push himself to his feet. "I'll give you both something to *bellyache* about!"

Without another word, Rolena drew the pine limb sideways and swung it with all her strength.

"Good Lord, Rolena!" cried Candy, staring wide-eyed at Buck as his head rocked back and forth before he fell facedown in the dirt. "You've hit him too hard. You've knocked him cold again! Now he'll be dead-weight getting in the saddle."

"Deadweight?" said Rolena, aghast. "You don't mean that now he really is . . . ?"

"No, he's not dead," said Candy. "But if we keep beating him, he's going to be! His head is hard, but *damn!*" She motioned for Rolena to give her the end of the rope. "Come on, let's get him tied and get going. We want to get back to town before dark sets in."

The first shot rang out in the afternoon heat as the ranger and Hadley Jones rode into Dutchman Flats on a narrow back-alley path. Three more shots exploded as both lawmen reined their animals sharply off the path and into the cover of some discarded wooden shipping crates piled high behind a mercantile store. Coming down from his saddle, Sam jerked his Colt from his holster and hunkered close beside his horse. Beside him, Jones grabbed his rifle from its boot.

Levering a round into the rifle chamber, Jones said, "I thought coming in the back way was supposed to keep something like this from happening."

"It always has for me." Sam ventured a gaze around the corner of the shipping crate.

"Then somebody better tell Deaks," Jones replied.

"I'm thinking this isn't Deaks doing the shooting," Sam replied. "If it was, I'm thinking at least one of us would be dead right now."

"Townsmen?" Jones asked, ducking slightly as a bullet thumped into the crate in front of him.

"Good thinking," the ranger said, having already

deduced as much, but wanting to see how quickly Jones figured it out.

Another shot rang out; then the alley path fell silent for a second. "Here's our chance," said Jones. He called out loud and clear along the backs of the buildings where the shots were coming from, "We are Arizona Territory Rangers. Hold your fire!"

The two waited for a moment, listening closely in the tense silence. Finally a voice responded from behind the town barbershop. "How do we know you're rangers?"

Sam and Hadley looked at each other and breathed a sigh of relief. "Who am I speaking to?" Sam asked.

"I'm Martin Coffee," the voice replied. "I'm the acting town constable today."

Jones and Sam looked at each other again. Sam called out, "All right, Mr. Coffee, I'm taking your word that you are who you say you are. I'm stepping out with my arms spread and my badge clearly visible. Keep your men from shooting at me."

"You heard him," Coffee shouted. "Everybody hold their fire, unless I say otherwise!"

Holstering his Colt and handing Jones his reins, Sam stepped out sideways, his arms spread, his duster hanging open, revealing his battered badge. "I'm Ranger Sam Burrack, from the Badlands ranger station." He gestured toward the shipping crates. "This is my partner, Ranger Hadley Jones."

A voice called out in a harsh whisper, saying, "Martin! I've heard of Burrack!"

"Shut up, Sudder, so have I," Coffee replied to the voice. Then to Sam he said, "You're the one who killed Junior Lake and his gang a while back?"

Sam gave Jones a thin, mirthless smile and called out to Coffee, "I am." He lowered his arms an inch and said sternly, "I'm letting my arms down now. Why don't you and your men come forward and tell us what's happened here?"

"Here we come, Ranger," said Coffee, stepping out from the edge of a building, a Spencer rifle at port arms across his chest. Behind him from both sides of the street, townsmen emerged cautiously and followed his lead.

"What's happened here is that we've been hit by Lonzo Greer and his whole damned Black Moon gang," said Coffee, wiping a hand across his forehead, letting his rifle slump at his side when he drew closer and got a better view of both Sam's and Jones' badges. Jones stayed close to the edge of the shipping crate a moment longer, protecting the horses should something suddenly go wrong.

"I bet that's who you lawmen are searching for, isn't it?" Coffee asked. "If it is, I wish to God you'd gotten here earlier. They've robbed the bank. Killed the owner. Killed our sheriff. Killed our blacksmith." He shook his head in sorrow. "Three good men gunned down for no reason at all except they dared to protect our folks and our community."

Sam had let Coffee speak and get his worries off his mind. When he'd finished, Sam said, "How much of a start do they have on us?"

Coffee looked a bit surprised. "You mean I'm right? It is Lonzo's gang you're looking for?"

"If it wasn't, it is now," said Sam. "How long?"

"Oh, four, maybe five hours," Coffee estimated. "They even have two loose-looking women riding with them. I believe we can all guess what they do for the gang."

As Coffee spoke, Sam and Jones stepped forward past him and a few of the townsmen, and led their horses out of the alley toward the street. The armed townsmen followed Coffee obediently, staring as if in awe at the two dusty lawmen.

Arriving on the wide, deserted street, Coffee pointed toward the bullet-riddled front of the town's brick bank building. "See what those scoundrels did? It's not enough they rob us! They have to vandalize the whole town! Kill innocent people for no reason!" Boards had been nailed up to replace the broken glass windows.

Sam and Jones let the man rage against the outlaw gang a moment longer. Then Sam asked, "Did a well-dressed lone rider come through here either before or after all this happened?"

"No," said Coffee, "but a *couple* of fellows did ride in and join them a little while beforehand. One of them was a bit *well-dressed* for that crowd."

"I see." Sam considered for a second. "The other one, was he a younger fellow, wearing range clothes?"

"Yes! That's them all right," said Coffee. "More members of the Black Moon Gang, I suppose."

"They are now," Sam said with finality. Sam had looked away for a moment, noting how low the sun lay in the west. He realized Jones and he would be riding in the dark by the time they watered their horses and got back on the trail.

Seeing what Sam was thinking, Jones turned to Coffee and asked politely, "Mr. Coffee, is there anything we can do for you folks? I see you seem to have things pretty well under control here."

"You're wanting to get right on their trail, aren't you?" Coffee asked.

Sam watched in silence, seeing how Jones was handling things.

"That's right, sir," said Jones. "If you don't need us here, we should get after them before they hit another town the same way."

"Then water down and go, fellows," said Coffee. "The sooner you catch these scoundrels, the better off we'll all be."

Within minutes Sam and Jones had led their horses to a water trough, loosened their cinches and let the animals drink. Thanking Coffee and the townsmen for a bag of food they brought to them, Sam and Jones climbed back into their saddles and got quickly back on the main trail out of town.

The two rode at a steady pace without overtaxing the horses. When darkness fell around across the land, they slowed their pace a bit but rode on for another full hour before the sound of horses' hooves clicking on the rocky trail caused the two to stop dead still and listen closely. In the light of a quarter moon, Sam motioned for Jones to step down from his saddle. Doing so in unison, the two led the horses silently off to the side of the trail and waited against the side of a large boulder.

A few minutes later, the sound of the hooves clicking growing closer, the rangers heard a woman's voice saying quietly, "If he tries loosening the rope, I'll have to hit him again."

Sam gave Jones a curious look in the darkness. They waited until they could see the two women riding slowly toward them on the trail, one of them leading a horse behind her. Sam saw the bootheels sticking out from the horse's sides and realized a man lay across its back. Sam gave Jones a nod, and the two lawmen sprang quickly into the middle of the road, holding their hands up before them.

"All right, ladies," Sam said, trying to keep his voice level so as not to frighten the women or their horses, "stop right there."

Rolena let out a short gasp; but the two women stopped and held their horses in place. "I'm armed, mister!" said Candy.

"So are we, ma'am," Sam responded. "But let's all keep our heads here. We're Arizona Rangers. Raise your hands so we can see them."

Candy and Rolena did so reluctantly. "We didn't have anything to do with those bastards robbing the bank and shooting up the place," said Candy. "We were headed back there to turn this one over to the law."

Sam leaned slightly sideways and looked closer at

the man lying across the saddle. Seeing that the women were holding their hands high and that Jones had the women covered, Sam stepped past them and around to the other side of the horse to where he could see the swollen, bloody knot on Buck Simpson's head. Gripping Simpson by both ears, Sam raised his head and looked at his battered face.

Purple eyelids opened narrowly, revealing Buck's bloodshot eyes. "Hel—hel—help me . . ." Buck moaned in a barely audible voice.

Chapter 14

———

Gathered around a small fire, Candy and the two rangers stared down at Buck Simpson, who lay with his battered head in Rolena's lap. Hearing Buck cough and gasp for breath, Candy said solemnly, "We didn't want to kill this poor stupid bastard. We just wanted him to go away and leave us alone."

"He *did* force you both to go with them?" Sam asked quietly, reaffirming what Candy had told him moments earlier.

"Yes, he did, Ranger Burrack," Candy said firmly. "You can ask anybody in Barstow. He dragged us out of the Silver Slipper kicking and screaming, right, Rolena?"

Rolena, with tears in her eyes, looked up from Buck Simpson's swollen, disfigured face. "Yes, he did force us to come with them . . . but I didn't mean to kill him. I never hurt nothing in my life, except *myself*, that is." She sobbed and dabbed Buck's cheek with a wet bandanna. "Ranger, isn't there something we can do to save him?"

"As soon as we get him watered down and rested a little, we'll take him back to Dutchman Flats." His voice lowered a bit. "But it doesn't look good, the shape he's in."

"Dutchman Flats," Candy said thoughtfully. "I hope they won't try to string us up for riding with the Black Moons."

"They are upset," Sam said. "We'll be with you, just long enough to explain things." He looked closer at Candy and asked pointedly, "Are you sure this wasn't all just a parlor game you girls were playing with these men?"

Candy didn't even have to consider the question. She said quickly, "It didn't start out to be, but as soon as we saw they were forcing us along with them whether we liked it or not, we tried to make like it was all a parlor game just to stay alive." She tilted her head high. "Can you blame us for that?"

"No, ma'am," said Sam. "I just need to know the truth on how things came about, if you want me to protect you from a mob of angry townsmen."

"Well, you can tell them we used the only weapons we had to stay alive," Candy said firmly. Nodding at the ranger's holstered Colt, she continued, "You have your gun. All we have is our bodies and our wits. Can you explain that to the folks in Dutchman Flats?"

Sam considered for a second, then said, "Ma'am, I'm just going to tell them you two were forced along.

Bringing us Buck Simpson will count a long ways for your good intentions, if the townsfolk will believe you."

"That's what I had hoped for," Candy said, breathing a sigh of relief. "If Dutchman Flats will settle down long enough to ask Thomas Drexal or Lady Bertha at the Silver Slipper, they'll tell you it's the truth. Lonzo and his men went on a rampage there. Forrest Bidson, the deputy, joined them. He's the one who killed Sheriff Goins."

"It'll all take some sorting out," said Sam. "Meanwhile we'll do our best to keep Buck here alive."

Regaining consciousness enough to hear the last part of the conversation, Buck moaned and said in a raspy, halting voice, "Something's all . . . busted up . . . inside my head. . . ."

At the sound of Buck's voice, Sam stooped and said, "Buck, tell us where Lonzo and his gang are headed from here."

"Can . . . I get some . . . help?" Buck asked, gazing upward through swollen, blood-filled eyes.

"We're going to take you back to Barstow, Buck," Sam said. "But first you've got to tell where the gang is headed."

"You promise?" Buck gasped.

"You have my word on it," Sam said sincerely.

"They're gone . . . to kill that other ranger," Buck said, looking up through slits of eyes at the dark sky.

"What other ranger?" Sam asked. He and Jones gave each other a knowing look.

Buck struggled to pull in a deep breath. "Eddie

Deaks killed one. Lonzo is gone to get the other . . . for killing Max Thurston. . . ." His words trailed as if he were exhausted.

Whispering, Jones said, "He doesn't even know it's us he's talking to."

"Yes," said Sam, "but I believe what he's telling us. I can see Calvin Thurston wanting revenge for us taking down his brother, Max. With a big gun like Deaks riding with him, Lonzo would be glad to do it, just to gain a reputation for his gang and himself."

"Then we need to get back to the ranger outpost and warn them," said Jones.

"Yes," said Sam, "we will . . . just as soon as we escort Buck and these women back to Dutchman Flats and clear the air so things don't go wrong for them."

"I'm more concerned with the outpost than I am this outlaw or these whor—" Jones stopped himself quickly and said, "These women, I mean."

"That's all right, Ranger," said Candy. "We know we're whores, same as you know you're a lawman. Still, we don't want to get strung up for just trying to stay alive!"

"I'm sorry, ma'am," Jones said humbly. "But the fact is, I have a wife back near the ranger post." He looked at Sam for understanding.

"We're taking them back to Dutchman Flats," Sam said with authority. "I know a good shortcut, an old stagecoach trail up through the hills."

"An old coach trail through the hills?" said Jones, sounding a bit shaky at the prospect of the Black Moon gang riding in the direction of his new bride.

"Don't you mean it's *good* provided rock slides haven't filled the trail in a dozen or so places?"

"That's always a risk," Sam said, studying Jones' eyes to see how well he was handling this new information. "But it'll cut the ride in half, maybe put us back on the lower trail right on Lonzo's heels." To calm Jones, he added, "The outpost is in no danger. Lonzo isn't stupid enough to take on a whole ranger garrison."

"I'm not even *thinking* about the ranger outpost," said Jones. "From here on, it's my wife I'm thinking about."

"Then let's get headed on back," said Sam, seeing the worried look that had shadowed the young ranger's face. "The quicker we get everybody back to Dutchman Flats, the quicker we can get back after Lonzo and his gang." He turned as if to gather his canteen from Candy Crawford and prepare to get the group under way. But Jones wasn't satisfied.

"We're partners in all things, right, Sam?" Jones said, his voice sounding tight.

"That's right," Sam replied. "We're partners all the way."

"On everything?" said Jones. "Including all the decision making?"

"That's right," said Sam, eying him closely. "Say whatever's on your mind. We're in a hurry here."

"I'm going on after the gang, Sam," Jones said with determination.

"Don't get rattled on me," Sam warned him. "I need you to be as calm on this as you would any other situation. If you ride after Lonzo and his gang, there's no way you'll catch up to them before I will. Even if you did catch up to them, there's only one of you. You'll be lucky if they don't kill you."

"I've got a rifle," said Jones, "and I've got the rocks and hills above the trail. It's what you would do if you were riding alone, isn't it?" His eyes took on a different expression. "Or do you figure you're the only man who can fight that way?"

"Time's a-wasting. Let's make our move," said Sam, seeing there was no way to talk sense to Jones under the circumstances. He turned and walked toward the horses, his canteen hanging from his hand.

Before he'd taken three steps, Jones bellowed angrily behind him, "Don't turn your back on me! Sam! This is my wife I'm talking about!"

Hearing Jones' Colt cock, Sam stopped cold and turned slowly, facing him, seeing the gun in his partner's hand, seeing Candy hurriedly step back out of the way. In an even tone, Sam said, "You'll need a spare horse to ride them down. I was going to bring you Buck's." He stared at Jones flatly. But Jones knew everything that flat stare was saying.

"Oh, Jesus, Sam," he said after a tense silence had passed. His arm lowered to his side. "I—I didn't mean this." His shaking hand made two tries before he managed to holster his Colt. "Look what they've got me doing!" He turned slightly and stared off into the darkness.

"I understand," said Sam. "If I had a wife out there, I'd likely feel the same way." But Jones knew what had just happened couldn't be undone. Sam knew it too. "Let me get that extra horse for you," he said with a bit of regret in his voice.

On the way to Dutchman Flats, Candy sidled her horse close to Sam and said, "What if you just gave us note, a letter or something, saying we had nothing to do with the Black Moon gang—wouldn't that do it? Then you could go on and meet your friend."

"I wouldn't feel right about it, ma'am," Sam replied quietly, still stung by the incident between Jones and him before Jones had taken the spare horse and left. Buck Simpson and he rode double on one horse, Buck slumped in the saddle, unconscious, leaning back against him. "I've seen townsmen out of control before. They might not take time to read a letter, let alone *believe* it."

Catching the stiffness in the ranger's voice, Candy said, "I'm only trying to think of a way for you to go on and join your partner."

"Obliged, ma'am," Sam said, changing his tone of voice a bit. "I'll take the old cut across trail, just like I said."

"I'm familiar with that old coach trail," said Candy. Cocking her head slightly, she asked, "Why didn't you tell him that old trail never gets covered by rock slides?"

Sam waited for a moment, then replied, "He had it set in his mind to go. It wouldn't have mattered what I said."

They rode in silence for moment, Rolena a few feet

ahead of them. Finally Candy said, "Boy, your partner sure loves his wife."

"Yes, ma'am, he does," Sam said.

"You can just call me Candy, Ranger," she said, "like everybody else does."

"Thank you, *Candy*," Sam said.

"It's short for Candice," she said.

"Yes, ma'am—I mean, *Candy*," Sam said, correcting himself.

Candy smiled in the darkness. "Can I call you Sam?"

"Sam is fine," the ranger replied, staring straight ahead into the night.

"It must really be wonderful having a man care that much for you . . . the way your partner does for his wife, I mean." She shrugged. "I have men say they care for me, but I know why they say it." She paused for a moment, then ventured quietly, "Do you have anybody you care that much for, Sam?"

Sam looked at her, sighed softly and said, "Candy, why don't you go ride beside your friend?"

"Gawd, Sam!" Candy exclaimed, "I didn't mean anything by it! I was only *asking*! You don't have to take it *that* way!"

"I'm not taking it any way, Candy," Sam replied calmly. Reining back a step, he reached a gloved hand around and smacked her horse on the rear, saying, "I've just got some things on my mind."

They rode the rest of the way to Dutchman Flats in silence. At the edge of the main street into town, Sam had the women stop beside him; then he stepped his horse a few feet in front of them and called out toward a campfire burning in the street before Coffee's mercantile store, "Mr. Coffee . . . It's Ranger Sam Burrack, back off the trail."

Dark figures stood up from around the outer edges of the fire and spread out, taking cover. "Ranger Burrack!" Martin Coffee called out. "Come forward and be recognized."

Keeping the two women close to him, the ranger led them to within a few yards of the fire and stopped. From the shadows a voice said, "Look, Coffee, it's them whores that was with the Black Moons!"

"Easy, men," said Coffee. "Let's hear what the ranger has to say."

"I don't have time to say a lot," Sam responded, "but here is one of Lonzo's men. I want him cared for, not lynched. If he lives, it's up to a judge to say what happens to him next. Understood?"

"Give him a hand with that man," Coffee said to some townsmen gathering around, "carefully too. He looks in bad shape. Get him over to Doc Thornberry's." Looking back up at Sam, he asked, "Where's your partner?"

"He decided to ride on," Sam said, offering no more than that on the matter. He handed Buck Simpson down to three of the townsmen, who carried him away toward an office along the boardwalk.

"Much obliged, Mr. Coffee," Sam said with a sigh of relief, seeing the attitude of the townsmen. Stepping down from his saddle and helping the women down one at a time, he said, "These two are Candice Crawford and her friend Rolena. They were snatched up in Barstow from the Silver Slipper and forced to come with Lonzo's bunch." As he spoke, he looked all around from man to man making sure everybody listened to him. "They *work* at the Silver Slipper. But understand this, they had nothing to do with what happened here."

"Ranger," said a short, stocky man wearing a brown bowler, "I know Candy. I've been calling on her a few times when I drummed household goods and notions over near Barstow." He tipped his hat toward the women. "Evening, ladies," he said.

"Don't worry, Ranger," said Coffee. "We're not an angry mob here . . . simply a town that has been crippled and stunned. But we're good folks. We'll see to it these women are treated cordially and that this outlaw receives no unfair treatment."

Sam felt even more relieved, seeing by the expression in Coffee's eyes that he meant what he said. "Good. Can I get the use of a spare horse? I need a good one. I've got a long ride ahead of me tonight."

"I own a black Morgan cross that can win a race or pull a draft wagon, either one, Ranger. He's yours indefinitely," said Coffee.

"If I ever live in town that gets raided the way this one did, I hope somebody like you is there to keep everybody cool-headed."

"We've lost a lot, Ranger. We'll do what needs doing in order to bring Lonzo and his men to justice." Coffee took up the reins to the women's horses and directed Sam and his horse toward a water trough while he sent a townsman to bring back the black Morgan cross, saddled and ready to go. As soon as his horse had drunk his fill, Sam climbed atop the black Morgan and, leading the other horse by its reins, cooling him down, Sam left Dutchman Flats at a quick pace.

PART 3

Chapter 15

Reverend Wilcox had circled wide of the Badlands ranger outpost and approached the small complex of modest plank-and-adobe buildings from the west. He rode alone, a well-worn, leather-bound Bible in his beefy hand. Dust and sweat stains mantled the shoulders of his black linen suit. His horse ambled along wearily in the midday heat, its chest and legs streaked with froth. At a small cantina along the trail he reined his horse up and swung down from his saddle, feeling the eyes of an old swamping woman upon him.

Draping his reins loosely over a sun-bleached hitch rail, he turned to the old woman, holding his Bible out toward her. "God bless you, old *Mother*, dear, and all others hereabouts." As he spoke, he turned full circle in a grand gesture, his arms spread wide.

"She don't speak," said a gravelly voice from the open-plank doorway of the cantina. "Comanch yanked her tongue out when she was no more than a baby."

Reverend Wilcox winced at the thought and said, "Then God bless her even more! I pray God those bloody heathens have long since died tasting the steel of a soldier's blade?" he asked, hugging the Bible to his chest.

In the doorway, the grizzled old cantina owner shrugged a bony shoulder and wiped a hand up and down the front of his grimy long johns shirt. "I don't know what they tasted and what they didn't." He nodded at the old swamper woman and said, "I bought her cheap that way a few years back. Mexicans around here say what happened to her caused her to be a *bruja*."

"A witch?" Wilcox stepped back, aghast, and shook his Bible toward the old woman. "God forbid and protect us all! Let no man seek the council of witches and sorcerers!"

"I put no stock in it," said the old man. "She's barely got enough sense to sweep up and dump spit buckets. 'Sides, I never believed in witches and such." He waved Wilcox inside the cooler darkness of the small, crumbling adobe hut.

"Oh! Then we'll have to pray for your struggling soul, my good man, for this holy book makes mention of witches time and again." He touched his fingers to his hat brim saying, "The most Reverend Vernon Wilcox, at your spiritual service."

"I'm Pecos Jack Hubert," the old man said as Reverend Wilcox stepped past him into the cantina, "and the fact is, I don't believe much in that book either."

Wilcox wiped his hand across his dry lips. "Then I can see why the Lord has led me here," he said. "My work is indeed cut out for me." He eyed three dusty bottles of mescal on the wall behind a makeshift bar. The bar was nothing more than a bowed oaken plank lying between two empty barrels, a dirty red-and-white-checkered tablecloth thrown over it. "Given the time, I could very well save your soul, my good brother."

"My soul's been saved and lost so many times I lost count," said Pecos Jack. Without being asked, he stepped around behind the bar, lifted a dusty wooden cup from beneath it, wiped it on his grimy sleeve and set it down in front of Wilcox. Turning, he took one of the bottles and pulled the cork from it with a soft *pop.* "Mescal is all I've got till the drummer comes through again," he said.

"Then mescal *it is,* my good brother," said Wilcox, dropping the Bible on the bar and wrapping his fingers around the cup even as Pecos Jack filled it. "I know you must be wondering what I'm doing, sojourning to this remote outpost," Wilcox said.

"I expect I am," Pecos said lazily, "but only if you want to tell me."

Stopping long enough to raise the cup to his lips and take a long drink, Wilcox shuddered slightly all over, set the cup down and continued, saying, "I have come here to bring salvation to one Edward

Deaks, for the cold-blooded murders he has committed."

"If that was your only business here, Preacher," said Pecos, "you may just as well turn around and go home. Stone Eddie Deaks got released. Hell, he's been gone a long time."

"Surely you jest with me!" Wilcox feigned a stunned look at the dirty cantina owner. "And how, pray tell, did those two young rangers take such news?"

"Rangers Sam Burrack and Hadley Jones?" Pecos shrugged again. "They took it in stride, I reckon." He offered a thin, greasy smile. "Leastwise, I heard no terrible wailing and gnashing of teeth." Seeing that the reverend didn't appreciate his humor, Pecos said, "I expect Jones is too busy with his new bride to care about Deaks one way or the other. I sure would be if I was him."

"A new wife you say?" Wilcox took another drink of mescal. "And where might I find these newlyweds so that I can stop by and lay my blessings upon their union?"

Pecos pointed off across the swirling heat in the direction of a stretch of low hills in the distance. "They've got a place over on the old Apache Fork Trail. The only place there. But they had a priest marry them proper like."

"A *priest?*" said Wilcox. "My God! All the *more* reason I need to get over. At least my sojourn will not have been in vain." He turned up the wooden cup, drained it and set in down firmly on the bowed bar.

Pulling a coin from his vest pocket and laying it down in front of Pecos Jack, Wilcox said, "Give me those bottles to take along with me. Then you can close your doors and rest until your drummer arrives." He gave Pecos a broad grin, the mescal already making him feel light-headed and friendly. "'Sweet is the rest of a laboring man,'" he said, misquoting a line of scripture.

Pecos reached for the bottles, scratching his disheveled head. "I reckon . . . if you say so."

With the bottles in a dusty, rolled-up burlap sack under his arm, Wilcox left the cantina and rode wide of the outpost once again and back along his trail until he saw the wavering outline of riders coming toward him at an easy pace. Stopping, Wilcox took out one of the bottles of mescal and slumped on his saddle horn with it hanging in his hand.

When the riders drew close and slid their horses to a halt, Wilcox pitched the bottle to Lonzo, who caught it, looked at it and smiled. "What did you find out for us, Reverend?" He pulled the cork and took a long swig.

Reverend Wilcox looked past Lonzo Greer and at Stone Eddie Deaks when he replied, "Word ain't back yet about Burrack being dead. Leastwise the bartender didn't seem to know it." He looked back at Lonzo and added, "That other ranger has taken a wife and they're laid up in a place over at Apache Fork. Should be easy pickings." He grinned slyly and caught the bottle when Lonzo pitched it back to him.

"Bless their hearts," he added. "They was married by a priest."

"Don't jump ahead of me on this, Reverend!" Calvin Thurston warned, pointing a gloved finger at the big, powerful-looking minister. "Deaks killed Burrack. I at least get this ranger all to myself!" He looked at Lonzo for support.

Lonzo grinned and said to Deaks, "Have you ever rode with a more *game* bunch of ol' boys than this?"

"It's inspiring all right." Deaks smiled. He turned his horse, following Lonzo and Metlet's lead, and booted the animal toward the distant hills.

Flora Cruz Jones finished wringing the last of the wet clothes and laid them atop the rest of the clothes she'd piled neatly in her new wicker basket. She then carried the heavy basket across the yard to the new clothesline her husband had strung for her before he'd volunteered to ride out in search of his partner. As she hiked the bulk of a damp sheet upon her shoulder and began spreading it out along the line, she saw the three riders approaching the house from the south.

She would have thought nothing of seeing three riders along the Apache Fork Trail had it not been for seeing two more riders approaching from the west when she'd finished hanging the sheet and turned slightly as she reached down for another piece of the damp wash. Seeing the other three riders caused her to immediately look all around. In doing so, she spotted three more riders east of the trail. Eight riders in all, she counted and her pulse began to quicken.

Forcing herself to stay calm, she laid the shirt she had just shook out back in the basket, then walked across the yard and into the house. In the small living room she stepped up onto a wooden chair and lifted the big Henry rifle from its pegs above the stone hearth. Stepping down with the rifle, she calmly checked it, making sure it was loaded. Then she walked from window to window closing the wooden shutters and latching them.

"Hadley, I hope these are some of your rangers," she said as if her husband were standing beside her; but something told her that wasn't the case. Looking out through a narrow rifle slot, she noted the riders coming at a faster pace. She crossed herself and cradled the rifle in her arms.

"Do you think she saw us and went to warn him?" Metlet asked Lonzo.

"Yep," said Lonzo, staring straight ahead.

"I would bet on it," Calvin Thurston said, riding on the other side of Lonzo Greer. "But it doesn't make any difference. If he's any man at all, he won't cut and run, leave his brand-new wife for us to paw over." Calvin grinned. "Right, Lonzo?"

Lonzo only grunted, staring ahead at the house, at the damp sheet rippling on the warm wind.

"For all we know, he might not even be there," said Metlet.

"That's all right too," Calvin returned. "If he's not

there, he'll come to see us for sure once he finds out
we've got his woman." Again he looked at Lonzo,
asking him, "Ain't that right, boss?"

"Shut up and get ready for some killing," Lonzo
said flatly.

The first three to arrive at the yard were Deaks,
Kid Lamb and Deputy Forrest Bidson, from the
south. Only seconds after came Calvin and Metlet
from the west. At almost the same time, Reverend
Wilcox, Owen Reager and Ernie Shay rode in from
the east. When the group had formed a circle
around the house and stopped a cautious thirty
yards from it, Lonzo nudged his horse a few steps
closer and called out, "Ranger! I'm Lonzo Greer!
Step out from behind your young wife and come
and say howdy!"

His request was met with silence. Calvin Thurston
rode a step ahead of him and said, before Lonzo
could stop him, "It was my brother you and your
partner killed like a dog! Your partner is dead. It's
time for you to join—"

"Gawddamn it, Calvin!" Lonzo shouted angrily,
jumping his horse forward and bumping it sidelong
into Calvin's horse. "I'm doing the talking here! Get
your ass back out of here before I bend a gun barrel
over your head!"

Inside the house, Flora listened, her hands beginning to tremble slightly upon hearing Calvin tell her
that Sam Burrack was dead. Could it be so? Was that
the reason her husband hadn't yet returned from

Quincy? She watched through the rifle slot and listened.

With Calvin back out of the way, Lonzo turned his attention back to the house, saying, "I saw you hanging clothes, woman, and you saw us coming. I believe if there was a ranger in there we would have heard from him by now." Lonzo stepped his horse back and forth, then forward a few more steps, signaling for his men to do the same. "The fact is, you're all alone in there, ain't you, woman?"

"Don't come any closer!" Flora called out in a shaky voice. "I'll shoot!"

"I bet you will too," Lonzo said, grinning, detecting the fear in her voice. "But all the shooting you do now, you'll have to pay up for later. We came here to do a dark piece of work, and we mean to get it done!"

"Go away! *Please go away!*" Flora sobbed aloud. "Don't make me shoot you!"

Lonzo looked all around at the others, his grin widening. "Now I've done it," he said. "I've gone and made the little lady cry!" He turned back to the house and said, "If you want to get this over with, woman, all you've got to do is—"

The big Henry exploded through the rifle slot. The bullet whistled past Lonzo's ear. His horse lunged sideways, spooked, almost spilling him from his saddle.

"Jesus!" Lonzo cried out, throwing a hand to his ear, making sure it was still there. Before he could even settle the horse, another shot exploded through the rifle slot. This one whistled past his other ear even closer than the first shot.

"Damn it, Lonzo!" Metlet shouted. "Get back here!" He had dismounted quickly and snatched his pistol from his holster. He fired three shots rapidly, each bullet thumping loudly into the thick plank shutters. But the shots didn't discourage Flora Jones. She fired again as Lonzo turned his horse and spurred it hard, getting it out of the rifle sights quickly.

"She ain't no shrinking violet, is she?" said Metlet, keeping an aim on the plank-shuttered window while Lonzo jumped down from his horse and behind the cover of a bare white oak.

"That damned woman needs her tail bobbed!" Lonzo said, looking around at the men who had all dismounted and taken cover where they could.

"She won't be as easy to take along with us as we thought," said Metlet.

"She's coming though," Lonzo said with determination. He looked off to the south, in the direction of the ranger outpost. "They've heard all that shooting, so we don't have time to fool around unless we want a whole swarm of rangers down our shirts. I expected to have the ranger killed and be on our way by now."

"Say the word, we'll burn her out of there," said Metlet. "They'll see the smoke too . . . but not until we've got her and gone on our way."

Lonzo considered for a moment. "All right then,

gawddamn it! Burn her out and let's go! We're too close to them damn lawdogs to suit me."

With a signal from Metlet, Calvin turned to Bidson, who stood crouched beside him, and said, "All right, Deputy, it's time you and me earned our keep."

Running to a small barn behind the house, the two raked together a bundle of hay. Bidson carried the hay back to the house. Right behind him Calvin ran in a crouch carrying two coal oil lanterns. "This stuff will bring her out of there, Lonzo," Calvin said, holding the lanterns up, shaking them.

"Good work, Calvin," said Lonzo. "Now get her smoked out before we start getting company." He looked off toward the ranger outpost.

Watching from behind the cover of an old sunbleached buckboard that sat off to the right of the house, Lamb raised his canteen to his lips, took a mouthful of tepid water and spit it out in a stream. "This is the kind of stuff I don't take much pleasure doing," he said to Deaks, who sat cross-legged in the dirt, leaning back on his hands as if relaxing at a picnic. A reed of wild grass stuck out of his mouth.

"Neither do I," he said, with a slight smile. "But I feel obligated to watch. After all, Lonzo is only doing it to show me how tough he can get."

"By roasting a woman?" Lamb asked with a trace of sarcasm.

"She won't roast," Deaks said confidently, taking the grass reed from his mouth, examining it idly and putting it back in.

"I hope you're right," said Lamb, turning back to

the house in time to see Bidson take one the lanterns from Calvin's hand and twist the top off its fuel tank.

Beside Bidson, Owen Reager looked at the other lantern and said to Calvin in an excited tone, "How about letting me hurl one of those in on her, Calvin?"

Calvin looked at him. "Are you sure?"

"Yeah, I'm sure," said Reager, wiping his palms up and down his trouser legs nervously. "I'm itching to do something to a woman. I don't care what it is."

"So am I." Calvin chuckled darkly, handing him the lantern. "But damn! I can think of something better than burning her house down." He pressed four sulfur matches into Reager's hand. "Enjoy yourself, Owen."

"Much obliged," said Reager, sounding more excited. He closed his hand around the matches and gripped the lantern handle tightly. "Here I go, Lonzo!" he shouted over to where Lonzo and Metlet crouched behind the white oak.

"Get your back against the house before you stop," Lonzo warned him. "This woman can shoot."

"Right," said Reager. But in his excitement, he ran toward the house and stopped short several yards away when a bullet grazed his right forearm and caused him to drop the lantern. Oil slosh out of the tank before he snatch it up, spilling oil down his leg.

"Damn!" Lonzo said to Metlet. "This is turning sour in a hurry. Give him some cover, men!"

Another rifle shot exploded. The bullet tore through Reager's thigh and spun him in a half-circle just as he struck a match and stuck it to the lantern's open wick.

"Don't throw it at us!" Lonzo shouted, seeing Reager flounder in confusion. Another bullet hit Reager in the back of his shoulder, turning him back toward the house. But before he could toss the burning lantern, flaming oil spilled down his raised arm, igniting his shirtsleeve.

"Good God almighty!" Lonzo screamed, seeing the flames jet down Reager's body and widen as the hapless outlaw screamed and spun and fell to the ground, rolling wildly as the fire engulfed him. Bidson and Shay started to run out and help Reager but a rifle shot from the window sent them scrambling back to cover.

Watching Reager scream and burn, Deaks shook his head and raised his rifle to his shoulder, saying, "This is disgusting." He fired one shot and silenced Reager. The rest of the men stared as the dead outlaw lay flaming in the dirt.

From the house, Flora Jones cried out in a tearful voice, reverting to her native tongue, "Go away! *Por favor!* Do not make me kill you! I beg you."

"*Por favor*, my ass!" Calvin growled aloud. "Give me that lantern, Deputy!" He snatched the other lantern from Bidson's hand and said to Ernie Shay, "Get around and guard the back door, Ernie. I'll get that little bitch cur out of there!"

Ernie led his horse around the house in a crouch and took a position behind a pile of wooden fence railing. He stared at the back door for a moment, listening to a rifle shot from the front of the house. He grinned to himself and said, "This is going to be too easy."

Leaving his reins dangling in the dirt, Shay sneaked closer to the house. Why wait for her to make a break for it when Calvin threw the lantern? he reasoned. All he had to do was slip inside and catch the woman from behind while she concentrated on the front yard. But before Calvin threw the lit lantern or Shay even had time to make his way to the back porch, Flora let out a scream and came running out the back door of the house, barefoot, the rifle blazing in her hands.

"*Yiii!*" Shay shrieked. He saw her coming, but startled, he only had time to throw up his hands to protect himself as she ran past him and batted his forehead with the rifle barrel on her way to the waiting horse.

"Well, I'll be *gawddamned*!" said Lonzo, standing up, slamming his hat to the ground at his feet. He watched the woman go racing away toward the ranger outpost, her skirt up over her bare thighs, her long black hair flying straight back. Without hesitation, she leaped on a horse grazing behind the house. In the yard Calvin saw her too, and he dropped the lantern to the ground and kicked it away. The lantern rolled across the hard dirt, stopped against the front porch steps and burst into flames.

"I've got her!" Calvin said with finality. He raised his pistol and took a long steady aim, using both hands. But when he pulled the trigger, the bullet fell short of the speeding horse and struck the ground five yards behind its pounding hooves.

"This looks bad, Lonzo," Metlet said just between the two of them.

Lonzo snatched up his hat from the dirt and slapped it against his leg. "You're mighty damn right it does."

Chapter 16

———

"Want me to ride after her?" Reverend Wilcox asked Lonzo, watching the woman and horse fade away into the dust lying high in the horse's wake.

"Hell no!" Lonzo shouted. "We've been here too long as it is!"

"She sure can ride," Metlet said, staring at the rising dust.

"Shut up!" Lonzo shouted, enraged and embarrassed, feeling Deaks and Lamb watching him. "Where the hell is Shay?"

"Here I am," said Shay, staggering around the corner of the house, a deep bloody welt across the width of his forehead. "I never saw her coming. She streaked past me quicker than—"

"Don't give us your sorry excuses, you stupid sonsabitch!" shouted Lonzo. "You let her get away! What more *is* there to say about it?" He looked at the men who had gathered in closer around the front of the house and stood with expressions of failure on their dusty faces. The body of Owen Reager lay burned and still smoking on the ground. "All of yas get on your damn horses, *if you can!*" Lonzo shouted with dark sarcasm.

"What about him?" asked Calvin Thurston, pointing down at Reager.

"Leave him!" shouted Lonzo.

But Reverend Wilcox took a moment in passing to remove his hat, bow his head and murmur a few words on Reagers' behalf while the rest of the men walked to the their horses, mounted and formed back around Lonzo and Metlet. When Wilcox said amen and joined them, the riders turned as one and rode away on the back trail west of the house.

A hundred yards along the dusty trail, Lonzo and Metlet half turned in their saddles and looked back at the house. Smoke rose from the burning front steps. But it appeared the fire was waning instead of spreading across the porch to the rest of the house. Lonzo shook his head in disgust. "All we've managed to do is burn their steps."

"Look on the bright side," Metlet said to Lonzo. "Maybe she's wounded. Maybe she'll die in the saddle before she ever reaches help."

Lonzo gave him a sour look. So did Calvin Thurston.

"How can you say something like that? You didn't see any blood anywhere, did you?" Calvin sat with his rifle across his lap, his hand tight, his finger inside the trigger guard.

"I'm just saying *maybe*," said Metlet, letting Calvin

see him rest his hand on his holstered Colt. "All the shooting that went on, how can you say she didn't?"

"You're crazy as hell!" said Calvin.

"Calvin, shut your mouth and get away from here!" Lonzo bellowed.

Tight-lipped, Calvin jerked his horse away and rode to the back of the line.

"He is strung too tight over this," said Metlet.

"Yeah, you both are," said Lonzo. He looked back at the house once more and shook his head. "This makes us all look bad, not being able to burn one lone woman out of her house."

"I don't understand why it's not burning," Metlet said, also shaking his head. "Think she's done something that caused it not to burn?"

Lonzo just looked at him bitterly.

Metlet shrugged. "We should have *shot* that place to the ground," he said.

"We could have," said Lonzo, "if we'd wanted to spend the rest of the day there and wait for the rangers to come."

Metlet nodded in agreement. "Then I say let's put it out of our minds, and to hell with her. It was her husband we wanted anyway."

"Yeah," said Lonzo, "but that hardheaded bitch— I wanted to see her get what she deserved, especially after what she done to Reager and all."

Metlet nodded in agreement again. "That would have been good, but look at it this way. If it was vengeance we wanted for what the rangers did to

Max Thurston, we got that sure enough, when Deaks killed Burrack for us."

"Some things are worse on a man than killing him," said Lonzo. "I just wish we could've all seen this ranger's face when he had to scrape his new little wife out of a burned house. That would have made everything right—for us and for Calvin."

Metlet sighed. "I expect Calvin will just have to settle for what we got for a while."

Lonzo shrugged. "If he ain't, he can come back to this ranger, now that he knows where he lives. He can face him down man to man out here, far as I care."

"He won't though," said Metlet. "He'd do better to catch him mounting his horse some morning and put a bullet in his back."

"That's his call," said Lonzo. "I've been thinking. After what we just did, it's best we split up for a while, lay low and let things simmer before we commence any more robbing."

"What about Deaks and Lamb?" Metlet asked.

"Deaks and Lamb can drop off where they want to, like the rest of us. They'll pick back up when we get started again. I figure all the rangers are going to be madder than hornets at us. We'd all be better off on the other side of the border for awhile." He gazed at Flora Jones' rise of dust farther away in the distance. "You're right though. She *sure* can ride."

At the head of the wake of dust, Flora Jones lay low on the horse's neck, still batting her bare ankles to its sides nonstop. She had no intention of slowing the horse until she reached the safety of the ranger post.

Retired ranger Chancy Edwards had been the first to hear the sound of distant gunfire. "Listen," he said, calling the blacksmith's attention to it. The blacksmith, Burton Morris, had been talking to him while repairing a wagon tongue. But he stopped talking and hammering and gazed off with Chancy, the two of them listening closely in silence for a moment until Chancy finally said, "That's coming from over at the forks trail—Jones' house!"

"Ain't Jones still out looking for his partner?" the blacksmith asked.

"That's right. He is." Chancy gave the blacksmith a wary look. "Do me a favor, Burton. Saddle a couple of horses for Captain Martin and me." Even as the old ranger spoke, he hurried off toward the command office.

"Hell, I'm going *too*!" the blacksmith said to his empty shop. He jerked his leather apron over his head and tossed it onto a peg near his workbench. By the time he'd hastily saddled three horses and led them toward the command office, Chancy and the captain met him halfway, the captain levering a cartridge into his Winchester rifle as he hurried along.

"What do you think you're doing, Burton?" Chancy asked the blacksmith, noting the third horse and seeing the blacksmith had shed his apron.

"There's no other rangers here today," Burton Morris replied firmly. "I'm going." He looked at the captain and added, "With Captain Martin's permission, that is."

Chancy started to object, but Captain Martin cut him short as he took his set of reins from the blacksmith's powerful hand. "He's right, Chancy. We're short on manpower. He's riding with us. Both of you bring extra canteens. We've got to keep moving until we get to Apache Fork."

They headed quickly and maintained a brisk steady pace across the flatlands, where a rise of wood smoke drifted sidelong on a hot breeze. Seeing the smoke, the men looked at one another but none of the three dared say what dire image the earlier gunfire, and now the smoke, conjured up in their minds.

An hour later, at the beginning of an upward slope where the trail meandered through scattered piles of rocks and sunken boulders, Chancy stood in his stirrups and craned his neck for a look over a low rise. "Captain! There's a horse!" he called out. "It's limping!" Dropping back into his saddle, he yanked his rifle from its boot and gigged his horse forward, the captain and the blacksmith right beside him.

"Spread out," Captain Martin said. "This could be a trick!"

They put thirty feet between them as they topped the low rise and descended on the exhausted animal. Looking all around, Chancy said, as he stepped down and walked up to the froth-streaked dun, "I've never seen this one before, Captain, but looks like it's broken a front leg."

Captain Martin looked warily off toward the

Apache Fork Trail, then back at Chancy. "Put it down quietly, Chancy. We don't know who might be listening." He looked all around on the ground beneath his horse's hooves for any sign of human footprints but saw none. "Burton and I will search around for its rider."

"Yes, sir, Captain," Chancy replied. He drew his long Bowie-style knife from its sheath behind his back and winced at knowing what he had to do. "Easy, boy," he said to the worn-out dun, running a gloved hand down its sweaty withers.

Only a minute later on the other side of a pile of rocks, Captain Martin and the blacksmith stopped suddenly for a second, then leapt down from their saddles and ran over to the right of the trail as Captain Martin called out, "Over here, Chancy! Come quickly! It's Hadley's wife, Flora!"

Having wiped the knife back and forth across the dirt and done the same across his trouser leg, Chancy sheathed the big knife, jumped back into the saddle and booted his horse to where the captain and Burton walked out from behind the rocks, Burton with Flora Jones lying limp in his arms. By the time Chancy arrived, the two had stooped down and propped the unconscious woman up against Burton's raised knee.

"I'm coming, Captain!" Chancy grabbed a canteen from his saddle horn as he sprang down and hurried over to Flora. Stepping down with the others, he yanked his bandanna from around his neck and wet it with cool water from the canteen. "That's a terrible blow," he said, touching the wet bandanna tenderly to the large purple knot on the side of Flora's head. Flora moaned only slightly.

"We've got to get her back to the post, to Doc Sanderson," said Captain Martin. As he spoke, he looked Flora over closely and said, "She appears to be all right otherwise. But the doctor will know better than us what shape she's in."

"What about the gunshots, the smoke?" Burton asked, looking out toward the Apache Fork Trail.

"That will have to wait," said the captain. "We know Hadley would have reported to the post before going home. I doubt if anyone else was there. If there was, whatever was going on is over now. The main thing is we have Flora." He looked at her face, seeing how deeply she seemed to have drifted away.

"Yes," said Burton, "thank God for that."

Standing as one, Burton picking Flora up easily, the three stepped quickly back over to their horses. Chancy said, "Should I ride on out, just in case Hadley doesn't check in at the post first? Make sure he knows that Flora is all right?"

"Good thinking, Chancy," the captain said to older ranger. "Yes, you do that, just in case."

But it was too late for Chancy to get to the Jones house in time to tell Hadley Jones anything. Jones had arrived at the house no more than an hour after Lonzo and his gang had ridden away.

Dropping from his saddle at the sight of all the horses' hooves scattered around his home, Hadley Jones ran through the empty house, first noting the burned steps with a puzzled, worried look. At the open rear door, he stared off in the direction Lonzo and his men had taken, seeing the horses' hoofprints headed west toward the border. Without even first watering his horse, he jumped back into his saddle and batted the tired animal's sides, sending it off in the same direction.

An hour later, Chancy Edwards rode up to the house, dropped down cautiously and led his horse around the house with his Colt drawn and cocked, taking a close look at the body of Owen Reager on the ground. Returning to the front of the house, he stared down at the burned steps and shook his head. When he holstered his Colt and started to turn back to his horse, he heard the sound of a hammer cocking and froze as a voice called out calmly, "Turn around slow like. Let me see your face."

"Mister, you're interfering with an officer of the law in pursuit of his duties—"

"Chancy?" Sam asked.

"Sam?" the older ranger asked in response, suddenly recognizing the younger ranger's voice. All the same he turned slowly, his hands still chest high. With a sigh of relief, he saw Sam lower his rifle. "We heard shooting out here and came as fast as we could, Sam. We found Flora Jones along the trail. Looks like she narrowly escaped something terrible here." He nodded toward the bullet holes in the front of the house and at the burned porch steps.

"Is she all right?" Sam asked.

"Captain Martin thinks she will be," said Chancy, "soon as they get her to the post and get the doctor to take care of her." Noting the dust caked heavily on Sam's hat, duster and face, he asked, "What's going on, Sam? Where is Hadley?" Behind Sam stood a horse covered with froth and dust.

"He's on the heels of the men who did this, Chancy," Sam replied, letting his rifle slump. "It's Lonzo and his Black Moons. We took one of them into custody and he told us they were heading here— vengeance for me and Hadley taking down Max Thurston."

"Then why is it you and Hadley ain't riding side by side?" Chancy asked. "You're partners."

"That's right," said Sam. "But he rode on while I took care of turning in the prisoner back in Barstow."

Studying Sam's face, Chancy said, "There's more to it than that, ain't there, Sam?"

Sam looked away, as if judging the distance between himself and Hadley Jones. "Not much more. We both knew they were headed here, and we knew his wife was alone." He gave Chancy an even gaze and asked, "What more needs to be said?"

"I'll tell the captain you're on the trail," said Chancy. "Whatever else he hears, he'll hear from you and Hadley when you return."

"Obliged," said Sam. As he spoke, he led the horse to the watering trough in the side yard. "As soon as I get back to the post and saddle Black Pot, I'm heading onto his trail."

"It's high time the Black Moons got put out of business," Chancy said. "I'd like to see them all stretching rope."

Sam stared off at the trail leading west. Realizing what Hadley Jones intended to do when he ran into any members of the gang, Sam said, "So would I, Chancy, for a whole lot of reasons."

Chapter 17

———

At a thin path leading off the trail, Lonzo brought the men to a halt and said to Ernie Shay, "Why don't you cut away from us right here and go visit your kin in Amberton Wells."

It wasn't a question—it was an order. Riding Reager's horse, Shay gave Lonzo a level gaze and said, "I ain't seen my kin there for the longest time."

"Then this should be a joyful occasion for every damn one of you," Lonzo said firmly.

Seeing that Lonzo was getting rid of him, Shay asked him outright, "Will you be coming back for me when we're ready to go do some more business?"

"We'll know where you are," Lonzo said, avoiding any direct answer.

Catching the sharp way Lonzo spoke, Shay responded, "What happened to me back there could have happened to anybody."

"I know that, Shay," said Lonzo. His hand rested on the butt of his Colt. "But not seeing you around for a while will sure make it easier not to put a bullet through your miserable head. Can you understand that?"

"It ain't fair," Shay protested half under his breath. But he turned the big roan and batted it away without another look toward Lonzo.

Turning their horses back to the trail, Metlet said quietly to Lonzo, "This puts him in a bad spot with the rangers. They'll see his prints and make Amberton Wells their first stop."

"Then he better hope his kin give a damn more about him than I do right now," said Lonzo. He reached a quirt back with his right hand and slapped his horse soundly on its sweaty rump. They rode on at a hard pace, knowing without question that by now they had lawmen on their trail.

On the smaller trail toward Amberton Wells, Shay kept the horse at a brisk clip, making his plans for staying alive on his own. His cousin Mallard Hazelit lived on a small spread near Amberton Wells with his two sons, Jedson and Philbert, and was widely known for giving shelter to members of the Black Moon gang over the years.

Instead of riding into Amberton Wells, he would find a rocky spot along the trail, jump off the horse and leave it on the trail into Amberton Wells for as long as it would stay there on its own. He would walk the remaining miles to his cousin's house and lie low until he figured out his best move.

Three miles later, riding a small stretch of trail through a slope of rocks, Shay wrapped his reins loosely around the saddle horn and leapt from the saddle without slowing the horse's pace. Carefully, he stood up, dusting the seat of his trousers, looking back toward the main trail. "You can just kiss my Missouri ass, Lonzo!" he said aloud. Then he shook a fist in the air in the direction of the ranger outpost and said, "And all you damned rangers! We'll just see how easy it is for you catch ol' Ernie!"

He took off his worn-down boots and walked upward over the hot rocks in his socks, careful not to leave so much as a scuff mark behind himself. On the other side of the rocks, he looked out along the trail he'd left and saw the horse as a speck on the distant horizon. He smiled and said, "Go, horse. Take the sonsabitches into Amberton Wells with my blessings!" Laughing, he sat down, put on his boots, then walked on in the direction of his cousin's house.

A half hour later, on the same trail, coming out of Amberton Wells, two riders spotted the big roan standing blown and sweaty beside the trail, nipping at a stand of wild grass. Reining their horses over closer, one rider chuckled and said to the other, "Look at this, Leon, a big roan with an empty saddle."

Beside him, Leon Maddox shook his head and said, "I don't know what's become of this country, Purple Joe. Folks will just turn a horse loose, saddle, tacking and all. Who the hell can afford to live that way?"

Purple Joe Croom nudged his horse ahead of Leon Maddox and replied, "Beats me, Leon, but I saw it first."

Riding up to the worn-out roan, then stepping down from their saddles together, Leon said, "Damn if that doesn't look a lot like Owen Reager's roan."

"You think?" Purple Joe asked, walking up to the horse, finding it too tired to try to shy away from him. "I never knew Owen to be so liberal with his riding stock."

"Put a posse on his ass, you'll see how liberal he can get," said Leon. He stood back while Purple Joe took the horse's reins and turned the animal sideways to them. "Uh-huh, look at that." He pointed at a brand on the horse's hip. "The Bar Kettle Y. It's Reager's all right. He stole it from the old Swede who ran that spread. Some say he might have killed the old Swede. Leastwise, the Swede disappeared, and Reager commenced riding his roan all over Wind River."

"Just so's this conversation don't take a bad turn in temperament," said Purple Joe, pulling the roan closer to him, "this horse mighta used to belong to Owen Reager, but it's mine now, from its hoofs up."

Giving Purple Joe a curious look, Leon said, "Damn, man, why are you getting so salty on me all of a sudden? I don't give damn about this spent-out roan. Far as I'm concerned it's all yours. Like you said, you saw it first."

"I never had a roan in my life," said Purple Joe. "When I was a kid that's all I ever hoped for. Now I got one handed to me free and clear, I guess you might say I am feeling a bit protective of it."

"Well, I'm pleased shitless for you," Leon said. "But I have to say, you'll be lucky this cayuse don't peter out on you before you get it to Lucille's and back."

"I ain't going to Lucille's now," said Purple Joe. "I'm going on back to Amberton, cool this fellow out and get him water-filled and grain-fed for a few days. To tell you the truth, I don't think much of Reager for wearing a horse into this kind of condition." He stroked a hand down the roan's gaunt flank.

"Again," said Leon, "let me make clear to you how hard pressed a man can get with a posse on his ass."

"I've had posses on me," said Purple Joe. "You don't have to tell me." He raised the roan's tired head and inspected its teeth. "Anyway, I ain't going to Lucille's now. You can take my turn with her."

"Suit yourself," said Leon. "In that case, I might just spend the night there. Lucille can get plumb sweet and romantic when there's just one man for her to accommodate."

"See?" said Purple Joe. "This fellow has brought us both *good luck* already."

"What are you talking about *good luck*?" Leon asked.

"Finding a roan horse is supposed to bring good luck to the one finding it," said Purple Joe.

Leon just stared at him. This was the first he'd ever heard of finding a roan horse bringing a man good luck. "I never heard of that," he said. "Where'd you hear it?"

"Hell, I've heard it all my life," said Purple Joe, as if it were a fact commonly known.

"I think you just now made it up," Leon said flatly. He spit and ran a hand across his lips.

Purple Joe turned a cold stare on him. "I think you best go on to Lucille's. I'll tell Bobby you're going to spend the night."

Leon nodded. "Obliged then." He turned his horse back to the trail. "Maybe your *good luck* will be getting that horse to Amberton Wells before it drops dead on you."

"If I was you, I'd ease up some on goading me about what I've heard about roans bringing good luck," Purple Joe warned him. "I know what I've heard, and I don't need you disputing it."

Leon saw that he had pushed Purple Joe a little further than he should have. Without another word he gave a slight raise of a hand in acknowledgment and rode away.

When he arrived leading the roan into Amberton Wells a half hour later, on a wooden bench out front of a ragged tent saloon, a one-eyed gunman named Bennie Stokes spotted him and said to Bobby Caesar, "Here comes one of your boys back, Bobby." Looking at the riderless roan he added, "Reckon the other one must've fell off and broke his neck."

Bobby Caesar squinted at the roan and replied, "That ain't Leon's horse, Bennie." He stood up and waited until Purple Joe stopped a few feet from him and stepped down from his saddle. Looking the sweaty roan up and down, he asked, "Joe, what have you got there, a stray?"

"I found him out along the trail on the way to Lucille's place. Just standing there picking grass, pretty as you please. I don't mind telling you I'm feeling really good about it."

Ignoring Purple Joe's excitement over the animal, Bobby Caesar stepped in closer, looked the tired horse over and said, "Hell, Joe, that's Owen Reager's stolen roan."

"All right, maybe it is," said Purple Joe, "but his loss is my gain, far as I'm concerned."

"Where's Leon, Joe?" Bobby asked firmly.

"He went on over to Lucille's. Said to tell you he'll be spending the night there."

"Damn it!" said Bobby Caesar. "I told you two knotheads to stick together. My bones tells me there's trouble coming."

"You don't have to call me names, Bobby," Purple Joe said, his tone turning dark. "I don't call you names. I don't appreciate you calling me—"

"All right, Purple Joe, forget it," said Bobby. "I didn't mean it. You're no knothead." He gave Bennie a look of disbelief. Then he said to Purple Joe, "Let me ask you this. Did you ever stop and wonder what it could mean, Owen Reager's roan horse roaming around out there by itself?"

"It means good luck," said Purple Joe.

Bennie Stokes tried to stifle a laugh, but it came out anyway. Purple Joe shot him a dark, angry stare. Bennie only shook his head and looked away, grinning.

"No, Purple Joe," said Bobby Caesar. "I think it means that Owen Reager might have somebody on his trail and had to dump that roan and light out on foot." He let his words sink in for a second. "The only kind of persons I can think of that might be after Reager is lawmen. And if they follow his horse, it stands to reason they're going to be coming here— don't you think so?"

Purple Joes's expression soured a bit. "That means they'll see where all three of our hoofprints came to- gether and maybe figure two of us rode back to Am- berton Wells."

"Damn right," said Bobby Caesar. "So you could say that bringing that roan here is about the same thing as bringing the law down on us."

"Hell, I didn't mean to do that, Bobby," Purple Joe said. "You know I wouldn't do something to cause us trouble."

"I know you wouldn't on purpose," said Bobby, "but I'm thinking you may have all the same."

"What do you want me to do to make things right?" Purple Joe asked.

"Get your *lucky* roan put away and we're all going to ride out to Hazelit's spread. Mallard Hazelit has a cousin, Ernie Shay, who rides with Reager and the rest of Lonzo Greer's Black Moons. If Owen Reager or any of them has brought trouble down on us, we need to know just how much and what kind."

The shoes on Jones' horse were still new enough to bear the trademark diamond of the Diamond Iron and Forge of Chicago, making it easy for Sam stay on the trail following the same tracks he'd been following all the way from the Jones house. At the trail where Jones' tracks turned off toward Amberton Wells, Sam had to stop and ask himself why Jones had followed the single rider instead of staying after the gang.

After a moment of consideration Sam said quietly to his Appaloosa and Morgan cross, "His horse is about to give out on him. He figures on overtaking the single rider and using his horse after he kills him."

Beneath him the big Appaloosa stallion stood in silence, so did the Morgan cross on the lead rope in Sam's other hand. But Sam continued speaking to them just the same, saying, "We've got to try to keep that from happening, don't we?" He patted a gloved hand on the Appaloosa's wet neck.

Following Jones' tracks, he hadn't gone more than two miles when he saw the body of Hadley Jones' horse lying dead alongside the trail. Riding on cautiously, he soon caught sight of Jones sitting slumped in the thin shade of a tall saguaro, his canteen lying in his lap with its cap off. "Jones, it's me, Sam," he called out, lest the heat, exhaustion and glaring sunlight cause Jones not to recognize him and go for his gun.

But even in his exhaustion, Jones did recognize him. Standing up unsteadily, Jones said, "Sam, thank God!" He eyed the Morgan with relief, seeing it already saddled and ready. "I'm done in here without a horse. They're getting farther away from me with Flora every minute I lose here."

As Jones reached for the Morgan, Sam jerked the horse away from him and said, "Listen to me, Hadley! These men don't have Flora with them. She got away. Captain Martin and Chancy found her along the trail. Her horses faltered and she took a tumble. But she's *all right.*"

"Don't lie to me, Sam!" Hadley blurted out, snatching at the Morgan.

Sam stopped cold and said, "I've never *lied* to you, Hadley. I'm wearing the same badge you're wearing, remember?"

"I'm sorry, Sam," Jones said, realizing he'd been out of line. He calmed down a little. "Flora is really all right? She's with Captain Martin?"

"That's right," Sam said, his voice softening some after having taken on a harder tone. "Captain Martin and the blacksmith took her on to the post for the doctor to look at. Chancy was at your place trying to catch you. He said Flora is going to be fine."

Hadley slumped and again said, "Thank God." Looking back up at Sam he asked, "Was she . . . I mean had they . . . ?" His words trailed, but Sam understood what he was asking.

"She wasn't harmed, other than from the fall from a horse," Sam said. "It looks like she fought the Black Moons to a standstill."

"My Flora? She fought them off?" Hadley looked proud and surprised.

"Now take this horse and get on back to her, Jonesie," Sam said, offering him a slight smile. "She's still been through a lot. She needs you there."

Jones hurriedly snatched his rifle from his saddle boot and leapt up onto the Morgan, leaving his own saddle and canteen where they lay in the dirt. But once atop the big horse, instead of turning on the trail, he said, "Sam, I'm riding on with you. Partners, right?"

Sam looked at him. "Are you sure about this, Jonesie? What about Flora?"

"Believe me, Sam," Jones said. "It's the way she'd want it if she was standing here to tell you so."

Sam didn't question any further on the matter. Instead he raised his Colt, checked it and slipped it back into his holster. "Amberton Wells can be a tough little settlement. For its size there are more outlaws and hardcases running through there than just about any town on the Badlands."

"That doesn't bother me," said Jones. He gestured down at the set of prints he'd been following. "There's only *one* outlaw there that I'm interested in."

Chapter 18

———

Mallard Hazelit and his sons, Jedson and Philbert, stood in the side yard dressing out a steer that hung upside down from the limb of a white oak when Bobby Caesar, Bennie Stokes and Purple Joe rode up. Startled, suddenly seeing the three staring down at him from only a few yards away, Mallard reached out and straight-armed his elder son, saying, "Gawd-damn it! Ain't either one of yas got enough sense to keep an eye on the trail?"

"For what?" asked Philbert, before he and his brother had turned around enough to see the three riders. When they did see them, their mouths gaped.

"Afternoon, Mallard," said Bobby Caesar, touching his hat brim. "Philbert, Jedson."

"Evening to you, Bobby," Mallard replied, feeling embarrassed for his lack of security. He saw the rifle lying across Bobby's lap. "Me and the boys were so busy butchering, we damn near didn't see yas." He wiped his bloody hands up and down his long rubber-coated butcher's apron, then pulled a dirty rag from his hip pocket to complete the job. "What brings you men out this way?"

Bobby went right to the point, saying, "Owen Reager is hiding out here. We found his horse out along the trail."

"*I* found it," Purple Joe cut in.

Bobby glared at Purple Joe. "All right, Purple Joe here he found it," he said to Mallard. "So we already know he's here—"

Before Bobby could say any more on the matter, Mallard cut in, "Owen Reager is dead. My cousin Ernie Shay rode that horse here. Ernie ain't been here a full day and he's already eat us out of staples." He gestured a blood-smeared hand toward the hanging steer. "That's why we're gutting market stock right now."

"Yeah, I'm here, Bobby," Ernie Shay said, stepping out on the wooden porch, barefoot, his gun belt hanging over his shoulder. He looked at Purple Joe and said, "Much obliged to you for catching my horse for me." He looked all around. "Where is it?"

"I didn't catch your horse for you!" Purple Joe said quickly. "That horse was wandering. He's mine now."

"Like hell he is," said Shay, taking a step.

"Hold it!" Bobby Caesar shouted, swinging his rifle from across his lap. "We're not here to deliver your damn horse! That horse is between the two of yas! I want to know who's on your trail so we know what to be expecting here before long!"

"There's nobody chasing me," Shay lied. "I just lost my saddle and ended up walking here for help. I intended to go retrieve that animal first chance I get."

Purple Joe blurted out angrily, "Shay, you're a lying son of a—"

"Damn it, Joe, shut up!" Bobby bellowed. He looked back at Reager, his rifle barrel lowering a bit toward him. "I'm not asking *if* somebody is on your trail! You and I both know there *is*! I'm asking you *who*, and if you don't answer me this time, I'm going to unbutton your shirt, Winchester-style." His thumb cocked the rifle hammer.

"All right, Bobby! Jesus!" said Shay. "I do have a little trouble that needs straightening. But it's nothing worth worrying yourself about. Lonzo and the rest of us went to settle some vengeance with a ranger over near the Badlands outpost. There's probably a ranger or two headed this way."

"Vengeance with a *ranger*?" Bobby gave a bemused half smile and shook his head as if to clear it. "I see Lonzo and Metlet haven't gotten any smarter since last I saw them. If you fools killed a ranger that close to home, every other ranger able to ride, walk or belly crawl is going to be coming after you."

"Crazy, huh?" Shay grinned. "But the fact is, we didn't kill him after all. He wasn't there. So we set fire to his house and went after his wife."

"That's even worse," said Bobby. "You burn down a man's house, assault his wife—you'd have been wise to go ahead and kill him first."

"The thing is," Shay continued as he scratched his

head, looking down sheepishly, "we didn't burn his whole house, just his front steps. We didn't actually *assault* his wife—we scared the *bejesus* out of her."

"Oh? You burned his steps and *scared* his wife?" Bobby Caesar looked dumbstruck for a moment as he tried to picture it in his mind. "What was this *vengeance* for, calling one of you a dirty name?"

"No," said Shay, "this was one of the rangers who killed Max Thurston. There were two of them, but Stone Eddie Deaks killed the one who carried that blasted list around with him. The one who killed Junior Lake?"

"You don't mean it!" Bobby Caesar's expression turned dead serious. "Ol' back-shooting Eddie Deaks killed *that* ranger, Sam Burrack?" Bobby let his hand slide down from the cocked rifle hammer. "I bet when he did, he ran off leaving a stinking brown trail behind him."

"I think you're discounting Stone Eddie some," said Shay. "He *did* kill him. And that's what started all this other stuff. Lonzo and us went to get the other ranger, a new fellow." Shay shrugged. "So now I come here to lay low and be with my kin."

Mallard Hazelit cut in, saying, "You never mentioned a damn word about killing a ranger! You jack-legged sonsabitch!" He started across the yard toward the porch, pulling a long skinning knife from behind him.

Bobby Caesar's hand went back up to the rifle hammer. Cocking it he said, "Mallard, stand down!" His eyes went to Philbert and Jedson. "You too, boys!" Then he said to everybody, "If we've got rangers coming to Amberton Wells, we best either get out of here or be prepared for them."

"I ain't leaving my spread," said Mallard. He scowled at his cousin. "I've been square and clean over four years, except for a little harmless rustling, some small robberies and a shooting or two. I can't give up all I've worked for here. You're my blood kin, Ernie, so me and the boys will have to stay and fight if that's what it comes down to."

"See what you caused, you rotten turd!" Bobby said to Shay. "Get your damn boots on. You're coming with us to Amberton Wells. If this thing plays down in the street, I want to see you right in the thick of it with the rest of us."

"Well, hell, yes," said Shay. "Where else would a hellcat like me rather be?" He turned to walk in and get his boots, but then stopped and said to Purple Joe, pointing a finger at him, "I *will* be gathering my horse when we get to town, Joe. You've been warned."

"I hope you *try* taking him from me," Purple Joe called out to the open doorway, Shay having already stepped inside the house. "That horse has been terribly mistreated and abused!"

"Quiet down, Joe," Bobby said sidelong to him in a lowered voice. "We've got more important things going on right now."

Before they turned their horses and left, Mallard Hazelit walked over closer to Bobby and said, "If you get my cousin killed, you better hope you die with him, Bobby Caesar."

"Don't make threats to me, Mallard," said Bobby, giving him a cold stare. "He brought this trouble down on you, not me. If you want a hand in this, saddle up and ride in with me."

"I ain't riding in," said Mallard. "But a Hazelit will avenge a Hazelit every time." He pointed a long finger for emphasis. "You've got my word on it."

Rounding a large sunken boulder alongside the trail, Leon Maddox stopped abruptly at the sight of the ranger standing squarely in front of him with the short-barreled shotgun pointed up at his face. "Get your hands up high!" Ranger Jones commanded him. Leon might have taken a chance and backed his horse away quickly while he ducked low in his saddle and made a run for it. But a voice behind him said, "Do like he says! You're covered."

With his hands chest high, Leon ventured a glance back and saw Sam aiming a rifle at him. Seeing the badges on both men, Leon sighed and rolled his eyes slightly, saying in a bored tone, "Can't you rangers find something better to do than to chastise and harass a poor working drover? What if my horse had spooked and bolted? I could have been injured or killed, for no reason at all."

Sam stepped around in front of him. "Who are they, Leon?" he asked bluntly.

Leon gave him a questioning squint. "Have we

met, Ranger? Because I don't recall ever being in-
trodu—"

"I recognize you from wanted posters I've seen between here and Texas. You're Leon Maddox, alias
Schoolhouse Pete Vesprez," Sam said.

"Oh, I see," said Leon, impressed and surprised. "I
haven't gone by Schoolhouse Pete for a *long* time.
Who are *you*, Ranger?"

"I'm Sam Burrack. This is Ranger Hadley Jones.
Now who are they?"

"Man, I have heard of you, Sam Burrack." Leon
grinned. "You've stirred up lots dust for yourself
these past months."

"Last time I'm asking, Leon," said Sam. He raised
the rifle butt to his shoulder.

"*Who?*" said Leon, acting a bit put out by the question. "I'm not given to reading minds!"

"The men who rode away from you less than three
hours ago," Jones said. "We followed a single set of
tracks and saw where that rider met up with two
other riders. We figure one rider was you. Who are
the others?"

"Beats the hell out of me," said Leon. "Folks just
come and go through here."

"Your belligerence just cost you a big toe, Leon,"
Sam said, taking aim at the tip of his worn-down
boot.

"Whoa, easy there!" Leon jerked his boot up from
the stirrup. "Damn! I'll tell you who they are! Let's
don't go clipping off toes! We're not savages, after
all!"

"You still aren't saying anything, Leon," Sam warned, keeping the rifle cocked and aimed.

"All right!" Leon saw the ranger's finger tighten on the rifle's trigger. "You're going to ride in there anyway. It was Purple Joe Croom and me. The other horse was a stray somebody left behind." He grinned. "We both recognized it as Owen Reager's horse, which makes me believe he just *Cheyenned* the two of yas somewhere along the trail."

"We suspected he might have," Sam said. "How many Black Moons are there in Amberton Wells?"

"Black Moons?" Leon looked surprised. "Hell, none that I know of, unless one snuck in while I was getting a bellyful of Lucille Daggett." He nodded back over his shoulder. "I'd have been there still, except she's too drunk and wild-eyed. Black Moons don't hang around the same places me and my pals do."

"Your pals being Bobby Caesar, Purple Joe and Hyatt Dickson?"

"Hyatt is no longer above ground," said Leon. "But yeah, Bobby Caesar and Purple Joe are pals of mine."

"Are they going to side with Owen Reager once we get into Amberton Wells?" Jones asked.

"I don't know," said Leon. "You're welcome to go ask them." He grinned.

After a moment of consideration, Sam said, "We will." He stepped in closer to Leon's horse, drew Leon's rifle from its boot and pitched it away onto the rocky ground. Leon winced at the sound of it and said, "Damn, that rifle is almost new!"

Drawing Leon's pistol from its holster, Sam pitched it away too and said, "You ride in and tell Bobby Caesar we're after Reager, and nobody else. Everybody gets a free visit this time, provided they don't interfere. Can you remember all that?"

"Well, I'll do my very damn best," said Leon, with blatant sarcasm.

"Now get," said Sam, giving Leon's horse a slap on its rump and sending it out along the trail to Amberton Wells.

Watching the outlaw hightail it away from them, Jones said to Sam, "Why is it I get a feeling there's more to it than this Reager fellow just running here to hide out? Why here? Why didn't he stick with the gang, or at least get farther away before splitting up?"

"Because Ernie Shay has an uncle near here who has helped the Black Moons in the past," Sam said matter-of-factly, staring at the disappearing outlaw. He lowered the cocked hammer on his rifle. "An old cattle rustler named Mallard Hazelit. He used to operate over in the Wind River country. Now he keeps to himself, rustles the high plains for beeves most ranchers would've cut out for wolves anyway. He's got a couple of half-wit sons who do anything he tells them. They're tough folks, the Hazelits. If you harm one, they all come after you, like a pack of dogs."

"Even *more* outlaws to deal with," Jones said, shaking his head.

"That's the nature of our business," Sam said with a half sigh.

"How do we know Reager won't just run, leave Amberton Wells before we get there?"

"He's had it," said Sam. "He'll figure if we're this close on his heels, he's better off sticking here with his kin than he is trying to make another run for it."

Jones shook his head. "Boy! Sam, I don't know how you manage to keep abreast of all this information on everybody, who's who and what they're likely thinking. You must spend every waking minute of every day figuring it all out."

"It's my job," Sam replied. "If it takes that much time, that's how much time I have to give it."

"I understand," said Jones, catching a bit of the edginess in Sam's voice. "This fellow Hazelit and his sons, are they fighters?"

"Probably so," Sam said. "If they think we came here threatening what they've built for themselves, they'll fight hard."

"Is that why you sent him back," said Jones, "to let Hazelit and his boys know we're not here to take what they've got?"

"Not just Hazelit," said Sam. "Bobby Caesar and his boys too. Everybody else will keep till later on. We're only after the Black Moons."

"It seems like one outlaw just leads to another," Jones said. "There's never any end to it."

"It ends when you walk away and go home, Jonesie," Sam said in a somber voice. "Why don't you think about doing that?"

Jones stared at him. "Why are you saying that to me, Sam?"

"Because you've got too much to lose, going into a fight like this."

"But you sent him in to tell them our intentions," said Jones. "They might listen to reason."

"Don't fool yourself into believing that," Sam said. "It'll only get you killed."

"Then why did you even waste your breath on him?" Jones asked in exasperation. "Why didn't we shoot him and leave him here—it'd be one less gun to worry about."

"I told him because we're lawmen, Jonesie," Sam replied. "We have to make an offer of a *peaceful means*, whether they accept the offer or not."

"I don't know that I agree with that after all that's happened, Sam," Jones said.

"I know you don't," Sam said quietly. "That's another reason why you ought to turn and go home."

Chapter 19

———

Leon Maddox rode straight to Amberton Wells at a fast pace, not slowing his horse until he slid it to a halt in front of the tent saloon. Jumping down from his saddle, he ran inside and looked all around for Bobby Caesar and the others. Not seeing them, he turned around and rushed back outside, just in time to see them riding toward him from the other end of the dirt street. Running to meet them before they arrived at the tent, Leon went to Bobby's horse, saying up to him, "We've got two rangers coming! I ran into them no more than an hour down the trail!"

"I already know it," Bobby answered without stopping, causing the dust-streaked outlaw to trot along like a dog until Bobby stopped at the hitch rail. "They've tracked Owen Reager's horse here." He gave a twisted nod toward Ernie Shay, sitting atop a horse between Stokes and Purple Joe. "Owen Reager is dead. Shay was riding his horse."

"What are we going to do?" Leon asked.

"We're going to kill them, if they come riding in here with their bark on."

"That's a fine idea," said Leon, "except that it might not be an easy thing to do! One of them is Sam Burrack! He's the ranger who's been thinning things out around here ever since he killed Junior Lake!"

Stepping down from his horse, Bobby stopped cold and stared at Leon. "Shay here said Burrack in dead."

"Then this ranger is lying," said Leon. "He identified himself as Sam Burrack, big as all get-out!"

"What about it, Shay?" Bobby asked as Shay and the others dismounted and walked over to him and Leon.

"I told you Deaks said he killed Burrack," said Shay, sounding a bit testy about the matter. "That's all I've got to say about it."

Bobby's temper flared. He snatched Shay by the front of his sweaty shirt and held him close. "That's all you've got to say about it? You bummer son of a bitch! Me and these men have had a good run here till your sorry ass showed up! If there's anything you're telling me that doesn't turn out jake, I'm gonna carve you into pieces small enough to feed birds!"

"Take it easy, Bobby!" Shay exclaimed, his testiness suddenly gone. "I'm not lying to you! Deaks said he killed Burrack! Maybe this ranger is claiming to be him just to rattle us! They do things like that, you know—Especially if they're scared and know they're outnumbered."

Bobby smiled slightly, releasing Shay's shirt. "Yeah, come to think of it," he said. "Two rangers against all of us—what's there to worry about? Even it *is* Burrack." He turned to Leon. "What did they say? How come they let you go?"

"They let me go so's I could come tell you that their only interest here is in a Black Moon rider." He gave Shay a cold stare.

"You can't trust nothing a lawman says." Shay sneered, returning Leon's stare. "They'll tell you that to get your guard down. First thing you know, you're stretching rope, wondering where it all went wrong."

"The one claiming to be Burrack said to tell you everybody gets a *free visit* this time."

"Well, that's mighty kind of him," Bobby said with contempt, "showing a little mercy on us poor ol' helpless boys." He gave Bennie Stokes a tight look. "Can you believe that son of a bitch?"

"Hmmph," Bennie grunted. "Yeah I can believe it. Every damn one of them thinks they're so all-fired tough a snake couldn't bite 'em."

"Maybe we'll just turn down his free visit," Bobby said, thinking things over. "Maybe we'll just be the ones to put this ranger underground."

"It'd be a feather in your hat sure enough," said Shay, trying to gain himself some support.

"Would it," Bobby asked, skeptically, "even though you're saying that Burrack is already dead?"

"Bobby, I don't swear to nothing," Shay said. "I just told you what Deaks said. If he lied about it, then

I reckon that just shows what a big thing it is, being the one who killed the ranger."

"How long before you figure they'll get here, Leon?" Bobby asked.

"Hell, anytime now," said Leon. "I rode hard, but they was already on their way."

"Everybody get ready," said Bobby. "I believe we'll just take their *free visit* and nail it to their coffin lids." He spread a nasty grin. "I've wanted to shoot myself a ranger for the longest time."

Thirty minutes later, standing in the shadows of a telegraph shack, Leon turned a sidelong glance to Purple Joe and said, "How lucky does that damn roan feel to you right about now, Joe?"

"That roan horse had nothing to do with this," Joe responded. "This is all the Black Moons' doings."

Leon studied Joe's dull eyes for a second, then said with feigned patience, "Joe, if Shay hadn't rode in on that roan, none of this other would be happening. Can't you understand that? The horse hasn't brought *good luck*. It's brought a shoot-out with the law."

"Yeah," Joe retorted, "and we wouldn't have been aware the law was coming if we hadn't found that roan out there grazing."

"Jesus, Joe." Leon shook his head in exasperation. "You just pick whatever it is you want to believe and to hell with everything else."

"So? What's wrong with that? Ain't that the way everybody else does?" Joe said, speaking but at the same time keeping watch on the trail leading out across the flatlands surrounding the town.

"Sure, I suppose so," said Leon, giving up on the matter. "Anyway, Shay seems to be dead set on taking that horse back, soon as the smoke settles."

"*Dead set* is what he'll be too," said Purple Joe, "dead set in the ground, if he tries to lay his hands on that roan, that son of a bitch."

Leon took a quick look back toward the ragged saloon tent; inside the open fly, he saw Shay standing between Bobby Caesar and Bennie Stokes, the three of them holding mugs of frothing beer. "I'll say one thing for the son of a bitch. He's managed to get himself in a better position than either one of us."

"If these rangers don't kill him, I will." Purple Joe swore under his breath.

Gazing out along the trail, Leon said, squinting against the sun's glare, "Then you best be ready to carry out your threat. Here they come."

Two hundred yards out, Sam and Hadley Jones approached Amberton Wells with the afternoon sun at their backs. Where the trail became the dirt street down the middle of the small town, the two stopped for only a moment and sat abreast. Sam raised his rifle from across his lap and held it propped up, the butt resting on his thigh. His gun hand lay in place, his thumb over the hammer, his finger on the trigger. Jones held his shotgun in same manner, but with both hammers already cocked, ready to fall.

"The street is awfully empty for this time of day," Jones whispered sidelong.

"Word travels fast," said Sam. "This is bad. It's a sign that Bobby Caesar isn't going to take my offer and stay out of things."

"Just like you thought," Jones said.

"There's Bobby Caesar now," Sam said, speaking softly, his gaze fixed on the tent saloon. "On your right there's two men beside the telegraph office."

"Onlookers?" Jones asked, catching sight of them without staring directly at them.

"I doubt it," Sam whispered. "Drop back and disappear. Make them worry some."

"Sam," Jones said, "I ought to be the one to take down Owen Reager."

Sam gave him a look that left no room for discussion as he as nudged the Appaloosa toward the tent saloon. Jones didn't like it, but he stepped the Morgan back, turned it smoothly and nudged it out of sight into a narrow alleyway.

"Where's the other one going?" Purple Joe asked, looking all around the alleyway entrance, knowing the alleyway could take a person in any number of directions without being seen.

"I don't know!" said Leon, sounding more concerned all of a sudden. "Keep an eye back that way. Watch out that he don't sneak up on us." He gestured his pistol barrel toward the rear of the telegraph building. Purple Joe stared back along the side of the building, but only for a second. He turned around and stared over Leon's shoulder, watching the ranger ride closer to the tent.

So intent were the two outlaws in watching Sam approach the tent saloon, neither of them heard a sound as Jones crept up the alley behind them. When Leon heard Purple Joe let out a grunt, he turned quickly. Realizing Joe had not been watching the back of the alley as he'd been told to do, Leon cursed, "Damn it, Joe!"

But then something sharp and cold hit Leon in the center of his chest, causing him to gasp and drop his rifle. For a moment his bulging eyes fixed on the solemn face of Ranger Jones standing before him. "Damn it, Joe," he managed to say again in a strained voice before sinking to his knee and pitching forward in the dirt.

Jones rolled him over and put his boot on the dead outlaw's chest, holding him in place while he pulled the knife from his chest. He wiped the blade in the dirt and quickly reached behind his back for a set of handcuffs as he stepped over and stooped down beside Purple Joe, who lay unconscious on the ground.

From the middle of the narrow rutted street, Sam called out, "Bobby Caesar." He stopped Black Pot again, this time less than fifty feet from the ragged tent. With his rifle in his left hand, he stepped down from the saddle.

Watching from inside the tent, Bobby stepped out slowly into the glaring afternoon sunlight. Noting that the ranger had the sun where he wanted it, Bobby sidestepped away from the open tent fly and adjusted his hat brim down an inch to relieve the glare.

"Yeah, Ranger, what can I do for you?" he asked. His voice sounded almost affable on the surface.

"You got my message from Leon Maddox, Bobby," Sam said firmly. As he spoke, he raised the big Colt from its holster and held it down his side, his thumb across the hammer. "I'm here to arrest one of the Black Moons, nobody else."

"So I heard," said Bobby. "But you see, I have a problem understanding just who you are. Leon says you told him you're Sam Burrack. But Ernie Shay tells me that Stone Eddie Deaks killed Sam Burrack. Now I'm wondering just which one to believe."

"Believe whoever you want to, Bobby," Sam called out. "I'm here to take Owen Reager in, either in his saddle or over it."

"I admire your confidence, whoever you are," said Bobby, stopping a few feet to the side of the tent. "But Owen Reager is dead."

Sam considered and said, "All right then. I want the Black Moon who rode in here."

"That would be Ernie Shay." Bobby grinned. "But you have to understand just how fond I am of ol' Ernie." Continuing his lie he said, "Why the ol' boy has been like a brother to me. I couldn't just turn him over to any ol' lawman, now could I? What kind of low-down dog would I be, treating my ol' pal that way?"

"I hear what you're saying, Bobby," Sam replied. "So let's get on with it."

"Whoa, Ranger," Booby chuckled. "All I want to do is talk a little, see if you really are Sam Burrack or some impostor."

"I am Sam Burrack," Sam said; and he offered nothing more on the matter. His thumb cocked the Colt but kept it resting down low at his thigh.

"There, you see?" Bobby offered a thin smile. "That didn't hurt, did it, telling me who you really are?"

"No more talk, Bobby," Sam said. "Give me the Black Moon or I take you with him."

"Hear that?" Bobby said toward the tent fly. "I've got Ranger Sam Burrack out here. Says he's going to take me in with you, Shay."

Ernie Shay stepped out of the tent and to the left, putting space between himself and Bobby Caesar. "I ain't going," he said in a low growl, his hand poised near his holstered pistol.

From the tent fly, Bennie Stokes stepped out of the tent with a rifle in his hands. "And you ain't taking him, Ranger," Bennie said.

Bobby Caesar said, grinning, "Well, well, Ranger, looks like you're outnumbered here, even with your other lawdog pal creeping around the alleys."

Sam didn't reply. He stared at Shay. Bobby didn't like that, the ranger seeming to disregard what he was saying to him. In a louder tone, Bobby said, "I'm glad you are Sam Burrack, Ranger. That makes me the man who finally killed—"

His words stopped short as he heard a pistol shot

explode and saw Shay sail backward, knocking down a corner of the tent before hitting the ground.

At the sound of the shot, Sam spun around enough to see Jones stand fifteen feet behind him to this left, his Colt smoking in his hand. Sam barely had time to spin back toward Bobby Caesar as Bobby got off a shot that nipped at Sam's duster. Sam's Colt bucked quickly in his hand and sent Bobby Caesar twisting backward and tumbling through a stack of wooden kegs to the ground.

"Sonsabitches!" Bennie Stokes shouted, getting off a wild rifle shot before both rangers turned and fired as one. Their shots hammered into Bennie's chest. The impact slammed him backward against the corner post of a building. But the post hurled him forward into the dirt. He tried to crawl, but his boots only scraped in the dirt for a second before they stopped.

Sam stepped over quickly to Bobby Caesar and kicked his gun away from his hand. From his spot amid the scattered kegs, Bobby looked up through fading eyes. "I . . . played this . . . all wrong . . . didn't I?" he said, blood spewing from his lips.

Sam didn't answer, seeing death spread its blank glaze across the outlaw's eyes. Turning, seeing Jones standing over Shay's body, he said, "What happened to the other two?"

"I took care of them," Jones said.

Sam stared at him.

"Sorry, Sam. But I should've been the one to take down Shay," Jones said. "We both know it."

Chapter 20

———

Inside the alley beside the telegraph building, Sam looked down at the body of Leon Maddox, seeing the large circle of blood on the front of his shirt and in the center of the blood the gash left by the blade of Jones' boot knife. A few feet away, Purple Joe sat with his hands cuffed in front of him, the side of his head swollen and turning blue.

"You rangers ain't going to stab me too, are you?" he asked nervously, casting a frightened glance at Leon's body.

"Settle down, Purple Joe," Sam said. "The fighting's over. You'll go to jail, but we're not going to stab you, are we, Jones?" he asked in a stern voice.

Jones caught his tone and said, "Sam, what's the difference? They were waiting here to ambush us, one of them the very man we turned loose right before we rode in here. What do we owe them?" He looked at Leon's body with contempt. "These lousy sonsbitches."

"That's the difference," said Sam. "They are lousy. They are ambushers and thieves, killers and thugs. But we're not, and we have to stop ourselves from becoming like them . . . if we expect to uphold any law worth upholding." He stepped over closer to Jones and helped him pull Purple Joe to his feet. "Ever since Lonzo and his boys made a move on Flora, you've been wound tighter than a spring clock. You've let these men get to you and you're taking this job too personal."

"That's my wife, Sam! You tell me how I can keep from taking it personal?" Jones glared at him.

"I don't know, Jones," Sam said. "That's the sort of answer no lawman can answer for another. All I can tell you is that you've got to let go of what *almost* happened to Flora. If you don't, this job will eat you alive."

Jones took a deep breath; he appeared to have listened to what Sam said. "All right, Sam. You're right. It did get to me, them coming so close to Flora. But I'll get back down to business now."

"I hope so," Sam said. "You're a good man to have wearing that badge. I'd hate to see you have to turn it in."

"You *won't* see that, Sam," Jones said sincerely. "From here on, I'm back to my usual self." He gave Purple Joe a slight shove toward the horses and asked Sam, "What are we going to do with this one?"

Sam thought about it. "There's no jail here. No sheriff either, for that matter," he replied. "It looks like we're stuck with him."

"He's going to slow us down," Jones said.

"Yep, I expect he will, some," Sam said.

"I'll try not to," said Purple Joe, hearing them. "Hell, I know I'm going back to Yuma Prison, once they get all my charges bunched together. But I ain't going to try no funny business on you rangers. You've got my word on it."

"Yeah, *your word*," Jones said with cynicism. "That makes me feel a whole lot better."

"I'll take you at your word, Joe," Sam said. "We're going to leave you in custody in the first town we come to that has a sheriff, Joe," Sam said. "Until then, you stay on your best behavior for me and I'll mention it to the judge for you."

"You've got it, Ranger," said Joe. "Only, one thing. Do you mind if I ride that roan I found out there?"

"Yes, Joe, you can ride the roan. We'll go get it for you right now." He gave Purple Joe a slight shove in the barn's direction. Twenty feet away, without having to be asked, three townsmen stepped cautiously over and began removing the bodies of Bobby Caesar, Bennie Stokes and Ernie Shay from in front of the tent saloon.

"Obliged, Ranger," said Purple Joe over his shoulder. "Finding that roan has been the best piece of luck to come my way in a long time. I tried to tell Leon it was lucky—he made fun of me for it. But look at him now and look at me."

"You're going to prison, Joe," said Ranger Jones. "I wouldn't call that too lucky."

"I call it luckier than getting stabbed in the chest

anyday," said Joe, rubbing the knot on his head with his cuffed hands. He smiled at his good fortune and walked along as if didn't have a care in the world.

Moments later they left the livery barn, Joe leading the roan behind him, saddled and ready for the trail. At the hitch rail where Sam had left his Appaloosa, he waited with Purple Joe while Jones went to bring back his horse from where he'd left it in the alley behind the telegraph office. Mounted, the three rode out of Amberton Wells, seeing the bodies of Bobby Caesar, Shay, Bennie Stokes and Leon Maddox stretched out in a row in front of the town barbershop. Townsfolk gathered and whispered and watched them ride away.

From the saloon tent, Philbert Hazelit walked over and looked down at the bodies with his thumbs hooked in his low-slung gun belt. He shook his head while the townsmen watched him expectantly. Then he walked to his horse, mounted and spurred it hard, leaving Amberton Wells in a rise of dust. "There'll be trouble a-plenty once Mallard hears what they done to his cousin," a townsman said to anyone listening.

"Those damn crazy Hazelits and their blood feuds," said another, watching the dust settle behind the rangers and their prisoner. "These lawmen better sleep with one eye open."

Darkness set in before the rangers and their prisoner reached the main trail and were able to resume tracking Lonzo and his gang. In the light of a full moon, they made a cold camp and spent the night in a small clearing on a rocky hillside. Aware of the threat Shay's cousin and his sons posed, the two spent the night sleeping in two-hour shifts until the first thin line of sunlight mantled the eastern horizon.

"So far, so good," said Jones when Sam awakened him quietly and they both helped raise the hand-cuffed prisoner to his feet. After a breakfast of jerked beef and tepid water from the canteen, the three men rode until daylight and stopped again thirty yards back from a shallow pool of runoff water at the base of the low hills.

"Wait here," Sam said, having noted no antelope or other animals at the water hole as they had ap-proached.

Drawing his rifle from its boot, Sam nudged Black Pot forward in the clear morning light. On the ground beneath him, he saw no fresh animal tracks even as he neared the water's edge. With a motion of his hand he signaled for Jones to stay put and get down from his saddle. Once Jones had done so, Sam stepped down from his saddle, his thumb over his rifle hammer. Stooping, he cupped a handful of water, sniffed it and tasted it.

Nothing wrong with the water, he told himself. That left only the presence of danger as a reason for ani-mals to shun their watering hole. That danger had to be man, he thought. "Easy, boy," he whispered to the big Appaloosa, whose senses seemed to be as alert as his own.

Stepping back into his stirrup, he started to ease himself up and into his saddle when rifle shots began exploding from a line of rocks twenty yards away on the other side of the water. One shot swiped Sam's sombrero from atop his head. Another kicked up mud at Black Pot's hooves. Sam crouched and slapped the Appaloosa soundly on the rump to get it out of the line of fire. Diving to the flat ground, he rolled into a sparse stand of wild grass, the only cover available.

Even as Sam threw his rifle butt to his shoulder and began firing, he heard Jones' rifle exploding behind him. Within seconds the two firing back caused the rifle fire from the rocks to diminish enough for Sam to call out, "Is that you over there, Mallard Hazelit?"

After a silent pause a gruff voice replied, "Yes, it's me, Ranger. Me and both my boys. I expect you know why we're here. Ernie Shay was my cousin."

"I don't care why you're here, Hazelit," Sam called out from within the grass. "You and your boys pulled a trigger on us. Now we've got to kill *you*."

"That's understandable, Ranger," Hazelit called out in response. "Let's get on with it."

But before a shot fired, Sam called out, "It's a shame though that you and your boys have to die over a snake like Shay. He was a murderer and a thief." Sam let his words sink in, then said, "I know you and your boys do a little rustling up here. It appears everybody does. But Shay brought us right here and served you up to us if we wanted to pursue it. What kind of kin is that to have to die for?"

"I know what he was, Ranger," said Mallard. "But

it makes no difference. Kin is kin. It's been that way since the beginning of time. Nothing can change it."

"But I had to try, Hazelit. It's my job," said Sam.

"Damn Ernie Shay to hell!" Mallard bellowed out in rage. "Why the hell did he do us this way? We had it good up here, the boys and me!"

"I don't know why he did it to you," Sam called out. "But like you said, if we're going to do this, let's get on with it." Giving a glance back over his shoulder, Sam saw no sign of Jones or his horse, only Purple Joe's roan standing off to the side, out of the line of fire. He knew that while he'd been talking to Hazelit, Jones had been slipping around trying to flank the riflemen.

Hearing renewed rifle fire from across the water-hole, Sam hoped he'd bought Jones the time he needed. His hopes were realized when shot after shot began to pound the Hazelit's rock cover from far left of him. "Damn it, Pa! I'm hit!" one of the boys yelled in agony.

The Hazelits stopped firing for a moment. Using that lull, Sam came up into a low crouch and ran splashing across the water hole. On the other side of the water he dropped behind a low rock just as two of the Hazelits' rifles started up again.

Hearing Jones' rifle return fire, Sam noted that Jones had gotten all the way around the stretch of rocks, breaking their cover, and was now firing in on the riflemen enough to keep them busy while Sam advanced.

"Pa! I'm hit too!" another voice cried out. But this time Mallard Hazelit didn't reply.

"Philbert, he's dead!" cried Jedson Hazelit as Sam hurried forward and dropped down against the other side of their rock cover.

"Give it up over there, boys!" Sam called out. "This fighting needs to stop before you all end up dead."

A moment of silence passed. It was broken by Jedson screaming, "They're dead, you murdering sons-bitches!" He began firing round after round repeatedly while sobbing and cursing aloud. "I'll kill you lawdog bastards!"

From his flanking position, Jones saw Sam spring up atop the rocks and fire one shot down, silencing both the rifle and Jedson Hazelit. Jones waited, tense, ready for anything. Finally he saw Sam stand atop the rocks and wave him in with a gloved hand. "They're dead," Sam called out.

Jones stood up and dusted his knees. But before he walked over to join Sam, the sound of a horse's hooves began pounding along the trail. Jones spun in time to see Purple Joe making a run for it on the roan.

Sam saw what Joe was doing; and at the same time he saw Jones' rifle butt come up to his shoulder. "Don't shoot!" Sam shouted with all his strength.

But it was too late. The rifle bucked in Ranger Jones' hands. The impact of the bullet picked Purple Joe up from his saddle and sent him rolling head over heels in the dirt, a stream of blood spewing from the bullet hole below his neck. Sam watched with his fists clenched at his sides.

Jones saw the look of anger on Sam's face when the two had gathered their horses and led them to the spot where Joe lay dying. "I'm . . . sorry, Ranger," Joe murmured, sounding more dead than alive. "I . . . felt lucky . . . riding that roan."

Sam and Jones watched the outlaw's eyes glaze over and turn upward in death. "He couldn't have gone far," Sam said in an even tone. "We would have overtaken him easy enough."

"He was getting away, Sam," Jones replied in the same tone. "I felt I had to do it." He paused. "Did I do wrong?"

"You might have brought him with you when you flanked them," Sam said. "He would've been less tempted to run."

"That's true," said Jones, "and if I had and he'd gotten shot by the Hazelits, would I have been any less to blame?" When Sam didn't answer, Jones continued. "Could I have moved as fast, gotten around and done what I did with a handcuffed prisoner beside me?" He took a deep breath and said, "Look, Sam, I didn't set this man up to shoot him in the back. He gave us both his word that he wouldn't run. He did. I shot him."

"It was his nature to run," Sam said.

"There was nothing to cuff him to," Jones offered. "He made his choice. He's dead. We're alive. It could have gone a lot of other ways. But this was it."

After a moment of consideration, Sam said, "You

made the call. I won't question it. But you were too quick to kill, Jones. We both know it."

"Me, quick to kill?" Jones asked. "What about you, Sam? There's lot of folks, rangers included, who say you're too quick when it comes to killing. What's the difference between us, Sam?"

"There's a difference," Sam replied with finality on the matter. Changing the subject, he gazed off along the trail and said, "There's a string of little towns like Amberton Wells between here and the border. I expect Lonzo and his men will be visiting as many of them as they can before they disappear into Mexico."

Jones saw that the conversation had ended. He shrugged slightly and began reloading his rifle. "Then it looks like we've got our work cut out for us."

Chapter 21

———

Near the town of Christi, without a word to anyone, Reverend Vernon Wilcox disappeared beneath a sky that had quickly turned dark and begun to rumble with distant thunder. "It was morning the last I saw him," said Paul Metlet. "But the reverend likes a storm better than any man I ever seen. He'll ride right off into one every time."

Sitting atop their horses on a trail reaching up the side a canyon, Lonzo smiled and said, "This is how the good reverend left us last time." Lonzo looked at Stone Eddie Deaks as he spoke.

"He don't say goodbye, adios or nothing else," Metlet added. "Once the storm moves out, he don't leave a trace of either man or hoof."

"He'll go lay low somewhere." Lonzo shrugged. "Maybe preach a little, shove some fire and brimstone down the throats of the local believers for a while. But as soon as his nose tells him the time is right, he'll find us."

"Funny thing about noses," said Deaks, "mine is starting to tell me the same thing Wilcox's must've told him. Maybe it's time I cut away too." Glancing at Norbert Lamb he asked, "What about you, Kid?"

"I can stay or go," Lamb replied. "But I've got to say, we haven't made any money to speak of since that last little raid where we brought the whores along with us."

"Which is it you're pining after," asked Lonzo, "the whores or the money?" Lightning flickered on and off in the distance.

"The money," said Lamb. "But the whores were a nice extra to have along for the ride." He looked at Lonzo squarely and asked, "What's our plan? When *are* we going to make some more money?"

"As soon as we know we don't have rangers hounding our trail for what we did back at Apache Fork," said Lonzo, not liking the way Lamb suddenly seemed to be questioning him. "But let me make something clear to you, Lamb. You're here because Stone Eddie brought you in with his recommendation. You're still a long ways from questioning me on how I run my business."

"The Kid knows that, Lonzo," Deaks cut in. "But since he brought the subject up, when are we going to make some more money? All I see us doing is dodging the law and frightening women." He chuckled a little under his breath, but no one shared his humor except for Lamb.

"You happened to join us at a time when we were just coming off a spree, Eddie," said Lonzo, not wanting to sound weak in front of his three remaining men. He gave a quick nod toward Forrest Bidson. "*Deputy* here is new with us. He understands it's going to take some time to get himself established."

"Yeah," Bidson cut in, staring at Deaks, "I'm new, but you don't hear me complaining."

"For what it's worth, *Deputy*," said Deaks, "coming straight from wearing a badge to riding owlhoot doesn't make you anything in my book except a sorry, weak-kneed failure. You couldn't make it as a lawdog, so you throw in with the opposition."

"Hey," said Bidson, "I don't have to take that kind of talk off no man!" His voice was angry, yet his hand made no move for the gun on his hip.

"No, you don't," said Deaks, smiling flatly. "But I'm betting you will. I can see you having nerve enough to splatter an old lawman with his own shotgun and burn his town down. But I can't see your nerve taking you much further than that." He stared at Bidson. "If you was going to make a move, you already would have."

"Everybody hold on!" said Lonzo. "We're all part of the same bunch here! There's no need in all this badmouthing among pals. We're just talking here."

"You're right. We're just talking," Deaks said, sounding bored as he turned his stare from Bidson back to Lonzo. "So, like the Lamb asked, when are we going to be making some money?"

Lonzo fumed, but didn't let his anger show. "Metlet and I are heading across the border, laying low awhile." He looked at Bidson, then at Calvin Thurston, then at Deaks. "You're welcome to stick with us or cut away for a while like you said."

"*Adios,*" said Deaks, backing his horse a step.

Beside him, Lamb said, "*And* goodbye," in a mocking tone. He backed his horse a step away as well, both he and Deaks keeping an eye on Lonzo and the others.

"You will be coming back, though, won't you?" Lonzo called out as the two began to turn their horses.

"We'll see how it goes," Deaks said, sounding a bit smug.

Lonzo and the other three sat watching the two riders put their horses on a thin trail leading down the flatlands. "Good riddance," Calvin Thurston said, spitting, as if clearing his mouth of a bad taste.

"Yeah, that goes for me too," said Metlet. "I never saw one thing to make me think he's anything special."

"He killed Sam Burrack for us, let's not forget," said Lonzo. He looked at Calvin Thurston. "He avenged your brother's death."

"Yeah," Calvin said grudgingly, "let's not forget he done that."

"I'm new here," said Bidson, "so maybe it ain't my place to say. But mostly all I saw him do was sit back and watch while everybody else did what needed doing."

Lonzo grinned, liking the way Bidson showed the kind of respect a new man should. "Deputy, you're going to do all right riding with us," he said, turning his horse back along the high trail. The men followed, raising their collars against the growing wind. "Wherever the good reverend is," Lonzo said over his shoulder, "I hope he's high and dry, waiting this storm out."

But ten miles southwest, Wilcox was not high and dry. He had pushed on steadily through rain so wind-driven he could scarcely see. He traveled straight up in his saddle, ignoring the rain, yet holding a hand down firmly atop his soaked hat to keep it from flying away. Beneath him the horse tried ducking its head against the wind and water, but Reverend Wilcox jerked the reins and made the animal bear up to the weather, as he himself did.

As the storm held on, lighting struck the trunk of a scrub oak on the hillside to his right, splitting the tree to the ground in a blinding spray of white fire. "Easy ol' horse!" Wilcox shouted, handling the spooked horse firmly to keep it from bolting away with him. "No elements of God's nature will destroy the righteous." Subduing the terrified animal he swept off his hat in a grand gesture, slinging water. "Let fall the wrath of God on the wicked!" he cried out to the broken blackened tree trunk as it tumbled down the hillside toward him.

Nudging the horse forward quickly, he watched the trunk bounce across the trail, where it was swallowed up by a powerful stream of water, and race away across the sloping land. "Pound the living hell out of this wicked, *wicked* earth, Lord! And lead me to do your bidding!" he said, laughing above the raging storm. He rode on.

By the time he had arrived on the outskirts of Christi, the wind and rain had slackened; the lightning and thunder had moved on, leaving a sodden land full of raging streams gorged with downed trees and debris in its aftermath. The first to spot him riding in were two mud-streaked townsmen who had ventured out and begun carrying boards from a pile where they lay stacked for just such occasions. "Lord have mercy, Ollie!" one of the men said to another. "Look who's coming here."

"My, my, Gerald," said Ollie Grayson, "what kind of man rides through this kind of weather?"

"That's what I asked myself," said Gerald Sandler, holding his slicker collar closed at his throat to keep the rain out. "Some *hardcase* afoul of the law would be my first guess."

They stood on the last board they'd thrown down and stared at Wilcox as he stopped his drenched horse, stepped down from his saddle and trod carefully along the boards toward them. The horse sloshed along in the mud beside him, Wilcox leading it by the reins, his Bible out and held tightly in his left hand. "Hello the walk boards, and God bless you good laboring fellows," he called out.

The two looked at each other, surprised. Rain streaked with mud ran down their haggard faces. "A preacher?" Ollie Grayson mused.

"Naw, can't be," said Gerald Sandler. But no sooner had he spoken than Wilcox's wet black riding

duster parted down the front enough to reveal the
white clerical collar he'd put on shortly after riding
away from Lonzo and his men.

"A preacher indeed," Wilcox called out, having
heard the skeptical townsman. Raising the Bible toward Gerald, he said, "Now the question is, can a
man of God walk these same planks laid down for
ordinary mortal man?"

"I reckon so," Gerald said, giving Ollie a wry grin.
"Otherwise you'd have fallen off!"

Stopping in front of the two, Wilcox reached out
with his Bible and thumped it soundly but good-
naturedly on Gerald's forehead. "I can see I'm going
to have my hands full saving your soul from hell."
Standing tall, he said bluntly, "I take you *are not*
saved . . . as I'm certain the rest of this town is *not!*"
He cast a subtle look of disdain over the town as he
spoke. "To whom am I speaking, gentle brothers?"
he asked.

"I'm Ollie Grayson, the town barber. This is Gerald Sandler. He runs the town land title company
and records office."

"Oh, a man of clerical skill," said Wilcox.

Yes," said Gerald, "that is when I'm not pitching
boards in the mud." He gestured a grimy hand toward the mud and puddles underfoot. "And who
might you be?"

"I am the Most Reverend Vernon Wilcox. You
might say I have weathered a storm most dark and
dreaded, in order to come here and bring hope to
this lost and suffering town."

"Well," said Ollie, scratching his head, "I wouldn't go so far as to say Christi is *lost and suffering*, Reverend Wilcox. Most folks here are good, honest—"

"Enough of that," said Wilcox, cutting him off. "I am a man of God, moved by the spirit to be here. If I say this town is lost and suffering, you can bet your ass it is!" He pointed his Bible down at the mud in front of them where the boards ended. "Now the two of you good brothers, go fetch some more boards and walk them right over to the saloon for me."

"The saloon?" Gerald questioned him.

"You heard me right, good brother," said Wilcox, "onward to the saloon. That's as good a place to start as any."

The two rangers had taken shelter out of the storm beneath a rocky shelf overhang. In the late afternoon when the storm had moved on, they stepped their horses out onto the muddy trail and looked down across the flatlands, where no dust stirred, and down at the mud beneath their feet, where all tracks had been washed away. "It looks like this is Lonzo's lucky day," said Jones. "Now what are we going to do?"

"We go on the same as we've been doing," Sam said, "There's not that many towns left between here and the border. Without any tracks to follow, we'll just have to hit each one and move quick. It's a sure bet Lonzo and Metlet will cross the border. We'll just have to come back for the rest if we miss them along the way."

Pointing down and across the muddy flatlands at a trail on the other side of a raging stream filled with brush and downed timber, Jones asked, "What's out that way?"

"Christi," Sam replied. "But it could take a while for the water to go down and the land to dry up. There's another trail that leads there. I'll show you when we get to it."

"Yeah," Jones agreed. "If any of Lonzo's men went there it would have been while it was storming. I can't see any of them doing that, can you?"

"Only one," Sam said, considering it. "A preacher by the name of Wilcox. He likes traveling in a storm, I've heard."

"Reverend Wilcox," said Jones. "Even I've heard of him. We can't leave Christi off our list if Wilcox is there," said Jones.

"I'm not saying he went there," said Sam. "But if any of them went there, they caught themselves a streak of good luck. We're staying on the trail after Lonzo and Metlet. Those two always cross the border and get away." He paused for a second. "But not this time."

They mounted their horses and rode down to the flatlands, where they set out on the main trail. With effort, the horses struggled along the deep muddy trail until the last long streak of sunlight sank below the western horizon. By then the land beneath them had turned rocky and hard once again, making it easier for the horses to negotiate.

At a point where two smaller trails snaked off in either direction, the rangers stopped and sat for a moment, sipping tepid water from their canteens.

"Here's the other trail I told you about that runs into Christi," said Sam.

"Okay, I'll take it," Jones said eagerly.

"Let me ask you this," Sam said, after careful consideration. "If we split up here for a while, and you ride into Christi alone"—he nodded toward a distant line of low hills—"will you *try* first to arrest any of the Black Moons you find before killing them?"

Jones gave him a look.

"It's an honest question," Sam said. "I've just got to know where you stand."

Jones took a deep breath, thinking the question over. "You're right, Sam. In light of all that's happened, you have a right to ask me that." He nodded and added, "Yes, I will try to arrest them first. If that doesn't work, I'm going to take them down however I feel necessary to do so. Is that fair enough?"

"That's fair enough," Sam replied. "You go to Christi. I'll go to Grant City. Tomorrow morning we'll meet back here and move on along the main trail. If one of us gets here before the other, we'll only wait an hour. Then we go on. This trail leads all the way to the border, so if we get separated, we won't stay separated long."

"Sounds good to me, Sam," said Jones. "I'll see you when we get back."

"Watch your back in there, Jones," Sam said. He turned his Appaloosa onto the smaller trail toward Grant.

"You do the same, Sam," Jones said, batting his heels to his horse's sides.

Chapter 22

———

Three miles along the back trail into Christi, Ranger Jones noted that a set of fresh wagon tracks came onto the thin trail from out across the muddy flatlands. Following the wagon tracks for the next mile he noticed that the trail had become grown over with wild grass and littered with mesquite brush. Staring ahead he saw the low skyline of the mining town in the distance. But of more immediate interest he saw the freight wagon sitting midtrail thirty yards in front of him, its rear wheel off, its left rear axle lying buried in mud. A few yards out in the wild grass off the trail lay the body of a horse, flies swarming above it.

Drawing his rifle from its boot, Jones nudged his horse forward cautiously until he saw boot prints in the mud leading around the front of the wagon. "Hello the wagon," he called out, stopping his horse fifteen feet away. When no one replied, he stepped down from his saddle, holding his rifle ready in his right hand. "Hello the wagon," he called out again. "Anything I can do to help?"

"Yeah," said a strained gravelly voice, "you can get your lawdog ass right back in that saddle and light out of here."

The voice sounded familiar. Jones tried to recognize it as he quickly raised his rifle to this shoulder and called out, "Show yourself, mister!"

"If I come out, I'll come out shooting!" the voice growled.

"So be it," said Jones. "Come on out!" Stepping away from his horse, he crouched a bit and cocked the rifle, ready to fire.

"Why don't you just go away and mind your own damn business?" the voice said, sounding less threatening now that Jones seemed to have called the man's bluff.

"Giles Pruitt?" Jones asked, lowering his rifle, but only an inch.

"All right, Ranger, it's me," Pruitt said, whining now as he stood up with his hands raised high. "You've got me again. I ain't armed, see?"

"Step around into view," Jones demanded, not taking any chances.

"Damn, all right," said Pruitt. He stepped out into full view, his shirtsleeves up, his forearms covered in mud. "I'm not armed. I lost my gun somewhere in that damned storm."

"I'll take a look and make sure," said Jones, stepping in closer, searching Pruitt with his free hand, seeing his holster filled with thick mud. Looking down at Pruitt's boot wells he saw no sign of a knife.

"I lost my knife too," Pruitt said. "I am about as unarmed as any miserable pilgrim you've ever seen out here. I'm lucky I haven't lost my hair, along with everything else." He nodded at a stub of an arrow sticking in the wagon.

Jones looked over into the wagon bed, flipped back a tarpaulin and said, "Where'd you get these two crates of whiskey?"

"Two crates?" Pruitt exclaimed, his eyes widening. "You're kidding! Let me see!" With his hands still raised, he pushed in beside Jones and stared down into the wagon bed. "I'll be double-dog damned," he said, letting out a tense breath. "I've been robbed by every low-down dirty son of a bitch in the Badlands."

"How much whiskey did you have?" Jones asked, looking the old drunkard up and down. "Where did you get it?"

"I never stole it, if that's what you're thinking!" Pruitt snapped at him.

Jones gave him a skeptical stare.

"All right, Ranger, maybe I did steal it, sort of," said Pruitt. "But I damn sure didn't kill the two bastards driving it!"

"You didn't? Then who did kill them?" Jones continued to stare, fishing for any information Pruitt might give up about himself.

Pruitt trembled and rubbed his lips nervously. "All right, damn it! I shot them, but it was in self-defense! I swear to God! And I never et them! That's the truth if I ever told it! I mighta had a little blood in my beard, but there wasn't no meat sticking between my teeth—"

"Hold it," Jones said, cutting him off. "What do you mean you didn't *eat* them?"

"I meant just what I said. I didn't eat them." Pruitt lowered his arms a bit. "I get pretty damn drunk but I've never been that drunk."

"Why did you even bring it up, Pruitt?" Jones asked, wanting to know more.

"Because I didn't want you thinking I might have et them, that's why," Pruitt responded.

Jones shook his head a bit, as if to clear it, and tried again. "But why would I have even *thought* you might have eaten somebody? Are you drunk?"

"I'm about as sober as I ever get, which ain't too much. But I'm no gawddamn cannibal!" Pruitt suddenly shouted. "I just thought I better make you understand that before you got any wrong ideas!"

"I see," said Jones, deciding to let the subject go for the moment. "How long ago did you *acquire* this wagon and its contents?" he asked, choosing his words carefully.

Pruitt thought about it, but couldn't get a grasp on time. Finally he shrugged and said, "I don't know. But it's been long enough to make me know that there is not a son of a bitch you can trust when it comes to whiskey. Everybody I've come upon has stolen from me. The last I recall was three Ute Indians."

"The Utes?" said Jones. "They're peaceable. They have been for years."

"Not these three," said Pruitt. "I traded them whiskey for two of their horses. They came back and stole one horse back, then shot arrows at me when I got away with the other." He nodded at the thin dead horse lying off the trail. "But they were no worse than anybody else I met. I've come to the notion that too much whiskey is a man's downfall."

"That's hardly a new idea," Jones said.

"Oh yeah?" Pruitt looked him up and down. "Where were you lawmen when *I* needed you?"

Ignoring Pruitt's question, Jones looked off toward Christi and asked, "How much farther is it into town?"

Without answering, Pruitt asked, "Are you going to help me get this wheel on?"

"Why? Your horse is dead," said Jones.

"Then you can take me somewhere to get a *live* horse, a mule or something," Pruitt insisted.

"I don't have the time," said Jones. "I'm tracking Lonzo and his men."

"Ha!" said Pruitt. "Not this way you're not."

"What are you saying, Pruitt?" Jones asked.

"I'm saying there's nobody to home in Christi," Pruitt said. "The mines all played out and Christi fell flat over a year ago. There's nothing left there but empty buildings and buzzard shit."

"Then why were you headed there?" Jones asked.

"I was going there to drink the rest of my whiskey

in peace," said Pruitt. "I'm tired of being on guard all
the damned time."

Jones ran it through his mind. Had he been sent on
a wild-goose chase while Sam rode into Grant City to
take care of any Black Moon riders who might be
there? Had his and Sam's differences grown that
great between them? Evidently so, he thought. To
Pruitt he said, "You can camp here and drink your
whiskey in peace. I've got to get over to Grant City."

"Grant City is where I'm wanting to go too," said
Pruitt. "We can ride double. I can get myself a horse
there."

"No," said Jones, "I don't have time to ride double
with you. I told you I'm in a hurry."

"You can't leave a man stranded out here like this,
Ranger," said Pruitt. "It ain't human! I need water, a
horse, food! I'll die out here!"

"You'll get by, Pruitt," said Jones stepping back up
into his saddle, anxious to get under way. "You've
done well for yourself so far."

"Damn lawdog!" Pruitt bellowed. "You've just the
same as killed me, leaving me like this!" He watched
Jones turn his horse and ride it away at a run. "My
blood is on your hands, Ranger! You murdered me!"
he screamed. When Jones had ridden out of sight,
Pruitt grinned drunkenly to himself, walked to the
side of the wagon and began taking bottle after bottle from one of the crates and shoving them inside his
shirt.

Cradling the whiskey bottles with both hands, he
turned one last glance along the trail in the direction

Jones had taken. He laughed and said aloud, "By God! Giles Pruitt's daddy didn't raise no fool!" Then he turned unsteadily in the muddy trail and staggered off toward Christi.

Sam kept the Appaloosa stallion at an easy pace all the way to Grant City. A mile from town he left the trail and circled wide in order to come in through a side street or an alley. Under the circumstances he thought it wise not to ride in straight down the middle of the main street and perhaps put innocent townsfolk at risk should one of the Black Moons see him coming. Having found an alley that ran the length of the town, he stepped down from his saddle, pulled his rifle from its boot and led Black Pot past the town dump to a shorter alleyway that led to the street.

From the shadow of the alleyway he scanned the town in both directions, looking for any signs of Lonzo or his men. At a hitch rail out front of the Jumping Coyote Saloon he spotted Stone Eddie Deaks' horse, and he let out a slight sigh of relief. "All right, Stone Eddie, I see your horse. Now let me see your face," he whispered to himself.

But seeing Stone Eddie didn't happen right away. Sam scanned the busy, mud-swollen street back and forth for a full twenty minutes before he finally saw Deaks step out of a restaurant almost directly across the street from him. Seeing Norbert Lamb step out right behind Deaks, Sam ducked back a step and watched the two walk along the boardwalk until they found a path of boards that crossed the street and led to the saloon.

Sam gave the town another searching look to make sure there were no other Black Moons around. Seeing no other familiar faces, he stood calmly staring at the saloon, judging how long it took Deaks and Lamb to get themselves a drink and settle in at the bar. When he felt he'd given them enough time, he walked Black Pot out onto the muddy street, hitched him at a nearby rail and went along the boardwalk to the bat-wing doors of the Jumping Coyote.

At the bar, Deaks and Lamb stood with their shot glasses of whiskey in hand. Sam slipped into the crowded saloon quietly, his duster closed to keep his badge from showing. Standing to the side for a moment, he watched the two throw back their drinks and set the empty glass on the bar. *Now,* he told himself. But before he could take a step forward, he saw Lamb turn away from the bar and work his way through the standing drinkers and out the back door to the outhouse.

Sam waited, watching the back door. Five minutes passed. He watched Deaks, saw his eyes scan the mirror behind the bar. Sam ducked away to keep from being seen. He waited a full five minutes longer, but still Lamb didn't return. Knowing he couldn't stand there much longer without being seen, Sam decided to make his move.

Deaks motioned for the bartender to fill the two glasses standing before him. As soon as the whiskey swirled down and around into the glasses, Deaks grinned and wrapped his fingers around the glass and raised it in a toast to the bartender. "Here's lice in your whiskers," he said.

The bartender's eyes widened; Deaks chuckled, thinking his toast had caused it. But before putting the drink to his lips, Deaks saw the ranger's face in the mirror—he was standing right behind Deaks. "Jesus!" Deaks said; he froze as if he'd seen a ghost.

"Stone Eddie Deaks," Sam said sternly, his Colt out at arm's length, cocked and leveled an inch from the back of Deaks' head, "you are under arrest for shooting an officer of the law."

"Shooting you?" said Deaks, trying to recover from seeing the face of a man he'd thought dead staring at him through the mirror. "I thought I killed you!"

"You missed," Sam said, not wanting to tell him what had actually happened, liking it better this way.

"You're lying," said Deaks, recovering quickly from his ghost scare. "I never miss." He appeared unshaken by the gun pointed at his head.

"Here I stand, Deaks," said Sam. "You tell me if I'm dead or alive."

"You're alive, *Sam*," Deaks said, making it a point to call him by his first name, his drink hand still raised and suspended in front of his face. "But I didn't miss. I don't know what happened, but my aim has never been at fault."

"Have it your way, Deaks," Sam said. "You've got the rest of your life in Yuma Prison to figure it out, provided they don't hang you."

"I'm not going to prison, *Sam*," Deaks said. He slowly placed the glass against his lips and took his drink. "Why don't you and me just walk us off some paces and turn and settle up? You wouldn't really want to see a man of my style and bearing wasted away in a cell or stretching bug-eyed on the end of rope, would you?"

"There's nothing I'd like better, Deaks," Sam said. Seeing the slightest twitch of Deaks' gun hand on the bar top, Sam ended the conversation with a sharp swipe of his gun barrel across the back of Deaks' head.

As Deaks sank to the floor, Sam lifted Deaks' gun from his holster and shoved it down into his belt.

"Are you really a lawman?" the bartender asked, having heard the conversation. As he asked, his hand crept slowly toward the shotgun under the bar.

Sam pulled back the lapel of his mud-streaked riding duster. "Yes, I am, so stop reaching for that scattergun before you get your fingers cracked.

"Sure thing, Ranger!" the bartender said. His fingers came off of the bar quickly. Drinkers had gathered in around the spot where Deaks lay knocked out on the floor. Wanting to keep an eye on the rear door for Lamb, Sam waved the crowd back, saying, "Give me room here. I'm not finished."

The crowd moved back quickly, faces looking all around, concerned about what *not finished* could mean. Sam turned back toward the rear door only to hear Lamb call out from the front door, "Ranger! Back here!"

Sam spun, his Colt out, cocked, ready. He saw Lamb's arm extended as well. But it wasn't a gun in Lamb's hand. It was a bright shiny badge pinned inside a leather wallet. "Don't shoot, Ranger," Lamb shouted, seeing the look on Sam's face. "I'm a lawman too!"

Sam was too far along to stop in time. His gun fired. But in that fraction of a second before the hammer struck the bullet he managed to throw the tip of the barrel down in time to send the shot slamming into the wooden floor.

"Oh God," Lamb said, his arm slumping a bit, the wallet and badge almost slipping from his hand.

"Who are you, mister?" Sam asked, raising the smoking Colt, still not trusting Lamb until he knew more.

"I'm Bert Stewart! I'm a detective with Midwest Detective Agency! Norbert 'Kid' Lamb is a name I took on to track down Deaks and any Black Moons I could find."

"Pitch that badge over to me easy-like, and keep your arm raised," Sam instructed him.

The detective did as he was told and gave the wallet a soft pitch. Sam caught it, looked the badge over good and held the wallet in his left hand as he asked, "What about the man Deaks said you shot?" He watched the young man's eyes closely.

"That was Dowdy Thompson, and I *did* shoot him down, true enough. But he was a man I'd been trailing for the past three months for train robbery. I got lucky. I killed him and managed to turn him in without revealing my cover to anyone." He took a breath and asked, "Ranger Burrack, can I lower my arm now?"

Sam pitched the badge back to him and said, "Yes, you can."

"Obliged," said Stewart. "I had been sent to get in as close as I could with Stone Eddie Deaks, knowing from reliable sources that Lonzo and his gang were interested in having Deaks join them. It sort of put a wrinkle in my plans when you showed up and arrested Deaks in Cottonwood. But I bided my time." He smiled. "Now it looks like everything is coming my way. I slipped out the back door under the pretense of going to the jakes, but I sent a telegraph to my office, telling them I had Deaks separated from the others. Now, if you'll allow me to share in arresting Deaks, I'll just turn in my report and mark his name off my—"

"Mark *yourself* off, you sneaking son of a bitch!" Deaks raged, swinging up on one knee. A small hideout pistol had streaked from beneath his coat and fired, in one lighting-fast move.

Sam swung his Colt and fired too. The shot nailed Deaks back against the bar. But his small pistol was still raised toward the detective. "Oh Jesus," Stewart groaned, his left hand grasping his bloody chest, his right raising his Colt at about the same time as Sam's next shot slammed Deaks even harder and left him dead on the floor.

Sam took a step toward Stewart to help him. The detective staggered in place, turning toward Sam with the Colt still raised in front of him. "I'm—I'm shot . . ." he said as if seeing it all from within a dream.

"Take it easy," Sam said, hurrying toward him.

"Look out, Sam!" Jones shouted, kicking open the bat-wing doors.

"No, Jonesie!" Sam shouted. But it was too late. Seeing the gun pointed at Sam, Jones fired. His first shot hit Bert Stewart and spun him around facing Jones, bringing the detective's Colt around pointed at the young ranger. Jones fired again. The shot hit Stewart and drove him back a step. The next shot sent him backward and pitched him on the floor beside Stone Eddie Deaks.

Jones stood with his pistol still raised and cocked, as if about to fire again. "Don't shoot, Jonesie!" Sam repeated. "He's dead!"

Jones turned facing him, saying, "Sam, are you all right?"

"I'm all right," Sam replied. He lowered his Colt, slumped and shook his head. "Jonesie, you just killed a lawman."

Chapter 23

———

By the time the townsmen had removed the bodies of Stone Eddie Deaks and the young detective, the crowd of drinkers had more than doubled at the Jumping Coyote Saloon. Once the word had spread that one of the rangers had killed another lawman, anger began to rise among the drinkers. Seeing their attitudes turn bristly with tension, Sam directed Jones away from the crowded bar.

In a small room off the side of the big clapboard building, the two rangers sat with a bottle of whiskey standing between them. A shot glass sat in front of them, but the only glass being used was the one Jones held tightly in his hand.

"I swear to God, Sam," Jones said softly. "It looked like he was out to shoot you dead . . . else I never would have fired."

Sam looked at him. "Go easy on the whiskey, Jones," he cautioned. Whatever else he had to say on the matter would have to wait. This was not the right time or place to say it.

"I know you think I fired too quick," Jones said, looking as if he hoped Sam would say otherwise.

"Not if he'd really been out to kill me," said Sam, giving his partner some consolation. He could have told Jones that he'd had no business jumping into the situation without Sam expecting him. But that wasn't the thing to say to a person who had just taken another man's life by mistake. Instead Sam asked Jones quietly, "What made you turn around and follow me here? You were headed into Christi."

Jones tossed back a shot of whiskey and poured himself another glassful. "That was my first terrible mistake, Sam," he replied. "I ran into the old drunk Pruitt on the trail. He said the mines near Christi had played out. Said the town had been abandoned."

Sam watched him drink with scrutiny. "So you turned right around and headed here," he offered.

"He played me for a fool, is what he did," Jones said bitterly, his hand tightening around the glass as if tightening around Pruitt's throat. "It—it came to me that maybe you'd sent me there to get rid of me while you rode in here, where you figured some of the Black Moons might be," Jones said, shaking his head, reflecting on his own foolishness. "I don't know why I thought that as soon as he told me Christi was deserted."

"Pruitt's a good liar," Sam replied. "They are *all* good liars. It comes built right into their character."

"And I fell for it," Jones said, staring down into the

whiskey glass. "I took his word and thought that my own partner had tricked me."

"I would never have done that, Jones," Sam said. "No matter what else might be going on between us, I wouldn't have thrown you off the trail that way."

"I know that now," Jones said. "But at that moment I wasn't thinking straight. This has been a hard trek for both of us. We've had our differences. I suppose Pruitt just caught me off guard."

"Their main job is to catch honest folks off guard," Sam said. "It's all that keeps them free and running."

Jones finished his fresh glass of whiskey. "And now I've killed an innocent man."

Sam turned and walked to the door that separated the room from the rest of the saloon. Peeping out, he looked at the drinkers standing three and four deep at the bar beneath a thick cloud of cigar and pipe smoke. "Get your drinking done, Jones," he said. "It's time we walk out of here."

Jones gestured his whiskey glass toward a rear door that led out to the alleyway behind the main street. "We could take this door, circle around and go get our horses," he said.

"Is that the way you want to do it?" Sam asked pointedly, staring at him. "You want to sneak out the back door?"

"No," Jones said, pushing back the shot glass and rising to his feet. "I did what I did. I can't change it. But it was as honest mistake. I'll walk with it."

"Good." Sam nodded his solemn approval and opened the door to the saloon. "After you."

"There they are!" a whiskey-fueled voice called out angrily from the bar as the two rangers crossed the floor toward the bat-wings doors, Jones in front and Sam walking behind him.

"What innocent man are you two lawdogs going to shoot next?" a man with a long, pointed mustache called out. He poked a stylish silver-tipped walking cane toward the two and said, "Bang! Bang!"

The rangers kept walking.

Yet a third voice shouted, "That's right. Act like you don't hear us! But we all *know* what you did!"

"Burn in hell for it," cried a woman who stood on the third step leading to a row of rooms upstairs.

"Tell them, Molly!" another voice said. "They're nothing more than killers themselves!"

"I say we string them up!"

"Or at least give them a sound thrashing!" shouted the man with the mustache and cane.

Jones had just stepped through the bat-wing doors; but upon hearing the last set of words spoken from the crowd, Sam halted and turned at the sound of footsteps stomping toward him. His Colt came up from his holster and he extended it at arm's length, the tip of the barrel jamming against the man's forehead. "Drop it!" Sam demanded.

On the floor behind the man lay the outer casing of his cane. Drawn back in his right hand, a thin hideout sword glistened. But upon feeling the cold steel gun barrel and seeing the look of resolve on Sam's face, he let the sword drop from his fingertips. It landed sticking up, swaying back and forth slightly in the plank floor. Sam gave a hard nudge of the gun barrel against the man's head.

"Don't any of you step foot out of this door until we are under way. Any complaints you think you have, send them to the captain at the Badlands outpost."

"That's Sam Burrack," a voice whispered in awe.

"I never thought he'd do something like this," another replied.

Having heard the commotion, Jones stepped back inside the bat-wing doors, his gun drawn and ready. "Ranger Burrack didn't do this! I'm the one to blame. Any of you who saw it already know that. I'm Ranger Hadley Jones, and this was all *my* fault."

"Get out of here, Jonesie," Sam said over his shoulder. "Go get our horses."

Without another word and with his Colt still drawn but held down by his side, Sam stood staring at the drinkers until their anger subsided, giving way to cooler thinking. When he heard Jones return with the horses, Sam stepped backward out the bat-wing doors, turned and stepped out onto the mud street, where Jones sat on his horse holding Black Pot by the reins. Climbing into his saddle, Sam gave a glance back at the Jumping Coyote and tapped Black Pot forward along the main street out of town.

"I have never left a town in that manner," Sam said, turning in his saddle and looking back for a moment as soon as they were clear of the town limits. "I never want to do it again."

Jones also gave a look back, but then turned and

rode in silence for a moment until Sam noticed him looking off in the direction of Christi and said, "We're riding on toward the border. That's where we'll find Lonzo and Metlet."

"What about Pruitt?" said Jones.

"Pruitt will keep, so will anybody else who happens to be there. We're finishing off Lonzo while we've got the gang thinned out."

"It doesn't seem right, letting Pruitt getting away with this," said Jones.

"He got you *bad*, Jonesie," Sam said, nudging the Appaloosa forward. "The best you can do is live with it and learn from it."

"Well, well," said Lonzo, smiling down from atop his tired horse, "look at the lovely senoritas. Just as pretty today as the day we left them."

"They look plumb sweet enough to eat," said Metlet, sitting atop his horse beside him.

On the flat banks of a shallow creek below them, the three Reyes sisters busily scrubbed their family's clothes on clean, flat rocks. The riders had gone unseen until the eldest of the sisters stepped out into the creek and raised a handful of cool water to pat on her face. Upon glancing up and seeing the four men sitting forty feet above them on a low cliff overhang, the young woman kept calm, but stepped back over to rest of the women and said, "Do not look up, Lucita, but the terrible men who tormented us are back."

"Oh no, Rosa!" Lucita crossed herself quickly and

hurriedly began piling the unfinished wash into a straw basket. Her hands trembled, but she did not look up toward the cliff overhang.

Beside Lucita Reyes, her sister Rosa reached out and tapped her younger sister, Consuela, on her shoulder, getting her attention. When Consuela turned her questioning gaze to Rosa, she saw the urgency in Rosa's eyes and at the same time saw her other sister hurrying the unwashed clothes into the basket. She started to look around to see what had caused her sisters such fear. But before she could turn her eyes toward the cliff overhang, Rosa had moved closer and taken her face into her hands.

Consuela, unable to hear or speak since birth, saw her sister shake her head no and understood right away. Without a glance in any direction, Consuela quickly helped her sisters gather the wash, stand up and begin walking calmly but quickly back toward the village over the rise.

Looking down from atop the cliff and seeing a few pieces of clothes left lying on the flat rocks, Lonzo grinned and said to the other three, "They've seen us. Let's round them up."

"Damn, Lonzo!" said Forrest Bidson, turning his horse and gigging it toward a downward path to the creek, "I *see* now why you think this is the best place to lay low awhile."

Lonzo laughed, his horse ahead of the others. "He's learning fast enough!" he said.

"See why we'd have to kill you if you ever told

anybody about this place, Deputy?" Metlet said over
his shoulder to Bidson.

"If I told anybody, I'd *deserve* to die!" Bidson
replied, his hat flying off as he hurried his horse
along behind the others.

In the weathered crumbling adobe-and-plank shack,
Grandfather Reyes heard one of his granddaughters
cry out, either in pain or in terror. He struggled into
his sandals and with the help of his long walking
stick limped over to the eight-gauge shotgun leaning
near the chimney. He recognized the voice of another
granddaughter, crying out, "No! *Por favor*, no!" as he
picked the gun up with shaking hands. It had been
months since he'd cleaned or checked the gun or
even made sure it was loaded.

But hearing his granddaughters cries, he wasted
no time checking the gun. Instead he limped out of
the shack and along the path leading over the rise
and down to the creekbank. "I am coming, Rosa!" he
cried out in a weak and trembling voice, his thin,
blue-veined legs looking ready to collapse with each
labored step. "Where are you?"

"No, Grandfather!" Rosa shrieked. "Do not come
in here!"

Her voice came from a small clearing just ahead.
He tried to hurry his feeble legs. "I come to you,
Rosa!" he cried out, ignoring her warning. "I come
to—"

But it was not Rosa's voice but rather that of
Lonzo Greer that cut him off, shouting back from the

clearing amid bracken and driftwood, "Do as she says! Stay out of here, fool! If you know what's good for you!"

Grandfather Reyes recognized the voice as he stepped around an oak log. Before he could stop himself, he caught sight of his three granddaughters lying naked, their thighs spread wide beneath the three half-naked men. Off to one side, Lonzo stood watching with his trousers down around his ankles, one hand holding his bushy crotch, the other gripping the butt of his big Colt pistol.

"I warned you, gawddamn it!" Lonzo shouted at the old man. Raising the Colt he fired a shot, aiming a bit to the right, clipping a chunk of wood off the downed oak, less than six inches from the frail old man's side.

"Run, Grandfather, run!" shouted Lucita, her voice broken by the harsh uninterrupted thrusts of Forrest Bidson atop her.

"Please do not kill him!" Rosa sobbed beneath Calvin Thurston. She tried to throw Calvin off her, but he grabbed her roughly and pinned her back down. "I ain't finished with your furry belly yet!" he growled.

With his Colt smoking, Lonzo turned his attention back to the others, saying, "Don't worry, little precious. I ain't going to kill him." His hand gripped his naked crotch again, even tighter this time. "After all, we're good, civilized people here."

On a rock no more than thirty feet from the terrible sight he'd just witnessed, Grandfather Reyes dropped down, exhausted and sobbing, and hurled the gun away from him. "What good are you?" he said to the gun. "You cannot fire without hitting one of my beloveds." While sounds not unlike the muffled grunting of pigs rose from the clearing behind him, he buried his face in his trembling hands and wept shamefully.

Chapter 24

Lonzo and his men spent the next two weeks terrorizing the Reyeses until at length the old grandfather could stand it no longer. He crept into the shack with the shotgun that Lonzo had let him keep, as a joke, and aimed it at Lonzo, who lay naked on a blanket on the floor, like the other men, with Rosa pressed naked against him. With his arm already around Rosa's neck, he tightened her against him and said with a dark chuckle, "Go on and shoot, old man. Kill me and her too."

"Grandfather, go outside! Right now! Go!" Rosa shouted.

On a blanket by himself, Forrest Bidson stood up, naked, in the darkness and walked over to where Lonzo and Rosa lay. "Ain't nothing like a little excitement to get a fellow's blood hot, is there?" He lay down on the other side of Rosa; he and Lonzo pressed her between their sweaty bodies.

Rosa sobbed and shook violently, watching the old

man amble slowly from the shack, the shotgun hanging limp in his thin hand. Listening closely even as the two men's hands moved over Rosa roughly and pulled her over on her back; she stiffened at the sound of the old man's shotgun blast and realized what he'd done to himself. "Grandfather!" she screamed loud and long, struggling to rise and run to him, the screams of her sisters splitting the darkness around her.

"Huh-uh, you lay down here!" Lonzo shouted at her. "You started something with the two of us—you've got to finish us up!"

In the morning, rising before the others, Metlet walked in front of the shack, naked except for the gun belt he threw around himself and buckled, leaving the tie down strings dangling along his leg. Standing beside the body of the old man, he relieved himself in the dirt. When he'd finished he stood for a minute looking down at the bloody corpse.

"All right, you brainless, faceless sonsabitch, let's get you away from here before you draw rats and get to stinking." He stooped down, grabbed the old man's cold blue arms and dragged him off into the weeds twenty feet from the shack.

Walking back inside the shack, he headed over to where Bidson lay sleeping with his face buried between Rosa's thighs. Nudging Bidson's leg with his foot, Metlet said, "Hey, Deputy! Wake up! Too much sleeping like that will make you simple-minded."

Bidson rolled off the woman and looked up at Metlet angrily. "Mind your gawddamn business!

You're just envious cause me and Lonzo is sharing her!"

"You crazy bastard," Metlet laughed. "Me and Lonzo has shared more than you'd even want to know about. Now get your nekked ass up from there. We're out of staples and whiskey."

"What happened to that last jug of mescal the old man had hidden?" Bidson asked, straightening up on his haunches and pulling on his dirty trousers.

"It's all gone," Metlet said, grinning. "I expect that might be why he blew his head off. About seven miles down the trail there's a village. They've got a cantina and some staples—poultry, produce and such. Bring us back enough to last a couple of weeks."

"What about some money to pay for it?" Bidson asked.

"Pay for it your damn self, *Deputy*," Metlet said in a harsh tone. "You've made yourself some cash riding with us." He pointed a finger at Bidson. "You mind your manners in that village. Don't bring no trouble down on us."

Trouble down on us . . . ? The drunken, stinking son of a bitch. Grumbling, Bidson finished dressing and walked out of the shack to where the horses stood inside a small rickety corral. Watching Bidson saddle, mount up and ride away, Metlet nudged Rosa with his toe. "Don't pretend you're sleep, little lady. One ol' boy leaves, another ol' boy just shows up to take his place." Metlet laughed, dropped his gun belt to the floor and lay down where Bidson had been lying only moments before.

Bidson cursed to himself and rode hard along the twisting dusty trail to the small village of Vista Luna, several miles away. Arriving at the village, he reined in his horse at the rear of the cantina and walked in, ready for a long drink of mescal to both clear and cool his head. He wasn't used to being treated the way Metlet had treated him. Metlet didn't realize it, Bidson told himself, but the son of a bitch had come dangerously close to getting his guts shot out.

Inside the cantina, after ordering a wooden cup of mescal from a squat elderly woman, Metlet downed the contents in a long swig and set the cup heavily back on the clay-tiled bar. "*Gracias, mamacita!*" he said, wiping a hand across his mouth. Pointing at the bottle he held up five fingers, saying, "*Cinco mucho.*"

"*Cinco?*" the old woman asked.

"*Sí, cinco,*" Bidson repeated.

Reaching down beneath the bar, the old woman began pulling up one dusty bottle after another, keeping an eye on Bidson as he walked over to a shelf filled with both airtights and bags of dried vegetables. Searching along the labels on the airtights, he pulled down can after can of peaches, sugar beets and chick peas, stuffing them in the crook of his arm until he could carry no more without dropping them. Then, with his other hand, he pulled down a large bag of dried beans.

Seeing him return to the bar with the food staples,

the woman stepped over to a small bin, filled a bag with cornmeal, brought it back and set it with the rest of the supplies.

"*Gracias*," Bidson said again, then added sarcastically in English for his own sake, "Nothing's any good to you beaners unless it's wrapped in a corn blanket."

The woman stared at him blankly.

Bidson chuckled, pulling money from his pocket and laying it on the bar top. "I bet if I cracked a pistol barrel over your head, you'd die quicker than a spindly bird, wouldn't you, ol' hag? I'd save myself a bunch of money."

"*Qué?*" The old woman looked puzzled.

"Forget it, gawddamn it!" said Bidson. "I can't bring '*no trouble down on us*,'" he said mimicking Paul Metlet. "Just sack this mess of shit up for me." Roughly separating the food supplies from the bottles of mescal with his forearm, he grinned. "I've got something warm and wet waiting for my return."

The woman stuffed the airtights into one burlap bag and the bottles of mescal into another. Balancing the large bag of beans on his shoulder, Bidson picked up the burlap bags and left without another word.

The old woman stared at the money he'd laid on the bar. It was far too much. She scratched her head and watched the doorway for a moment. When Bidson didn't return, she shrugged, picked up the gold coins and dropped them into a tin box beneath the bar.

Bidson didn't make it a full mile before stopping

his horse long enough to pull a bottle of mescal from
the burlap bag and swig from it for the next two
miles. When he'd drained the last drink from the bottle he flipped it away into the hot sand and pulled another from the bag. *To hell with Metlet*, he thought,
feeling the mescal wrap soothingly around his brain.
If he wanted more, he could pay for it himself. He
took an even longer swig from the new bottle and let
out a long, gurgling belch.

It was afternoon when he returned with the supplies. As soon as Bidson stepped down from his saddle, Metlet and Calvin stepped forward, both of them
dressed now and acting cross and jittery, suffering
with hangovers. "What the hell took you so long?"
Metlet asked angrily, jerking the top of a burlap bag
open and running his hand down among the mescal
bottles.

"I ain't been gone that long," Bidson said in his
own defense, his tongue thick with mescal. "Next
time *you* can go."

"What kind of bullshit is this?" Metlet growled,
pulling up a bottle of mescal with one hand and with
his other hand the remaining two. "Three bottles!
Three lousy bottles?" Both he and Calvin glared at
Bidson. "Jesus, Deputy! My old mama could've drank
three bottles of this horse piss fixing breakfast!"

"Next time your mama can go!" Bidson shot back,
his temper flaring.

"You're drunk, ain't you, you son of a bitch!"
shouted Metlet.

"He got drunk and there went all our mescal," said Calvin.

Inside the shack, dressing himself while the three sisters sat huddled in a corner wrapped in serapes, Lonzo heard the bickering out front and cursed aloud, "Damn it to hell! Can't I get my clothes on in peace around this lousy shit hole?"

He turned and stomped out of the shack, leaving one of his two hideout pistols lying on a rough wooden table against the wall. No sooner had he'd left the shack than the young women looked at the pistol, then at each other, then at the rear door that Calvin had nailed shut with some rusty nails, using his pistol butt as a hammer. "No, Lucita!" Rosa said, grabbing her sister's arm before she could made a grab for the pistol. "It is too risky, and there are too many of them!"

They sat in silence, listening to drunken cursing and threats among the three men. Finally, Lonzo said, "All right, that's enough! No more of this arguing and bickering among ourselves!" His tone of voice softened a bit. "Boys, look around you. We've got a little piece of heaven right here. Let's enjoy it, damn it!"

Consuela stared at her sister's frightened faces. Unable to hear, she did not understand why Rosa had stopped Lucita from reaching for the pistol. Even as Lonzo's footsteps neared the open front door, Consuela rushed to the table, snatched up the pistol and hurried back to her spot beside Lucita.

"Oh no!" Rosa whispered close to Lucita's ear. "She has killed us!"

Still cursing, but chuckling with dark laughter, Lonzo walked in, carrying a bottle of mescal in his hand. Lucita and Rosa held their breath; but Consuela sat calmly, her serape drawn around her, the pistol poised in her hand, her thumb over the hammer.

They expected Lonzo to look at the table, then at them, knowing they had the pistol. Rosa watched him, having to force herself not to make the sign of the cross. Not yet. But when Lonzo looked up from the table, instead of missing the gun and flying into a killing rage, he turned up a long drink of mescal, wiped his hand across his mouth and said, "All right, beautiful little angels, which one of yas can cook us up something without poisoning the lot of us?"

"Coo—cook?" Lucita said haltingly, almost in disbelief that the three of them were still alive after Consuela had stolen the madman's pistol. Perhaps God was with her and her sisters after all.

"Yes, *cook*, gawddamn it!" said Lonzo. Making a gesture of spooning food into his mouth, he said, "You know . . . *el food-O*, damn it! There's more to life than laying around on your lazy asses fornicating all the gawddamn time!"

Lucita swallowed a gulp of air and calmed her voice. "I am the one who cooks."

"All right then, off your ass and get to cooking," said Lonzo, swigging again from the bottle of mescal. "I could eat the head off of a live muskrat."

"*Rat?*" said Lucita, looking confused. "*El rodento?*"

"No, damn it, woman! I don't want to eat no gawddamn rat!" Lonzo bellowed. He stepped forward and kicked her to her feet. "There's grub out there! Go get it and get it cooked, you stupid woman!"

Lucita hurried from the shack holding the serape around her bruised naked body.

Chapter 25

No more than an hour after Bidson rode away from the cantina in Vista Luna, Sam and Hadley Jones reined their tired horses to an iron panther's head hitch post and slapped dust from their shirts with their hats. "Well," said Jones, "I can now say that I have been to every town between the outpost and the border. I've learned my way around."

"Trouble is, half of them will be gone and a few new ones will have sprung up if you wait six months," Sam replied. He'd kept his partner under close observation for the past week. He was relieved to see Jones starting to recover from killing the young detective. For all their differences and with the difficulty they'd had tracking the Black Moon gang, Sam could now see Jones turning into a strong, competent lawman.

"Good," said Jones. "Every time I ride through, there'll be something new to see." He smiled. "I'll never get bored."

"You can count on that," Sam said, the two of them walking into the cantina out of the midmorning sun.

Before the rangers even got to the tile-topped bar, the elderly woman saw that they were Americans and hurried around to them holding out the gold coins Forrest Bidson had left lying on the bar. "Here, *senors*!" she said, sounding afraid. "I did not mean to keep the money. Your friend left so quickly, there was no time to stop him!"

Sam and Jones looked at each other. "No, ma'am," Sam said, calming her. "Whoever that money belongs to, it is no friend of ours."

"Oh . . . ?" She gave them a questioning glance, noting the badges on their chests beneath their riding dusters. "You are lawmen, *sí*?" she asked.

"Yes, ma'am," Sam replied. "We were just about to ask you if you have seen any of the men we're after." He nodded at the gold coins in her hand. She closed her hand quickly, now that she knew she had nothing to fear. "Was this man an anglo?"

"*Sí*, he was an Americano," she said, nodding vigorously as she spoke. "He is *loco*, this one! He talked like a madman. He did not know that I understood his language. I am not *stupido*." She tapped the side of her head and added, "I did not want him to know that I understood his *loco* words." Her eyes widened a bit. "I think he is a bad *hombre*, this one." She made a gun with her short, weathered fingers and held her hand against her hip. "His holster is tied down here."

"I see," said Sam. "And what sort of items did he buy from you?"

"He bought five bottles of mescal and food for only a few days," she said.

"Five bottles of mescal." Sam pondered for a second. "Which way did he ride when he left here?"

She pointed south, toward a stretch of low hills beyond a sandy basin. "He has not been gone long," she said. "I think if you hurry you will catch him."

"*Gracias*, ma'am." Sam said, "As soon as we've eaten and watered and rested our horses, we'll be on our way."

"I will prepare a meal for you while you attend your *caballos*," the old woman said. "It will be ready when you return."

"Much obliged, ma'am," Sam said, Jones echoing his words.

As soon as they walked out of the small cantina, Jones said in a lowered voice, as if having to contain his excitement, "Sam, this is it! I can feel it! We're getting ready to put this whole Black Moon bunch out of business this time."

"This could one man, or it could be half a dozen," Sam said. "What makes you so sure this time?"

"Just a feeling, Sam," said Jones. "Something big is about to happen. I think we'll soon be headed home."

"I am home, Jonesie." Sam stopped beside the Appaloosa, took down his canteen and began leading the stallion toward the village well a few yards away.

"Not me," Jones said. "I'm going home to Flora and do some serious thinking about things."

"Oh, about what?" Sam asked, but he already had a feeling he knew what Jones was about to say.

Jones offered a thin smile and said, "Maybe you didn't think I was listening to you, Sam, but I was." They walked on, leading their horses. "I've heard every word you said: about these men, about this job, what it is and what it does to a person."

"You're turning in the badge?" Sam asked.

"Yep, I am," said Jones. "As soon as I get back to Flora, I'm giving it up. I've seen what it does to me, and I don't like it. This job brings out all the worst things in a man." He caught himself and quickly amended himself. "I didn't mean it about *you*, Sam. You make it all work some way. It doesn't do the things to you that it would to most men. Somehow you manage not to be broken by it. But I can't."

"If that's how it is for you, Jonesie," Sam said, "then this is the time to get out."

"As soon as we're done, Sam," Jones said.

But Sam stopped abruptly in the street and said, "No, Jonesie. Stop right now, right here. Water your horse and head back."

"No, Sam, not right now," Jones said, having stopped beside him. "I wouldn't leave a job unfinished. You're my partner. I'm keeping up my end of it."

"Don't jinx yourself, Jones," Sam warned. "If you're quiting, *quit*. Don't risk riding out there and getting yourself killed."

"I'm going, Sam," Jones said firmly. "It's still my job as long I've got this badge on. Besides, what if I turned back now and something happened to *you* out there?" He smiled to lighten the grim conversation a bit. "I won't let you leave something like that hanging on me the rest of my life."

Sam looked at him, considering his words. "No, I reckon not." The two turned and continued toward the well.

"Anyway, nothing is going to keep me from going home to Flora, Sam. So put any talk about jinxing and dying out of your mind."

"Consider it done," Sam said with finality.

When they'd watered, grained and rested the horses, and eaten a hot meal of beans and goat meat, the two resaddled their horses and rode on, finding the fresh tracks of a single horseman starting right from the side of the cantina easy to follow.

Less than a mile along the trail, the tracks stopped where the horse had stood still long enough for its rider to pull out a bottle of mescal. A mile farther along, the tracks began to weave as if the horse were no longer receiving any guidance from the man behind its reins. Another mile passed and Jones spotted the empty mescal bottle lying glistening in the sand.

Stepping down from his saddle, Sam picked up the empty bottle, touched the tip of it and found it dry. Pitching the bottle away he said, "He didn't stop and drink it all in one spot. There must be others waiting for him." He stepped back into the saddle, pulled his rifle from its boot, laid it across his lap and nudged Black Pot forward, Jones riding right beside him.

In the corner of the shack, Consuela had spent the day with the serape drawn tightly around her. In spite of the heat and the beads of perspiration on her forehead she shivered and stared blankly at the men when they moved past the open door and looked in on her.

"Whatever she's got, I hope she ain't passed it around to the rest of us," Calvin said. He spit and took a drink of mescal, as if to wash a bad taste from his mouth.

"Damn her if she has," Lonzo cursed. "I'll kill any sow who passes me a fever or anything else." As he spoke, his hand instinctively brushed the butt of his holstered pistol.

"That goes the same for me," said Metlet, who stood twirling his pistol idly on his finger. He stopped twirling and held the pistol as if ready to fire.

"My sister is not ill," Rosa ventured in broken English. "She is only frightened."

"Frightened? Of us ol' boys?" said Metlet, grinning cruelly, continuing his pistol twirling. "Pray tell, *why?*" He and Calvin Thurston cackled with dark drunken laughter.

"She'll have cause to be frightened if I catch anything from her," Lonzo warned. He wiped his thumb around on his empty tin plate, mopping up any last morsel of bean gravy, sucked his thumb and said, "I hate a woman with unsanitary habits."

Calvin Thurston turned back a large swig of mescal, swallowed it and said, "I don't know about the rest of yas, but I'm about ready to put this place behind me."

Metlet, Lonzo and Bidson all looked at one another as if in disbelief. "Well, now." Lonzo stood up, sucked his teeth and stepped over to Calvin with his hand out for the bottle of mescal. "How long have you been suffering from this condition?"

"What condition?" Calvin asked, passing the bottle to him.

"Of being a gawddamn idiot," said Lonzo. He took a swig of mescal and passed the bottle over to Metlet.

"I ain't no *idiot!*" said Calvin. "I just get my fill of a place and know when it's time to get up and get on down the trail. I like seeing new things."

Metlet and Bidson muffled a laugh. "Oh, do you, now?" said Lonzo. He lunged over to where Lucita and Rosa stood huddled in their serapes. Reaching out, he snatched Rosa's faded serape from her and left her standing naked in front of the men. Metlet and Bidson whistled and cheered.

Lonzo grabbed Rosa down low and shook her roughly. "Tell me, Calvin. What the hell do you expect to see down the trail that's going to look any better than *this?*"

Metlet called out, "Yeah, Calvin, is there something wrong with you? Something we oughta know about?"

"The hell's that mean?" Calvin asked, instantly taking offense.

"Whatever you want to take it to mean," Metlet said harshly, his attitude turning as sour as Calvin's, both of them goaded on by the venomous bite of mescal. Again Metlet's pistol stopped twirling.

"Both of yas, stand down!" Lonzo commanded. "I ain't having no more fighting or bickering among—"

His words stopped short. Beside him Rosa gasped. Lonzo and Rosa had just caught sight of Ranger Hadley Jones stepping slowly into view from behind a pile of mesquite kindling. He held a shotgun aimed at the backs of Metlet, Bidson and Calvin. "Don't anybody move," Jones said calmly.

"Jesus Christ!" said Metlet, startled—not so much by the sound of Jones' voice behind him, but rather by the sight of Ranger Sam Burrack stepping into view ten yards behind Lonzo and the woman. "It's Burrack—that ranger Deaks said he *killed!*"

"Deaks, you *lying* son of a bitch," Calvin growled under his breath. He continued to stare coldly at Sam, knowing that this was the man who killed his brother.

"Drop your guns," Sam said, seeing the big Colt in Metlet's hand.

"Whoa now, Rangers," said Lonzo. Slowly reaching an arm behind Rosa, who stood naked beside him, he drew her against him and asked with a sly grin, "Which is it? *'Don't make a move'* or *'Drop our guns?'*" he taunted. "We can't do both at once."

"Turn the woman loose, Lonzo," Sam demanded, his gun hand hanging down his side and gripping his big Colt loosely, but with the hammer already cocked.

"Damn, more orders!" Lonzo grinned, holding Rosa tight, half hidden by her trembling naked body. Lonzo raised his gun from his holster and started to cock it. "Now you listen, Ranger! Unless you want to see this pretty little senorita's brains blown all over this shack, you better—"

Sam's Colt leveled up and bucked once in his

hand, cutting Lonzo off. The bullet hit him squarely in the center of his forehead and sent both him and the screaming woman flying backward against the front of the shack. The other three men flinched for an instant as a mist of blood and brain matter filled the air.

No sooner had Lonzo hit the front of the shack than Rosa rolled away screaming and scrambled away across the hard sandy ground in Sam's direction. Lucita screamed also, hunkering down at the corner of the shack for protection. Metlet, his gun in hand, leapt sideways as he turned toward Jones, firing.

Jones dropped the hammer on the shotgun. The blast of buckshot flung Calvin Thurston across the yard, his face and chest torn to shreds. But only a few pellets nipped Metlet in his arm as he hit the ground rolling toward the corner of shack, where he snatched Lucita and threw her between himself and the rangers.

At the same time, Bidson had dropped into a crouch and raced across the yard into the shack, his gun hand thrown back, firing wildly behind him. A shot from Sam's Colt slammed into his shoulder.

Lucita screamed, crawling quickly across the yard for any kind of cover she could find. Bullets ripped through the air above her like angry hornets. Then the guns fell silent; Metlet rolled over on his back and stared up blankly at the sky, Sam's last shot having struck his heart. Sam stepped back into the cover of a broken-down wagon whose one rear wheel lay sunk in the sand. He raised his free hand toward Jones, as if to hold him back, as he called out to the shack, "Your pals are dead. You're wounded. Toss out your gun and surrender. We'll see to it your wound gets treated."

"You mean before taking me to rot in Yuma Prison?" Bidson called out with a dark, insane chuckle. "To hell with you, Rangers! I'm going down bloody! I'm taking you both with me, and I'm taking this *dummy* too!"

Dummy . . . ? Bidson's words caught Sam by surprise. But only for a second. A shot rang out, followed by a strange, muted-sounding lament.

"Consuela!" Rosa shouted, running naked across the yard toward the shack.

"No, wait!" Jones shouted, running over, intercepting her quickly and taking her to the cover of some mesquite brush.

"My sister! My siser Consuela!" Rosa shouted hysterically.

Jones quickly jerked his riding duster from his back and threw it around the naked woman. "Sam! There's another woman in there! I'm going in!"

Jones turned and raced to the open door of the shack even as Sam called out, "No, wait, Jonesie!"

Seeing that Jones wasn't about to stop, Sam hurried forward himself, his Colt cocked and ready. Racing across the dirt, he saw Jones disappear into the shack. Another shot rang out from inside; but Sam kept running, giving no thought to taking cover.

In the dirt in front of the shack, Sam slid to a halt, seeing Jones reappear in the doorway, a look of surprise and anguish on his suddenly tight pale face. "She . . . shot me, Sam," he said. "See?" He nodded down at the blood oozing through his fingers where he gripped the center of his chest.

"Jonesie!" Sam hurried forward and helped him sit down and lean against the doorframe. Quickly, Sam looked inside the shack, seeing Bidson lying face-down dead in a puddle of blood, a small bullet hole in the back of his head. Rosa rushed past Sam and into the shack, going to her sister, jerking the smoking pistol from her hand and comforting her. Consuela sat sweating heavily, a wild terrified look on her face.

Sam turned back to Jones. "Sit still. Take it easy, partner. I'll get you some water."

But before he could leave, Jones gripped his arm and said, "She . . . didn't know I was . . . here to protect her, Sam. Imagine that."

"Let me get some water, Jonesie!" Sam said. We need to take a look at that wound!"

"Aw, Sam," Jones offered a weak smile, "this isn't so bad. It doesn't hurt much. I believe I'm going to be all right."

"That's good, Jonesie." Sam settled down, seeing that there was no hurry. Nothing he could do would make any difference now.

Jones chuckled weakly under his breath. "I should have waited . . . like you said. Right, Sam?"

"It's okay, Jonesie," Sam said. "I don't know everything." He'd whipped Jones's bandanna from around his neck and begun blotting sweat from his dying partner's face.

"I think you do, Sam," Jones whispered, his voice fading. "That's why . . . I always wanted to do a good job."

"You did, Jonesie," Sam said, feeling his own voice tighten in his throat. "You're the best. The best I've seen."

Jones looked surprised. "Do you mean it, Sam? The best?"

"That's right, Jonesie," Sam said. "The very best."

Jones let out a long sigh, turning his head sideways and resting it against the doorframe. "I can't wait . . . to tell Flora. . . ."

"Jonesie?" Sam said quietly, giving only a slight nudge to his shoulder. "Jonesie . . . ?" He sat looking at his partner's face for a moment, then shook his head slowly, stood up and stared out across the endless desert floor.

"She did not mean to shoot him," Rosa said, sounding excited; Lucita and she drew nearer cautiously. "She had a gun she stole from one of theses pigs! She cannot hear or speak. She did not know what was going on out here! These men drove our grandfather to kill himself and dragged his body into the brush!"

"I understand," Sam said, without turning to face them. "I'll just take a minute here. We'll see about gathering the dead and going on."

A stillness had set in as Sam helped the woman bury their grandfather and place a wooden marker above his grave. When they had finished, Sam dragged the bodies of the last of the Black Moon gang to their horses, and pitched them over the animals' bare backs. "You and your sisters sell their tack and saddles and keep what money you get to live on," he told Rosa. It wouldn't be much, but those women were used to very little.

"*Gracias,*" Rosa said. She stood silent for a moment, then said, "Maybe this will help you. If not for you and your *amigo,* I think my sisters and I would not be alive much longer."

"Much obliged, ma'am," Sam said quietly. "That *does* help me."

He linked the dead outlaws' horses together with a lead rope. But he left Jones' horse saddled and wrapped Jones in their two riding dusters and laid him carefully across his horse's back. Keeping Jones' horse beside him, reins in hands, he said to the big Appaloosa, "All right, Black Pot, let's take our friend home." He nudged the stallion toward the trail leading back to the Badlands. Soon all Rosa and her sisters could see of him were the drifts of dust rising and swirling as one from the horses' hooves.